STILL WATERS RUN

A deeply immersive suspense thriller

MARK WEST

Published by The Book Folks

London, 2022

ISBN 978-1-80462-048-9

www.thebookfolks.com

For Nick, who shared those 80s seaside adventures with me.

Prologue

Late August, 1985

The lock slammed into place and Dan heard the scuffle of footsteps as the killer dragged a struggling Charlie away.

He felt angry and powerless but if he didn't get out of the derelict seafront building quickly something terrible was going to happen to her and then it would be his turn.

Charlie screamed and he tried to focus. He took a steadying breath and looked around.

The room was dusty with a lot of pipes and what looked like boilers. There was a fire escape on the opposite wall. He rushed over and pushed the safety bar.

The wind caught the door and slammed it against the outer wall. The storm was raging and the tide was in. High waves filled the air with spray as he looked down. If there had ever been a fire escape ladder, then it was long gone and he couldn't see any other way of getting down the wall.

The swell of the tide receded to reveal hidden rocks beneath the wall.

If he wanted to escape, then this was his only option. The horrifying reality of that made his bones feel heavy. To be able to help Charlie he had to jump into the sea and try to swim for it.

It was madness. He wasn't a good swimmer and even looking at the white-tipped waves scared him almost senseless. He didn't know how deep the water was or how high the other rocks were.

He went back to the main door and tried to open it again but it wouldn't move an inch.

Dan bit his lip hard enough to draw blood.

There was no other choice, and the longer he thought about it the more he risked the life of Charlie. He felt sick and leaned forward until the sensation passed. His heartbeat thudded in his ears.

It was now or never.

Dan pushed away from the door and ran across the room. With a yell he launched himself through the open doorway.

The water seemed to rush towards him and the rain instantly soaked him.

His momentum carried him over where he'd seen the rocks but he was falling all the time and then the cold water took his breath away.

He went under.

Chapter 1

"Welcome to fabulous Seagrave."

Dan glanced up from the roadmap as they passed the road sign his mother had just read. The car crested a hill and the town was laid out before them, bathed in sunshine. There were docks off to the right, a large funfair, a long stretch of golden beach and two piers that extended out to sea.

"I'd say it looked pretty fabulous," his mum said and the quiver in her voice made him look at her. She gave him a big smile that didn't quite hide the sadness in her eyes.

"I think you're right," he said and gave her a big smile that seemed to lift hers a little.

Dan was sixteen and this time last year his dad promised they'd all go to Spain on holiday. But that was before they knew what his dad had been doing and things seemed so much better, even if the poisonous effects had been already spreading, unseen, through their lives.

Money was tight and he had no idea how his mum managed to find enough to come away here even if it was only for a few days at the tail end of the season. She'd put on a brave face as they packed her old Fiesta that morning and he'd matched it because he really wanted her to have a break.

However much his dad had hurt his son, he'd hurt his mum so much more. Some nights, Dan heard her crying as she sat in the kitchen and drank a bit too much wine and smoked too many cigarettes. Once or twice he'd heard her mutter "forty and on my own" and never quite knew how he'd respond if she ever said it directly to him.

"Do you really?"

"Oh yes," he said. "I mean, even if the town's rubbish, it'll have us in it."

That surprised a genuine laugh out of his mum and made her eyes sparkle.

They followed the steep hill down into the town where shops sold everything a tourist could possibly want and amusement arcades did a roaring trade.

She had written detailed directions in her precise hand for this leg of the journey – she'd never been to Seagrave before – and Dan directed them to Marine Drive. Across the junction was a large pier with an entrance covered by posters for acts that had appeared during the summer. Dan recognised some of them that had been big in the seventies but then shunted off television with the new wave of comedians taking their place. On the beach he could see adults sitting behind windbreaks and little kids splashing in the sea.

"Turn left here," he said. "Then it should on the right."

His mum followed his directions. The houses on the left seemed to get larger and larger with the first dozen or so converted into hotels. Expensive cars sat in driveways and most of the upstairs had balconies, some set with chairs so the owners could sit out and enjoy the unimpeded sea view.

"Wow," said his mum, leaning forward to look at them out of the windscreen. "Lots of money there."

"Uh-huh," said Dan and glanced across the road at a small park and some ornamental gardens before a hedgerow blocked the view of the sea.

"That's us." She turned off into a wide driveway.

Stone gateposts painted a glistening white and linked by a high metal arch marked the entrance to the holiday camp. The road went around a large rectangular lawn with a pitch and putt course set into it and beyond was a two-storey white building with a clock tower in the centre of it. 'Holidaze Seagrave' was written in neon tubing above the large clock face.

A girl stood on the kerb of the first corner looking into a hedge and holding an expensive-looking camera close to her chest.

Wow, he thought. She was very pretty and about his age and height. Her shoulder-length black hair stood out against her white Blondie T-shirt.

She glanced at him and then his mum who raised her hand as they drove by. The girl returned the gesture absently. As they drove around the corner Dan resisted the urge to turn in his seat.

"You thought she was pretty too, eh?" his mum asked.

Dan felt his cheeks heat with colour. "Mum," he groaned.

"What? I just mean it'll be nice for you to have other teenagers about."

"She's not going to be interested in me."

"Of course she is. You're a handsome lad and you've got a great sense of humour."

"I think there's a rule you have to say that, but it's not right."

"You watch," his mum said. "I'll be right."

Midway along the building was a porch with steps leading up to a wide glass door that had 'Reception' written on it. His mum parked in the nearest bay and switched off the engine.

"We'll go and get signed in," she said after a moment. "Unless you want to stay and watch the pretty girl."

"Very funny," he said and hoped he wasn't blushing.

"I try," she said and got out.

The reception was cool and bright with a couple of sofas and a rack of pigeonholes on the back wall. A counter split the room and a young woman stood behind it. She looked up as they went in and smiled.

Dan couldn't help staring. The girl by the hedge was pretty but this woman looked like she'd stepped out of a magazine. In her early twenties, she wore a green blouse with a few buttons undone that showed a necklace resting against her sternum. Blonde hair draped to her shoulders.

"You're catching flies," his mum whispered and Dan quickly shut his mouth.

"Hi," said the woman with a big, sincere smile. "Welcome to Holidaze Seagrave. My name's Mia, how can I help you?"

"Hello, Mia, I'm Jude Moore and this is my son Dan. We've got a caravan booked."

"Excellent," said Mia. "I'm pleased to meet you." She checked a ledger book on the counter then unhooked two keys from one of the pigeonholes. "You're in caravan E12. Drive down by the left side of reception and it's in the first block of caravans on your left."

She turned the ledger so his mum could sign it. After she had done so Mia gave her the keys.

"Thanks."

"You're welcome," said Mia with a dazzling smile. "I hope you enjoy your stay here."

She tipped Dan a wink and he felt his cheeks blush.

* * *

The girl with the camera had gone and a young family were now on the pitch and putt course.

His mum drove around the building and the camp spread before them with rows and rows of caravans stretching into the distance until the furthest away were almost a blur against the blue sky.

As Mia had said, the E block was off to the left on a narrow lane that ended at a high hedge. The first few caravans were small, probably no bigger than an estate car and grubby with it, as if no one had cleaned them during the summer. Dan groaned inwardly.

The caravans got bigger the further they went.

"E12," said his mum and pulled into a space between two caravans. "Well, as our home away from home it looks okay to me. What do you reckon?"

The caravan was a good size and seemed to be clean and tidy with three large windows on this one side as well as a half-glass panel door. Even if it didn't look better than he'd expected he wouldn't have burst her bubble. She needed this holiday even more than he did.

"It looks good."

Her face seemed to crumble for the briefest of moments then she cupped his cheek. "Thank you, Danny." Her eyes glowed as if she was about to cry.

"You open up," he said quickly. "I'll get your case and my rucksack."

"Yes, sir," she said and mock saluted him.

She gave him the car keys and went up the brick and slab steps while he unlocked the boot. He held the door so it didn't bounce up too quickly and pulled out her suitcase first then the oversized rucksack he'd borrowed from his grandad. As he pulled out the carrier bag of groceries his mum had brought from home in case the stuff was too expensive on the camp, Dan became aware of someone standing beside him.

"And what do you think you're doing, laddie?"

Chapter 2

Jude opened the door into the narrow hallway. The caravan smelled like it had just been cleaned and looked tidy. The kitchen was across from the bathroom, and across from her was a small room with a window and twin single beds. The master was to her right with cupboards over a double bed that almost filled the room.

Was it too small? Would Dan hate his room? He'd never say anything but that somehow made her feel worse. He'd already had to put up with so much crap this year from all the shit her ex-husband Neil had created, but apart from one or two moments at school he seemed to have coped so well with it all.

Fucking Neil, she thought. None of this was their fault yet here they were in a borrowed caravan on an east coast camp rather than the Spanish holiday they'd been looking forward to. And she could barely afford this as it was.

A raised voice drew her attention and she leaned out of the doorway. The Fiesta boot was up and obscured Dan and the other person from view.

"I'm here with my mum," Dan said.

"A likely story." The unseen person sounded annoyed. "Did you think you could get away with nicking all this luggage?"

"I wasn't…"

Brilliant, Jude thought. They'd been here less than five minutes and it was already going wrong. It wouldn't surprise her if Dan begged to go back to Hadlington straight away.

"Excuse me," she said and went down the steps. "Can I help you?"

The person who moved away from the back of the Fiesta was tall, slim and handsome. He had a strong jaw and dark hair greying slightly at the temples. His angry look slid away as he took Jude in.

"I'm Jude Moore. I've rented this caravan for the week and this is my son, Dan. That's our luggage."

The stranger put a hand to his chest and smiled. He looked attractive when he smiled.

"Then I apologise profusely, Mrs Moore, to you and your son."

He looked at Dan and held out his hand. Dan shook it.

"No hard feelings?" the man asked.

"No," said Dan.

The man walked to her and the sunlight caught his stubble. "I'm Paul Reid," he said and shook her hand. "This is my caravan."

"Of course." She recognised his name from the rental paperwork one of her teacher colleagues had organised.

"I hope it lives up to your expectations."

"I'm sure it will."

"I'd been waiting for you actually. I was over at Neptune's Palace." He jerked a thumb over his shoulder towards reception. "It's the club on site and they do a decent meal in there too." He turned to Dan. "There's also a decent amusement arcade, assuming you like shooting things or driving race cars."

"Sometimes," Dan said.

"You'll love it." Paul took a business card out of his wallet and held it between two fingers for Jude to take. "It's got my home number on so give me a ring if you need anything at all."

"I'll be sure to."

He looked at her for a moment too long then said "Okay" and nodded at her. "I'll let you lovely people crack on and hopefully we'll see one another again while you're here." He gave her the full effect of his smile again then walked down towards the road.

She watched him go.

"I'm sure we'll see him again," said Dan with distaste.

Jude thought that might not be such a bad thing.

"He seemed alright," she said. It was the first time anyone had paid her attention like that in a long time.

"Yeah, if you like Don Johnson."

"He didn't look anything like Don Johnson."

"Didn't you see his designer stubble? I'll bet in the evenings he wears pastel jackets with the sleeves rolled up like he's in *Miami Vice* or something."

"I thought you liked *Miami Vice*."

"I did, but I'm a teenager, he's…" He stopped and looked guilty. "He's old enough not to be copying a TV show."

"You weren't impressed then?"

"He thought I was nicking our stuff."

He sounded so indignant it made her chuckle and that made him laugh. Thankfully, with Dan, any annoyances were quick to dissipate.

"Come on," she said and grabbed her suitcase. "I'll show you around."

Chapter 3

His only memory of a caravan was the one his gran and grandfather once had in Skegness but that seemed tiny compared to this.

"What do you think?" his mum asked.

"It looks alright," he said as he took in the kitchen and lounge.

"I thought so too," she said with a bit too much enthusiasm and he felt guilty for using the word 'alright'. "That's the bathroom with a toilet, shower and sink."

"All mod cons then?"

"Indeed. This isn't the caravan in Skeggy where you had to nip out in the night to the toilet block."

Had that worry been playing on her mind too?

She opened the bedroom door and he peered in. The window overlooked the hedge and field beyond the camp.

"The beds are a bit narrow but hey, you've got a bedside table."

"Just what I've always wanted."

"If only I'd remembered how easy it was to please you," she said. "If it's too small you can have the double room or we can fold down the table in the lounge and covert it to a bed."

"This'll be fine," he said. It could have been worse — there could have been bunk beds.

She squeezed his shoulder and he saw the glint of a tear in her eye. She'd told him a couple of weeks ago that she was fed up with crying and he tried to think of something to say that would distract her.

Someone knocked at the door. His mum raised her eyebrows.

"Who could that be?" she asked and went into the hallway to answer it.

Dan sat on the bed across from the window. There was a brief exchange of conversation he couldn't quite hear then, "It's for you, Dan."

"Me?" How did that make any sense?

He went into the hallway and the girl who'd been standing by the hedge looked at him. She didn't have the expensive camera now but was carrying an Instamatic instead.

"This is Charlotte."

Dan felt his cheeks heat up.

"I prefer to be called Charlie."

"This is Charlie," his mum corrected herself then introduced him.

"Hey," Charlie said. "I saw you drive in and thought I'd come by and say hello."

"That's very nice of you." His mum dropped him a wink that Charlie couldn't see.

"Not really, Mrs Moore."

"Hold on, love. If I'm to call you Charlie, you need to call me Jude."

"I love that name," Charlie said with a smile that lit up her whole face. "I'll be honest, I'm being a bit selfish. I've been at the camp for a while and there aren't many people here my age."

"Are you going to talk, Dan?" his mum asked.

He wanted to but couldn't think of anything. A very pretty girl had come to speak to him and he didn't want to mess up but this seemed like just the kind of occasion he would.

"Hi," he managed.

Charlie tilted her head to one side as if curious and Dan felt a tingle in his belly.

"I know you haven't settled in yet," she said, "but I haven't got anyone to speak to around here and it's driving me mad. How about I show you around the camp or something?" She looked at his mum. "If that's okay with you, Jude?"

"Of course. Go off and enjoy yourselves."

Things were moving a bit too quickly for Dan to keep up with. How insanely bored and lonely would a pretty girl have to be to want to spend time with him?

"Are you sure?" he asked. "Shouldn't I help you unpack?"

"I can deal with that," Jude said and made shooing motions at him. "Go and have a good time."

* * *

Charlie led him down to the road and back towards the reception building.

"How old are you?" she asked.

"I'm sixteen. What about you?"

"Same."

It seemed as if they both mentally breathed a sigh of relief. How awful would it have been to find out you were stuck wandering around with a fourteen-year-old?

"Where are you from?" she asked.

"Do you always ask this many questions?"

"No. But how else would I find out the answers?"

He laughed. "I'm from Hadlington."

She looked at him blankly.

"It's a few miles from Northampton."

She shook her head. "Haven't heard of that either."

"So where are you from?" he asked.

"Sheffield."

"I've heard of that," he said and cringed inwardly at how needy it sounded. Some of his mates could chat to girls like it was the easiest thing in the world but whenever Dan tried, he basically forgot syntax and everything lapsed into an awkward silence.

When his mum told him they were coming here he'd made the decision to try harder. He was miles from home and nobody knew him here, so why couldn't he become in real life the cool kid he was in his mind?

"So have you been here long?" he asked and cringed again. Why was he shooting himself in the foot like this? He sounded like someone's dad trying to make conversation.

"A few weeks," she said as if she didn't think it was a stupid question. "My dad works here for the summer but he lives in town so I stay here on my own."

"Oh." It didn't make enough sense for him to respond. Even cool Dan would have been stumped.

"It's alright," she said quickly. "It gets me used to being independent and living on my own, but it can be boring and it's nice to have company." She looked directly at him. "Don't get any funny ideas though, okay?"

He felt both frustrated and relieved. "Okay."

"Why did you come down today rather than on Saturday?"

"It was a last-minute thing," he said defensively.

"Perhaps it was a cancellation," Charlie said then paused. "Oh…"

"I don't know," he said and felt a flare of embarrassment. He didn't want Charlie to think they were poor. "Mum's always doing things on the spur of the moment." That didn't even sound convincing to him. "We just met the owner actually. He thought I was nicking our bags."

Charlie laughed. "Well that's a good start. I don't think you look much like a thief."

"I look better than him. He seemed to think he was Don Johnson's little brother."

"Ah, you mean Paul."

Had his description been that good? "Yes, Paul Reid. Do you know him?"

"I've taken photographs for him. He and his partner are doing up the lido."

"I've never been to a lido before."

"You haven't lived," she said and her quick smile told him she was winding him up. "I love it there and it photographs beautifully. I'll show you it when we go into Seagrave."

"Do you take a lot of pictures?"

"Loads," she said and held up her Instamatic. "This isn't the best camera but I keep it with me so I'm always ready. You never know when you're going to come across that Kodak moment."

They crossed the road. The reception was to the right and a line of buildings ran along to the left. Charlie went through the gap between the two onto a large patio where several picnic tables were set out with Cinzano umbrellas folded in the centre of each. The back of reception belonged to Neptune's Palace according to a large neon sign over the wide portico. The main doors for it were propped open and someone was running a vacuum cleaner just inside.

"Sin city." Charlie smirked. "Lots of smoke and sexy people dancing. It's like you're in the best disco you've ever heard of in London."

"Is it?"

"No, of course not." She laughed. "This is Holidaze Seagrave. Are you always this easy to wind up?"

He wanted to kick himself for falling for it. How exciting was a nightclub on a holiday camp catering for families going to be?

The patio opened onto a lawn with a bandstand in the centre. Rows of deckchairs filled with pensioners catching the sun radiated away from it in waves even though no one was playing at the moment.

The line of buildings was a row of shops and Charlie walked down the path in front of them. The amusement arcade doors were propped open to emit a steady trill of electronic sounds and kids laughing and shouting. Younger kids were sitting at the Kentucky Derby and throwing balls into the slots that moved their horses in the game while a man with a money belt behind the counter shouted encouragement as if he were commentating on the Grand National.

There was a newsagent, a hairdresser's with a 'back in 5 minutes' note taped to the window, a general store and a chip shop which was doing a good trade this close to lunchtime.

The shops and lawn ended at the curve where the road headed back up to the other side of the reception building. A line of tall conifers blocked his view of whatever was behind them.

Charlie walked across the road and through the maze of caravans. He quickly got lost with her zig-zag route.

"Great T-shirt, by the way," he said.

"I love Debbie Harry."

"Me too. I had a poster of her on my bedroom wall for years."

"We might have loved her in different ways."

"Maybe," he said. "I had Blondie's greatest hits and played it so much I wore the tape out."

"When Dad bought me a stereo a few years back he got *Eat to the Beat* for me to play on it."

"Is that your favourite album of theirs?"

"Nope," she said. "It's *Parallel Lines*."

"Cool. That's mine too."

"You see," she said, "we're clearly destined to be friends. What are you listening to now?"

"I've got *Hits 3* in my Walkman."

"I've been listening to this new band called INXS. They're bloody brilliant."

"Never heard of them."

"Remind me and I'll lend you the tape."

The caravans ended at a large playing field that overlooked the sea. Several football games were underway refereed by young people wearing green T-shirts and orange shorts.

"They're camp workers in the Holidaze colours," Charlie explained.

Charlie walked across the field to narrow fence. A well-trodden footpath separated it from the edge of the cliff.

"Apparently you can walk all the way from Yarmouth to Happisburgh on this path," Charlie said. "I've never tried it."

The cliff edge was sandy and ridged with thick seagrass. A wooden staircase led down about thirty feet to the beach.

"And apart from the bikes and the golf, that pretty much concludes our grand guided tour."

"Very thorough," he said.

"Why thank you, sir," she said and gave him a mock curtsy.

They walked back into the caravans and this time she veered to the left towards the area hidden by the conifers.

"What's behind there?"

"The staff chalets," she said. "They're not very glamorous."

"How do you know?"

"Because I've been in there? Did you want to have a look?"

"Are we allowed?"

She pulled a face. "No, because we're not staff. But we're also not eight, so we can do things we're not supposed to."

He decided the Dan he wanted to be wouldn't worry about it. "Okay, let's go."

Charlie walked up a gravel path to a slatted wooden fence with a gateway in the centre of it. A sign pinned to it proclaimed 'Private – Staff Only: No Admittance'.

"Last chance to chicken out," Charlie said quietly and pushed open the gate before he could say anything.

The gravel path branched. One arm led to another gate while the other went down to a field that had been marked up as a car park. The cars there all looked the worse for wear.

"Staff car park," she said and put her hand on the latch of the second gate. As she did, it opened from the other side. With a surprised "Oh", she stepped back.

A young woman came out, wearing shorts and a bikini top under an oversized shirt. A large floppy hat hid most of her face. She had a sprinkle of freckles on her shoulders and clearly wasn't expecting to see Charlie. She squeaked out her surprise and someone Dan couldn't see laughed. The woman pushed her hat back to reveal a pretty, pale face with more freckles across the bridge of her nose. A flick of red hair fell across her forehead.

"Bloody hell, Charlie," she said. "You nearly scared me to death."

"Sorry, Becky, I didn't mean to."

As Becky came onto the walkway the person who'd laughed stepped through the gate. She too wore a bikini top and cut-off shorts but no hat and Dan recognised Mia from reception instantly. He didn't quite know where to look and didn't want her to catch him staring at her cleavage or firm midriff or her long and tanned legs. It wouldn't have surprised him if his blush ran all the way down his neck. Mia's necklace caught the sun, and this close he could see it was a circular piece of sea glass with a sunset painted on it.

"Hey, Charlie," Mia said.

"Hey," said Charlie brightly.

Mia turned her attention to Dan and something went ping in his chest. "I know you, don't I?" she asked with a small frown then clicked her fingers. "I booked you in this afternoon, didn't I?"

He nodded without saying anything, terrified of what gibberish might come out of his mouth.

"Dan?"

"That's me," he said and felt a quick burst of joy in his belly that she remembered him. "That's my name."

Charlie glanced at him with pursed lips.

"So what're you two up to?" Mia asked.

"I showed him around the camp and he asked what was behind the conifers…"

"And you told him this was where the magic happens?" asked Becky and Mia laughed.

"Nah, I told him the truth. Are you two off to the beach?"

"Yes," said Becky. "Our shifts just ended so we're going to get some sun before we start this evening. This one's singing in Neptune's at ten."

"You're a singer?" Dan asked.

Mia waved her hand as if she was scoffing at the notion. "I can carry a tune."

"She's very good," said Charlie.

The gate clattered open behind them and Dan turned to see a man in his early twenties almost filling the space. His bleached blonde hair looked almost white in the sun and his legs were tanned and muscular. He wore a pale-yellow T-shirt and Speedo trunks.

"What's this?" he demanded, narrowing his eyes at Dan and Charlie. He bunched his fists and veins stood out on his forearms.

"Give it a rest, Tommy," Mia said wearily. "They're friends of mine."

"Yeah and I've had to tell you the rules often enough. No fucking grockles back here."

Chapter 4

"Hey."

The voice took Jude by surprise and she turned to see Paul behind her in the queue of the shop. He was holding a loaf of bread.

"Hi. Small world." She held up her pint of milk. "I brought enough food to feed an army and forgot the milk."

"These things happen." He ran a hand through his hair and his cuff slipped down to reveal an expensive-looking watch. She saw him glance at her ring finger. "I'm glad I caught you."

"It's nice that you did," she said. His ring finger was clear too. It had been a long time since she'd checked anything like that and it felt a little thrilling to be looking.

"I've been at the lido all morning. Thought I'd use this shop on the off chance of catching up with you again."

"You work at the lido?"

"Kind of."

He had a wonderful lazy smile that produced a pleasant tingling in her chest. It was the most alluring smile that had been directed at her in a while.

"I'll bet you can't guess what I do though."

"I can't see you collecting money at the gate." She looked him up and down. It really was a nice suit. "You're perhaps a bit old for a lifeguard."

His mouth widened into an 'O' as he feigned shock. "Under this bespoke suit I have the figure of Adonis."

"I'll take your word for it but that only leaves me with the man who mops up in the changing rooms."

He laughed and she liked the sound of it. "You guessed wrong because I co-own the place with my business partner Andy. I'm a real estate developer and we're doing the place up."

"Sounds impressive."

"I hope it will be. Anyway, I hoped to bump into you because I wanted to ask a question."

"Go on."

He cleared his throat. "Are you married?"

"You're very forward, Mr Reid."

He smiled. "Mr Reid, eh?"

"No. I'm recently divorced."

His smile held. "I'm sorry to hear that."

"Don't be. I'm not."

Jude put her pint on the counter and the girl behind the till rang it up.

"Are you seeing anyone?" Paul asked.

The girl on the counter raised her eyebrows but kept her focus on the till.

"I wouldn't dare guess your age," he said, "but I'm in my early forties and I'll be honest, if I see someone attractive, I want to know straight away if they're available or not. Dating doesn't get easier as you get older."

Her mind snagged on 'attractive' and the tingling in her chest intensified. "I've not started dating again but I can imagine."

He looked genuinely surprised. "I can't understand why someone hasn't snapped you up."

"Well they haven't."

The girl behind the counter handed Jude her change and turned her attention to Paul.

"So as neither of us are attached and it's your first day in a new town, how about I take you out tonight? No pressure, we'll just go as friends."

It felt like a good idea. It had been a while since anyone showed any interest in her and she felt like she deserved a bit of happiness on that front, especially after Neil's foul-up.

"Where would you take me?"

"How about here?" he asked. "Neptune's Palace has a decent bar and live music." The girl handed him his change and he walked Jude to the door. "Dan can obviously come along too if he wants."

"He might have other plans."

"If he does, he does. I'll see you at eight."

Chapter 5

Mia squared up to Tommy and the air between them seemed charged. Dan suddenly felt horribly anxious and took a step to put himself between them and Charlie. She gave him a quick glance then looked back towards Mia.

"They're my friends," Mia said. "Charlie's been here almost the whole summer so she's as good a permanent resident of this camp as you are."

"But they're not workers. Come on, Mia, for fuck's sake. How many times do you need telling?"

"Not more than once, you should know that."

She almost spat the words at him and the viciousness in her tone seemed to throw Tommy for a moment or two. Then he regained his composure and stood taller to use his height as a weapon.

"No grockles, Mia."

Dan took another step forward. He was scared and could feel the threat of violence in the air but he wasn't going to stand by and let this happen. He'd had enough of bullies after this year. Tommy gave him a quick glance.

"You haven't got the high ground here, Tommy," Mia said. "You shouldn't use that word in front of the guests and anyway, in Norfolk we call holidaymakers furriners or visters. You're the grockle, you're from fucking Devon."

Tommy clenched his fist again and Dan wasn't sure how far this would go.

"But before you get your knickers in a twist," Mia said, "we were just leaving."

"Fine." Tommy's shoulders dropped. "Do whatever you want, Mia, as always."

"That's not fair," she said.

"Nothing ever is," he muttered and pushed past her.

She tried to stand her ground but he knocked her shoulder with his and she stumbled back a step.

"Hey," said Dan and felt anger rush through him. His heart raced.

Tommy turned on his heel and held up his finger in Dan's face. "Not another word."

"You didn't have to bump her," Dan said.

Tommy glared at him then left through the gate.

"He's such an arsehole," said Becky.

"Who was it?" Dan asked. He felt shaky.

"Tommy Mackintosh," Mia said. "He's in charge of the staff but he only got the job because he's Old Man Mackintosh's nephew and spent all of last summer nicking everyone's good ideas."

"Old Man Mackintosh is the camp director," said Becky.

"Tommy's not worth our time thinking about him," Mia said. She clicked her fingers and pasted on a big fake smile. "There you go, out of our lives."

Dan felt his heartbeat slowly return to normal.

"We need to make a move," said Becky.

"Sorry I caused the trouble," said Charlie.

"Don't worry about it," said Mia. "It took my mind off the fact someone told me there's a talent agent in tonight."

"Coming to see you?" Charlie asked.

"I hope so."

"So what do you sing?" Dan asked.

"Anything they want me to in Neptune's because it's fantastic practice and extends my range. I used to do a lot of Suzanne Vega kind of indie stuff but pop is what sells so I'm focussing on that. I've learned most of the *Like a Virgin* album which goes down well and if it gets me spots on open mic nights then I'm happy."

"Mia's going places," said Becky.

"Just London," Mia corrected her. "I'm heading down there," she said to Dan, "once I've got enough money together."

"The bright lights of fame and fortune," said Becky and the easy laugh she shared with Mia suggested it might be something that was often said.

"Which reminds me," Mia said. "Are we still on for tomorrow morning at the beach?"

"Yes," Charlie said.

"Good, I need some up-to-date headshots and I can rely on you."

"You really can," said Charlie and her cheeks went pink.

Becky pulled the gate open and held it for everyone to go through.

"Come and see me tonight, Dan," Mia said.

"I will."

Dan watched her and Becky walk away then became aware Charlie was speaking.

"Earth calling Dan. You're catching flies."

He was embarrassed at being caught out but couldn't think of anything to say.

"Come on, Romeo," she said. "I'll show you the pitch and putt."

They walked up the road side by side.

"I thought you were cool standing up to Tommy like that."

"He's an arsehole," he said but enjoyed the compliment and the fact Charlie thought he'd done something cool. "He shouldn't get away with that kind of thing."

"He rules the roost here and thinks he's a big man but he's really just a twat with a bit of power. He's seen me almost every day this summer but hardly said more than a dozen words."

"Why's he so down on Mia?"

"There's history. They went out for a while and it was getting serious but he did something and it all fell apart and now she's about the only person who stands up to him."

"What did he do?"

She shrugged. "It must have been bad, whatever it was, to force her away like that."

* * *

It normally cost fifty pence to hire the golf clubs and balls but Charlie knew the girl working on reception who let her have them for nothing. The first three holes went well for Dan.

"We should play for ten pence a hole," Charlie said.

"Okay. So you owe me thirty pence."

"Uh-huh," she said and took her shot without apparently aiming. It stopped an inch from the hole.

"Have you conned me?" he asked.

"Butter wouldn't melt," she said with a sweet smile.

His next shot hit something in the grass and stopped so far away from the hole it was almost as though he wasn't trying.

"Do you fancy her?" It was asked as a straight question but Dan caught her tone.

"What?" he asked, playing for time. Who wouldn't fancy Mia? She was gorgeous. But Dan was smart enough to realise now probably wasn't the best time to admit it to. "I mean she's pretty and all that…"

"She's gorgeous." Charlie pinched her lips together. "That's fine."

"What is?" He didn't understand. Hadn't Charlie told him earlier not to get any funny ideas? "I don't fancy her, Charlie."

"I told you it's fine." She tapped her ball into the hole. "You have played golf before, haven't you?"

"Yes," he said and tried to sound hurt.

She grinned at him which lightened the mood. It seemed whatever had been on her mind had apparently cleared.

Charlie won over the nine holes and Dan paid her twenty pence as they handed back in the clubs. They walked down the roadway and the smell of the conifers was heavy and sweet. She swung her arms with each step and he wondered how it would feel if their fingers touched. He was really starting to like her. Not only was she pretty but her sense of humour seemed to match his.

"Penny for them?" she asked.

Had she caught him looking at her? "Yes, why?"

"You're just being quiet. Did you want to come to the club tonight?"

"The club where all the sexy people go to dance?"

She laughed with surprise. "That's the one."

"Did you want to meet there or shall I come and pick you up?"

"Wouldn't that be a bit like a date?"

Would that be so terrible? he thought. "I don't know."

"It might be and anyway, my dad usually drops round on a Monday. How about we meet in there?"

Was he was going to have to meet her dad? "Okay."

They got to the point where the road curved and she stopped.

"Shall I walk you back?" he asked.

"It's daylight, Dan. I'm hardly going to get mugged by some young thug who wants money to play the Kentucky Derby."

He knew she was making light but it still stung and it must have shown in his face because she touched his arm.

"I appreciate the offer but I'd better not. I have nosey neighbours and one of them will grass me up to Dad that eligible lads have taken me home."

She smiled with enigmatic cool and gave him a little wave as she walked away.

* * *

His mum was reclining in a deckchair in front of the car. A glass of wine stood on the grass next to her book and she'd closed her eyes against the sun. A cigarette burned between her fingers. She'd changed into a vest top and shorts and her bare feet rested on her discarded flip-flops.

"Hey," she said.

"How did you know it was me?"

"I can tell by the way you walk." She opened her eyes and shielded them with her hand. He moved so the sun wasn't behind him. "How did it go with Charlie?"

"Great. She's a laugh."

"I'm glad to hear it. I like that you've met a new friend."

"Well, it's time for a new me."

Something crossed her face for the briefest of moments and if he hadn't been paying attention he probably wouldn't have seen it. She'd told him one evening after a glass of wine too many that she knew the divorce and his dad's actions had affected him badly. He'd let her hold his hand tightly and said he knew it had affected her badly too and it seemed to be the best thing he could have said. She tried to laugh off her tears and blame the wine but the next day she thanked him for having the maturity to see.

"Did you and Charlie eat?"

"No, have you?" Since the divorce she often seemed to survive on coffee and Benson & Hedges and it worried him.

"Not yet but I will. Time for a new me too, I think. Speaking of which, guess who I bumped into earlier?"

He only knew four people here and she didn't know three of them. "I give up."

She shook her head. "You used to be much more fun at these guessing games when you were little. Why did you have to grow up so quickly?"

"I think it's biology."

"Smarty-pants."

"So who did you see?"

"Paul. He's asked us to go to something called Neptune's Palace with him tonight."

"That's good. Charlie already asked me if I wanted to meet her there. She said it was a proper sin city, with lots of smoke and neon light and sexy dancing."

His mum smiled broadly. "The more I hear of Charlie, the more I like her."

Chapter 6

Jude looked at her reflection in the small mirror on the dressing table. The sun slanted through the window at an angle that picked out the grey in her otherwise dark hair and showed the lines around her mouth and eyes where the stress had taken its toll. The lines were made worse by the weight loss that made her cheekbones more pronounced.

"Nope," she said. "Not today."

Every now and again she had to remind herself this was her new life. She'd spent too long worrying about what had happened and couldn't be changed rather than looking to the future and starting again as a forty-year-old divorcee. Tonight might be an opportunity to start. Paul hadn't called it a date but she still had butterflies and a little bit of fun might put her back on track.

There was a gentle tap on the door. "Hey, Mum? I'm just heading out to meet with Charlie. I'll see you later."

"Have a good time, Danny."

"You too, Mum."

Jude took off her dressing gown and looked into her suitcase. She hadn't really packed for going on a date which meant she had plenty of T-shirts and shorts but only one skirt and blouse and two dresses. But then again, who cared about her clothes? How Paul felt was his own business and she couldn't change it. She'd spent too long in a relationship that had rotted from the inside out however much she had tried to repair things, and she wasn't going to go down that rabbit hole again. It was easier said than done but she had to be comfortable in her own skin now.

She'd wear a dress and put on some make-up then go and enjoy herself.

* * *

Jude was at the door when Paul arrived and parked his Jaguar behind her Fiesta. He straightened his jacket when he got out and she smoothed her dress over her belly and thighs.

"Hi," he said. He hadn't gone full *Miami Vice* but was wearing a pale sports coat with jeans and a pastel grandad shirt. His sleeves weren't rolled up. "You look fantastic."

"So do you."

"Is Dan coming with us?"

"No. He's meeting up with a girl called Charlie."

"I know a girl called Charlie. She does some work for us and is a cracking little photographer."

"She did have a camera with her," said Jude. She slipped on her only pair of heels and locked the door behind her.

He moved closer and she enjoyed the quick thrill of anticipation that he might kiss her. Instead he took her arm and helped her down the steps.

* * *

The foyer at Neptune's Palace was brightly lit and noisy with chatter. A girl in camp uniform sat behind a desk trying to tempt people to buy raffle tickets. Paul put his hand in the small of Jude's back to guide her through a set of double doors on the far wall.

The club room was busy and a lot of tables were occupied as people took part in a game of bingo. The bar took up most of the right wall and the stage was against the left with a wooden dance floor between. A spotlight trained on the mirror ball hanging over it which cast reflections across the room.

He led her to a table near the stage and pulled out a chair. "What did you want to drink?"

"White wine would be lovely."

"I'll be right back."

Jude sat and lit a cigarette as she watched Paul stop at a couple of tables to speak to the people there. Someone called house and a young woman bounded out from behind the stage to shout the numbers to the caller. The person who'd won seemed very excited to have done so.

Paul came back with a large glass of wine and sat opposite her then held up his pint in a toast. "That's better," he said. "Nothing better than wetting your whistle after a warm and busy day."

A reflection from the mirror ball caught the side of his face and as it raked across the plane of his jaw she wondered what it would be like to kiss him there.

"Or an afternoon of relaxing after a long drive over," she said.

He licked froth from his top lip. "So you came a long way?"

"It's a couple of hours' drive but the traffic was fairly light."

"So what do you do?"

"I'm head of year at our local comprehensive school."

"Better watch my language then, hadn't I?"

"Are you in the habit of swearing in front of teachers?"

"Not usually but I think you're the only one I know. What do you teach?"

"Economics for the sixth form and English literature for the main school."

"A reader then?" He shook his head. "Sorry, that was a stupid thing to say. I'm not normally this nervous."

"I'm making you nervous?"

"Are you kidding?" He leaned back in his chair. "You're very attractive and I want to make a good impression but I'm blabbing on like an idiot."

She felt a boost to her self-confidence. "You're not, but thank you."

He leaned forward with his elbows on the table. "I should have taken you somewhere in town but I didn't want you to think I was making a move. If tonight goes well, next time we'll go to a little Italian place I know in Seagrave."

"That would be nice," she said and meant it. "You said before you were doing up the lido?"

"That's right. I'm a businessman and entrepreneur who's fully embracing Maggie's philosophies. The lido's been derelict for years and the council have been happy to let it sit and rot so me and my partner got it at a knockdown price. It's prime real estate on the beach and we're putting in luxury flats."

"And you're a landlord too?"

He leaned forward as if to impart a secret. "I had spare cash and I'll be honest, I watched one of the *Confessions* films and thought that was the kind of business I'd like to be in."

"Did it pan out that way?" she asked with amusement.

"Not really. It's more like an episode of *Hi-de-Hi!*"

The bingo caller tapped his microphone. "It's now time to hand you over to our musical trio for an evening of singing and dancing. Ladies and gentlemen, boys and girls, put your hands together for The Sultans of Swing."

The crowd applauded as the bingo caller left and three men in late middle age wearing sparkly jackets and trousers with a bit too much flare in them made their way onto the stage.

The keyboard player leaned into his microphone. "Thank you very much, you're wonderful. On with the show and we'll start with a hit from the last few years."

As they went into a Human League song Jude was only barely able to identify, Paul leaned back and raised his hand. She turned to see a couple standing at the doors.

"That's my partner Andy," Paul said. "Would you mind if they joined us?"

"No, of course not." So maybe it wasn't a date after all.

Chapter 7

"This is Andy Sykes and his wife Fiona," said Paul when they reached the table. He gave Fiona a quick, oddly stiff hug then shook Andy's hand heartily. "This is Jude."

Fiona was medium height and thin with a tidy bob and a perky face. Andy was shorter than Paul and his thick hair had been styled to hide the bald spot the lights were mercilessly exposing. His suit, shirt, tie and slip-ons were light grey and his watch was very big and flashy. He looked close to fifty.

"Hello," said Fiona as she next to Jude.

"Hi."

"Andy Sykes," he said and held out his hand. In a smooth movement he turned hers and kissed the back gently.

"You'll get used to him," Fiona said. "He tends to be a bit overexcitable."

"Nonsense," Andy said and sat next to Paul. "What are we all drinking?"

"I've already–" Paul started.

"Nonsense, nonsense, a pint for you and what's that, a white wine for the lady? Be right back."

Fiona watched him go and the lights caught her face. Jude thought she might be in her late twenties or early thirties.

"That's fine," Jude said. "I like a little exuberance."

"He'll be right up your street then," said Paul.

Since The Human League hadn't roused the crowd, The Sultans of Swing went into *March of the Mods* and the dance floor filled as soon as the first bars rang out.

"So are you here on your own?" Fiona asked.

"No, my son's here too."

"And how old is he?"

"Sixteen. He's off to sixth form for his A levels."

"Sixteen?" asked Paul. "How old were you when you had him? Twelve?"

Fiona tutted and tapped his arm. "Easy tiger," she said.

"I was twenty-four," Jude said. "Do you have any?" she asked him.

"None I'm admitting to," Paul said with what he clearly thought was a winning smile.

"I don't yet," said Fiona. "But I'm planning to."

Andy put a laden tray on the table. "Who's planning what?" he asked.

"We were talking about children. Jude's son is sixteen."

Andy feigned surprise. "That can't be possible. You're surely not old enough."

"Your charming colleague already tried that approach," Jude said and Fiona laughed.

Andy sat down. "So where is this strapping lad of yours?"

"He's out with Charlie."

"Our Charlie?" Andy asked, glancing at Paul who nodded. "She's a lovely lass."

Jude saw Fiona make a quick motion with her hand, rocking it from side to side.

"She's been helping us out at the lido," Andy said to Jude. "She's a very accomplished photographer."

The *March of the Mods* finished with a flourish from the drummer and the keyboard player leaned into his microphone again. "Now we know which of you lot were mods back in the day, eh?" He continued over good-natured laughter. "But now I'd like to welcome onstage a great singing sensation…"

Fiona reacted as if she'd received a little electric shock and leaned across the table. "Did you know she was singing tonight?"

"Of course not," said Andy. He looked worried.

"You know I wouldn't have come if I'd known," Fiona said.

"Seriously, Fi, I had no idea."

"For fuck's sake, Andy."

Jude caught Paul's eye and mouthed "who is she?".

"Mia Garwood," he said. "She works here but it turns out she's a great singer."

Mia came through the wings and the drummer saluted her with one of his sticks as she walked to the front of the stage. Her knee-length black strappy dress complemented her figure beautifully and her blonde hair was tousled and held back with a thick black ribbon. Her eyes were a dark smudge and her lips were vibrant red. She had several multi-coloured bangles on both wrists and her sea glass necklace shined with the lights reflecting off the mirror ball. Jude thought she looked incredible and carried herself with real assurance that didn't veer into arrogance or that over-the-top mugging holiday camp entertainers often used.

"She's such a tart," Fiona said and venom seemed to drip off each word.

Jude glanced at her but Fiona was staring at the singer.

"No she's not," said Andy and Fiona hit him on the arm. She might have pretended it was a love tap but Andy jerked his arm away. "Ouch. What'd you do that for?"

"Seriously, Andy?" Fiona demanded.

"I was only complimenting her."

"Well don't. She hardly needs the encouragement."

"She's young," Paul said, without looking away from Mia. "Let her enjoy herself."

"She's a tramp," said Fiona. "What does she think she looks like?"

"Oh come on," Paul said. "The lead singer of that group last week wore a leotard and fishnet stockings with no underwear and you didn't say anything about her."

"How do we know she's a tart?" Jude asked but had to look away from Fiona's glare.

Nobody answered her.

Jude watched as Mia took her microphone off the stand and nodded to the keyboard player. "Well I think she looks good," she said, unsure if anyone was listening. "I wish I could have carried off a dress like that when I was her age."

The keyboard player counted the band in then played the intro to *MacArthur Park*. Jude brightened because the Donna Summer version was one of her favourite songs and that was the one Mia was doing. Her voice soared and she really did light up the room.

Fiona leaned in close to Jude. "She's not all that, is she?"

"I think she's incredible."

Fiona gave her a pitying look. "She maybe thinks she looks incredible."

"I don't know about that, Fiona, but listen to her. I love this song and she's really handling it."

The song built and The Sultans of Swing did their best but Mia never faltered. When she finished, Jude happily joined in the applause.

"She's so good," said Paul.

"I can't believe she's not a professional," said Jude.

"Thank you, Holidaze Seagrave," Mia said and somebody in the audience whooped and made her smile. She shielded her eyes against the glare of lights. "That must have been my boss, happy I got a plug in." Several people laughed at that and someone clapped. "I've only got time for three songs tonight and following that wonderful Donna Summer epic, here's something from a very new artist. I hope you like it."

The band started playing *Material Girl* and several teenaged girls dressed in close approximation to Madonna made their way to the dance floor.

Fiona stood up quickly making her chair tilt back and Paul caught the top of it so it didn't fall over. "She does my bloody head in and this song choice takes the biscuit."

"It's Madonna," Jude pointed out.

"It was lovely to meet you, Jude, and I hope we can get together another day but I need to go now because she makes my skin crawl."

Andy got to his feet slowly and Jude couldn't tell if it was because he was embarrassed by his wife or just wanted to hear and see more of Mia.

"See you tomorrow," he said to Paul and clapped a hand on his shoulder. He leaned down to Jude. "Lovely to meet you and please forgive Fiona. She's feeling a bit under the weather at the moment."

"No problem," said Jude. "I understand."

He held Fiona's arm and they moved away. Paul looked at Jude and raised his eyebrows.

"What was that all about?" she asked.

"It's a long story," he said and looked as though he wanted to tell her but really shouldn't.

"She's not a big fan of Mia, is she?"

"Nope." He finished his beer. "Sometimes Fiona gets a bee in her bonnet about things and makes up her mind and that's pretty much it. The lady is not for turning, as Maggie said. Not that Andy helps."

"What do you mean?"

Paul spread his hands. "He's that type of bloke, you know? Little bit loud, little bit lairy and likes the ladies. He's a great salesman because he oozes self-confidence."

"A bit greasy, you mean?"

"That makes him sound worse than he is. He loves Fiona but he has an eye for the ladies and they respond to him. I like that he's very sure of himself because it's great for business. In fact, I wish I'd met him years ago when I was starting out because he could have taught me plenty."

It felt to Jude like she was missing a key piece of information but didn't want to push it.

"Enough about them though. What do you have planned for your holiday?"

"I want to relax and get some sun and catch up on my reading. Danny's of an age now where he can go off and do things himself and we'll just have breakfast and dinner together."

"I could take you around the place if you want."

"As my chauffeur and tour guide?" she asked straight-faced.

He gave her a slow smile and something tingled through her chest and belly. She liked the sensation.

"If that's what you want," he said and stared into her eyes. "I can do that."

It had been a long time since anyone flirted with her and she felt hopelessly out of practice. She was worried she'd seem awkward.

"I might like that."

"Excellent."

Material Girl finished and Mia stood at the lip of the stage. "Last song for tonight, ladies and gentlemen, and this is one of my favourites. The drummer's also a big fan too." He said something that made her laugh. "*Say Hello, Wave Goodbye*," she said.

"I love this song," Jude said.

"Would you like to dance?" Paul said.

"Depends on who's asking."

"What if it were me?"

"I might be tempted."

"I like the idea of you being tempted," he said and stood up.

He held out his hand and she took it and they walked to the dance floor with several other couples. She enjoyed the contact of his skin.

They found a space and she felt awkward again, then his hands settled on her hips and she rested her arms on his shoulders.

"I'm glad you decided to come out with me," he said. His face was so close their cheeks were almost touching.

"So am I," she said and closed her eyes, enjoying his proximity and Mia's voice.

Chapter 8

Charlie looked fantastic. She was wearing high-waisted jeans and a checked blouse and her hair was bundled on top of her head. Dashes of colour marked her eyes and lips.

"Dad's got us a table," she said.

Dan followed her through the foyer and into the club. Mia was on stage singing a Donna Summer song his mum loved and the band sounded like they were trying to keep up.

Charlie led him around the dance floor to a table where a man in a dark blue polo shirt sat on his own. Charlie dropped into the seat next to him.

"This is my dad," she said.

Dan sat down as the man leaned over to shake his hand. "Simon Fraser," he said. "I'm pleased to meet you, Dan."

"Pleased to meet you, Mr Fraser."

"Call me Simon," he said. "They call me Mr Fraser at work and it makes me sound like a dinosaur."

"You are a dinosaur," Charlie pointed out.

"Thanks for that." Simon looked him up and down. "Charlie tells me you're here with your mother? Have you had a good first day?"

"I have," Dan said.

Charlie leaned close to her dad. "He doesn't need the third degree," she said then looked at Dan. "He's very nosey. It's a real problem."

"It's not being nosey," Simon said. "I'm just taking an interest."

The music finished and Simon drained his pint then checked his watch. "Sorry to love you and leave you," he said, "but I've got to get going."

Charlie looked surprised. "You're leaving already?"

"I've got a couple of things to do before I go back to the flat."

"At this time?"

"Don't worry about it," he said and patted her hand. Her expression shifted into disappointment. He stood and pushed his chair in. "It was nice to meet you, Dan. Sorry it had to be so brief but hopefully we'll see one another before you head off."

"I hope so," Dan said.

Simon dropped a kiss on his daughter's head. "Take care, Charlie. I'll see you soon."

They watched him go and Dan could almost feel the tension coming off Charlie.

"Are you okay?" he asked.

"Not really," she said with a tight smile. "Mondays are supposed to be our night. He comes over, we eat and come out to the club and catch up. And now he runs away."

She looked glumly to the stage and Dan wished he could think of something to say that would lift her spirits. Nothing occurred to him.

Mia began to sing *Say Hello, Wave Goodbye*. Dan watched several couples make their way to the dancefloor then looked at Charlie. She looked at him. His mouth dried up. With her dad gone, did this technically count as a date?

"Did you want to dance?" he asked before he could mentally talk himself out of it.

"No," Charlie scoffed in surprise.

"Okay," he said and felt about an inch tall. "I just thought you might."

"Oh," she said and blanched. "Well we could if you want, I really don't mind."

That didn't make it any better and he wished he'd kept his mouth shut now. Why did girls have to be so bloody complicated?

They both looked towards the dance floor and he caught a glimpse of his mum dancing very close to Paul. He was kind of glad Charlie had said no now. He definitely didn't want to be dancing if there was any chance he'd bump into them.

The song finished and Mia left the stage to great applause.

"I told you she was good, didn't I?" Charlie asked.

"That was Mia Garwood," said the keyboard player. "Isn't she great? When she's on *Top of the Pops* next year just remember you saw here her first at Holidaze Seagrave. But now it's time for The Sultans of Swing to bring a bit of action to the evening."

"This should be fun," said Charlie as the band began a weird interpretation of *A Town Called Malice*. "They tried *I Want to Know What Love Is* last week and the dance floor emptied in seconds."

A sense of tension seemed to have settled over the table that made Dan uncomfortable. Charlie didn't seem that happy either and neither of them spoke. When the band moved on to *Come On Eileen* people around them began to leave.

"Did you want to go?" he asked.

She brightened as he spoke to her. "We can stay if you want. I don't mind."

"The music's not getting any better," he said and she laughed. "Come on."

There was a slight chill in the air now and a ground mist covered most of the lawn. Some kids were chasing around through it and a couple were snogging in the bandstand.

"Did you want me to walk you back?" he asked.

"You're persistent, Dan, I'll give you that," she teased.

"I'm just trying to be a gentleman," he said, playing along.

"It doesn't suit you." She stood on tiptoes and kissed his cheek quickly. "I'm sorry about what I said in there."

"Don't worry about it."

"I'll try not to then. Are you about tomorrow?"

"Of course."

"I've got my photo shoot with Mia first thing so I'll call for you after that."

"That sounds good."

"Take it easy, Dan," she said and walked away. She glanced back when she reached the bandstand and gave him a wave then disappeared into the mist.

Her apology had helped him feel slightly less embarrassed about his mess-up. She was giving him another chance and he should stop worrying. He took a deep breath and decided to take the long way back to the caravan to clear his head a little.

Spotlights were dotted among the conifers and cast a diffused light across the roadway. The mist got thicker closer to the building and he could feel the chill of it on his arms. The streetlights on Marine Drive were pale shimmers.

A footstep scuffed off to his left and made him jump. Someone came from behind the conifers shining a torch at the ground. The person stopped and shined the light in Dan's eyes. He put his hand up to shield himself.

"I know you, don't I?" asked Tommy Mackintosh.

"You saw me this afternoon."

"That's it. You're the new grockle with Charlie Fraser. What are you doing wandering around here?"

"I've been in Neptune's and I'm going back to my caravan."

"No caravans up this way, mate. Don't even think about going into the staff area again."

"I won't. I just wanted a bit of a walk."

"Planning to put up some graffiti were you?"

The ludicrous suggestion took him by surprise. It seemed like Tommy was desperate to accuse him of something.

"Of course not."

"So you say." Tommy cast the torch beam along the side of the building as if checking for damage. "I don't like kids wandering around here in the dark."

Dan wanted to point out he wasn't a kid but knew it wouldn't be worth the hassle. "I won't do it again."

"You better not. Don't let me catch you out here again."

Tommy turned on his heel and went back behind the conifers. Dan felt a little short of breath now the confrontation was over. A car started up but the sound echoed between the building and trees and he couldn't make out where it was.

He walked around the corner of reception and heard a door open. Light reflected off the glass door momentarily and then Mia came out into the night. She'd changed into a short pale dress and her hair was loose. Even in the thick mist she looked gorgeous. She ran across the pitch and putt green as a car came up from the other side of the building. He couldn't tell what make it was but the headlights caught her dress and made it glow. She looked, for a moment, like a ghost rushing across the grass.

Brake lights flared and a door opened and the soft mumble of voices drifted to him. The door closed and the car drove the wrong way around the pitch and putt.

* * *

He found his mum sitting on the caravan steps with her coat over her shoulders. The smoke from her cigarette drifted into the mist around her.

"Hey, Danny. Fancy seeing you here."

"I know, weird eh?"

"How was your evening?"

"Pretty good," he said. "I met Charlie's dad and we listened to Mia."

"So did I. She's an incredible singer."

"How did your date with Paul go?"

She smiled and flicked ash by pulling her thumbnail over the filter. "It wasn't a date, but I enjoyed it. I also met his business partner whose wife really didn't like Mia."

She patted the space next to her and Dan sat down.

"I didn't think you'd be back this early," he said.

"Or me. He said he had to go and do something so we called it quits early." She took a deep drag and tipped her head back to exhale the smoke in a plume at the sky.

"Same here," Dan said.

The neighbouring caravan was in darkness and hid most of the lights from Neptune's as well as blocking most of the noise. It seemed, for a moment, that they were alone in the quiet night and it felt nice. She obviously thought the same and tapped his knee gently.

"This is what our holiday should be, Danny. A chance to forget ourselves for a while."

Chapter 9

The sun hadn't yet burned through the haze that hung over the camp and made the sky look almost sandy-coloured.

Dan had been to get a newspaper and the caravan door was open when he got back. He looked around quickly for Paul's Jaguar but couldn't see it. He didn't really fancy spending time with the bloke that morning but it was nice to see someone paying attention to his mum. She'd withdrawn into herself since the divorce and he often wondered how loneliness felt for an adult who hadn't expected to encounter it.

She was sitting at the table with Charlie as he went in. Charlie's T-shirt had 'Frankie Says' written on it and it looked way too big for her.

"Here he is."

"Hey, Dan," Charlie said with a crooked smile. "How're you doing?"

"I'm okay." He put the paper on the table and leaned against the kitchen counter.

"You should ask me how I'm doing. Girls like it when boys say it and you never know, it would make you a babe magnet."

"How do you know I'm not already one?"

"Because you didn't ask me."

His mum laughed. "She's got a point."

"Oh right," he said and joined in the fun by throwing his arms up. "So now you're ganging up on me?"

"Don't look at it like that," his mum said. "We're trying to help you."

"Is that so?" he asked sarcastically.

"Well," she said. "Sometimes we are."

Charlie laughed.

"Did you finish the photo shoot already?" he asked.

"No," Charlie said. "Mia didn't turn up which is weird because she normally lets me know. I dropped by her chalet on the way here but there was no one in."

"Are you two off somewhere nice today?" asked Jude.

"I took some pictures at the lido yesterday morning and want to get them developed so I thought I'd show Dan the sights of Seagrave."

"Paul told me last night you were taking pictures for them."

"I love it," Charlie said. "The whole place is so photogenic. It must have been great fun when you could actually swim there."

"I remember a lido from my dim and distant past," Jude said.

"She means the sixties," Dan said in a stage whisper.

Jude threw him a pretend frown. "Thank you, Danny. In the best decade ever we went to a lot of lidos and it was great fun. I remember the water was always freezing but I was a teenager so it was more a case of posing and having a laugh than swimming."

"We'd better go," said Dan. "Before she starts singing sixties classics."

"I like songs from the sixties," protested Charlie.

"I told you I liked her," his mum said. "She's got taste."

"What about you, Jude?" asked Charlie. "Are you doing anything?"

"I plan to get outside and soak up the sun, make a start on my book."

"Sounds good," said Charlie. She stood up and put on a small and colourful shoulder bag. Her Instamatic case was clipped to the strap and one orange foam ear cushion from her Walkman had escaped from the zip.

Jude kissed her fingers and pressed them to Dan's forehead. He made a show of rubbing his skin as he followed Charlie out of the caravan.

"I like your mum," she said.

* * *

Becky was unfolding the Cinzano umbrellas as they cut across Neptune's Palace's patio.

"Hey," said Charlie.

"Hey, you two. I'm sorry, I can't stop and chat."

"Is everything okay?" Dan asked.

Becky shook her head. "Not really. Mia didn't come home last night and Old Man Mackintosh is going mental because she hasn't turned up for work."

"Oh," Charlie said. "Is she alright?"

"No idea, she didn't leave a note and it's not like her to just disappear."

"I think she was going out somewhere last night after the show," Dan said. "I saw her getting into a car."

"Perhaps she met a friend from off camp," Becky said. "But I'd have thought she'd let me know."

"If she had a heavy night she might be sleeping off a hangover," Dan suggested.

"I've never seen her drink," said Becky.

"If we see her in town, I'll let you know," said Charlie.

"That'd be great," Becky said. "I'll see you later."

"That's weird," Charlie said as they walked to the roadway. "But I'm sure she'll get in touch."

"Of course she will."

"So did you want to walk into Seagrave or go in style?"

"Go in style, of course," he said even though he had no idea what it could mean.

* * *

The bike hire was behind the conifers across from the pitch and putt. A long rack held a mixture of adult and child size bicycles, all painted in the Holidaze colours with the camp name written on the crossbar. Behind them was a variety of Surrey bikes with orange frames and green canvas roofs. A dark-haired man in his early twenties sat in the small hut next to the rack. He was reading a copy of *The Home Computer Advanced Course*, which he quickly tucked behind him when he saw Charlie approaching.

His eyes were big behind thick-rimmed glasses. "How're you, Charlie?"

"Doing well, Ade. This is Dan. He's here for the week."

"Hi, Dan," Ade said and barely gave him a glance.

Dan felt ignored. "Hi."

"Can you lend me a bike to go into town?" Charlie asked.

"I really shouldn't," Ade said. "You got me into real trouble the last time."

"Did I?"

"You signed the bike out as Cyndi Lauper."

Charlie smiled sweetly at him.

"That's not going to get you out of it," Ade said. "I got a proper bollocking. And with the mood Old Man Mackintosh was in at briefing this morning I don't want to piss him off today."

"I promise I won't do it again. If you lend us a bike now we'll get it back before anyone notices and you can sign the book."

He regarded her like a pesky kid sister he couldn't resist helping out even though she was bound to get him into trouble. "Back before I close. Understand?"

"I understand."

"I'm not kidding, Charlie."

"Would I let you down, Ade?"

"You surely don't want me to answer that, do you?"

Ade gave in and they got on the bike.

"Did you really sign one out as Cyndi Lauper?" Dan asked.

Charlie nodded. "It wasn't really my fault. I'd just heard *Girls Just Want to Have Fun* on my Walkman."

They cycled away and it didn't take Dan long to get used to the Surrey bike even though he hadn't ridden one in years.

"I'll steer," Charlie decided, "and we'll both pedal."

The haze had gone now and the sky was almost cloudless but the canvas roof shaded them as they rode along Marine Drive. Other bikes in Holidaze colours went by and the riders waved at one another.

Dan couldn't resist watching Charlie and hoped she didn't notice. She looked beautiful in the sun which caught highlights in her hair and made her tan look darker. If he'd seen her at school or glimpsed her at the camp he would never have dared speak to her and yet here he was, sharing a bike and off to the excitement of a seaside town.

They passed an ornamental garden and a small go-cart track and she pulled in to the kerb.

"What's wrong?" he asked.

"Kodak moment," she said and slipped off the seat onto the pavement. "Come on," she said.

"Where are we going?" He got off the bike and walked around.

She flicked the lens cap off her camera. "Can I take a picture of you?"

"Why would you want to do that?"

"Because you're here with me and it's a lovely blank page of a day. Plus the sun is wonderful. Come on, you'll look good."

Did she just say he'd look good? Wow, the day was getting better.

"Okay."

She took a couple of pictures before he'd properly had a chance to pose then slid the lens cap back into place.

"Have you finished?"

"Uh-huh. We can go now."

She got back onto the bike and waited until he'd sat next to her then started to pedal.

"Do you collect these pictures or something?"

"Why wouldn't I? These are the real life most of us don't pay much attention to. Think about it. Everyone we pass from that bloke walking his dog to that lady pushing her pushchair has a life as full as mine and yours and that amazes me. They pass us by and then they're gone. I like to try and catch some of it if I can." She glanced nervously at him as if expecting him to laugh. When he didn't she looked back at the road. "I sound right up my own backside, don't I?"

"No, you sound…" He searched for the right word. "Is passionate a good word?"

"Yes it is. I'm passionate about photography and catching a moment that would otherwise be lost." She shook her head embarrassedly. "I sound even worse now."

"No you don't." He liked the brash side of Charlie who could wander up to a stranger's caravan and introduce herself because she was lonely and bored but there was something really nice about this quieter one too.

"Good. Once I get my A levels I'm planning to go to Huddersfield Poly because they have a photography course."

"That's cool."

"So what are you going to do, go to work or go on?"

"I'm going into the sixth form and doing computer science."

"Is that a thing?"

"Of course. Programming and stuff like that. I enjoy messing around with computers and writing little games programs and I think they're just going to get bigger and better in the future."

"You and Ade should get on well together."

"Nah, I finished The Home Computer Advanced Course ages ago."

She laughed. "Did you really?"

"Are you kidding? There were like a million parts to collect and I only bought the first few."

She steered them off Marine Drive when they reached the pier and onto a long road filled with tourist shops.

"Regent's Row," she said. "It runs up to the old town."

"I didn't realise there was an old town."

"You have much to learn, Grasshopper."

He laughed. "Yeah, like how much you need to work on your impressions."

"Oi." She tried to sound offended but it didn't quite work.

Regent's Row was on a slight hill and Dan began to feel the pressure of the incline in his legs.

"Is that where the Co-op is?" he asked.

"What Co-op?"

"The chemist's where we're getting your film developed?"

"Do you take your films to the Co-op?"

"Unless I send them off by Truprint."

"We're going to a proper chemist's shop," she said. "I'm going to develop them myself because it's the last part of the process. If I misframe an image or mess up a composition I can repair it in the darkroom. Plus if I take the world's greatest picture that has Ansel Adams looking over my shoulder" – she looked at him as if he'd know who she meant and he nodded even though he didn't – "I don't want some idiot in a lab somewhere messing it up."

Her passion animated her and he liked to see it. "So where do you work your magic?"

"Patterson's on Market Street. He likes me and loves that I'm going to study photography so he's happy for me to use his darkroom. Plus Andy pays me ten pounds to develop and print each roll I shoot for them so I'm making money too." She grinned. "He told me the secret to business is finding an angle and that's one of mine."

Chapter 10

Jude's bare feet were cold.

She'd sat in the deckchair in the full glare of the sun earlier but it was lunchtime now and the shadow of the neighbouring caravan was encroaching. She went into the caravan and tilted her neck from side to side until the tendons creaked. In the bathroom she applied more sunscreen.

The caravan felt empty and she hoped Dan was enjoying himself with Charlie. She was starting to enjoy being away from home and sitting in the sun without a worry as she read *Lace*. Her old life wasn't here and now was the time to start making changes.

Jude slipped on her deck shoes, grabbed her handbag and wrote a quick note for Dan then went out. She walked through the camp to a large playing field that overlooked the sea. A light breeze ruffled her fringe and it felt like blessed relief.

A footpath at the cliff edge ran north to south and she didn't know what was north so she went that way. The path followed a winding trail as far as she could see and the fields on the left were full of greens and yellows. Some way ahead was a building with terracotta-coloured tiles and what looked like a pub sign. If it was a pub, she decided, she'd have lunch there then walk back.

It was a leisurely stroll and she enjoyed the smell of salt in the air and the warmth of the sun on her arms and legs. Occasionally she'd hear laughter from the beach or the screech of seagulls.

Someone shouted "Hey!" from behind and she looked down to see someone in a colourful summer dress waving with one hand while the other shielded her eyes. Bangles on her wrist caught the sun.

Jude assumed it was someone being friendly and waved back. "Hi," she shouted.

"Jude! It's me." Fiona dropped her hand briefly as if to prove it.

"Hi, Fiona!"

"Where are you heading?"

"Towards that pub if it's a pub. What about you?"

"Would you mind some company?"

"Not at all," Jude said. A bit of company might be nice.

Fiona stuck up her thumb. "Keep walking. I'll come up at the next staircase."

The next stairs weren't far and she waited by the top as her new friend came up the wooden steps.

Fiona's face shined with sun cream and she fanned herself with one hand. "Hot one today."

"It really is," said Jude and they fell into step on the path.

"That was a stroke of luck seeing you," Fiona said. "I'd been thinking about getting some lunch too. I take it you were heading for The Smugglers Rest?"

"Unless it's a biker bar."

Fiona laughed. "I can assure you it's not."

It didn't take long to reach the pub. There were half a dozen cars parked outside and a knackered-looking horse stared at them dolefully from where it had been tied to a post. Fiona gave it a wide berth and Jude did the same.

The pub snug was bright and almost empty. The dark wood panelling had a sheen of age and the floor felt uneven as if generations of feet had created grooves in the boards. A small chiller unit on the bar held a selection of sandwiches and although none of them looked particularly appetising, Jude's stomach rumbled. The barmaid looked at them expectantly.

Jude chose a ham and cheese sandwich. Fiona went for one that said 'egg and cress' on the handwritten ticket but didn't look like it contained much of either.

"I'll get them," Fiona said. "Did you want a drink? I'm going to have a glass of wine."

Jude had planned to have a coffee but a chilled glass of vino after walking in the midday heat was very appealing.

"I'll join you," she said.

"Good."

Jude sat at a small round table by the window overlooking the sea. A light aircraft flew by trailing a banner that exhorted people to visit the Seagrave Hippodrome. Fiona brought over two generously filled glasses and the barmaid followed with the sandwiches on paper plates.

"Cheers," said Fiona and held up her glass.

"Cheers." Jude toasted her.

The wine was dry and crisp. Her sandwich was limp and felt chilly but it tasted better than it looked.

"I should have said this earlier," Fiona said, "but I'm sorry about last night. I was in a shitty mood and really rude."

Jude agreed but thought it best not to point it out. The woman had, after all, just bought her lunch.

Fiona bit into her sandwich and looked as if she'd chewed on cardboard.

"It wasn't the best first impression to give you, as Andy told me on our way home."

"You were harsh on the singer."

"I know but I just don't like her."

"Is there any reason?"

"Yes, I think she's trying to get her hooks into Andy." She paused and Jude met her gaze but didn't say anything. "I know it sounds mad, but he seems to attract that kind of attention."

Considering Mia was half his age there must have been something about Andy Sykes that Jude couldn't see.

"Is that right?"

"It is, and always with younger girls. Maybe it's a daddy kind of thing but…" She let the sentence fade.

"How long have you been together?" Jude asked.

"About ten years. I met him when I was in my early twenties. Probably the same age as Mia is now, thinking about it. I keep warning him but he says he doesn't see it."

"What do you see?"

"A young woman with a bit of talent and no money who wants to get out of Seagrave and catch a break." She shook her head. "Now I just sound bitter."

"No," said Jude. "I understand the dynamics."

"He's too bloody trusting, that's his problem. We're solid though and I shouldn't worry but she's so transparent it gets on my wick."

"Have you caught her saying anything to him?"

"Oh no, she's too clever for that. We got friendly a while back and I felt sorry for her. Her home life's nothing to brag about and she's got too much talent for the holiday camp but that's the way it goes sometimes." Fiona sipped her wine. "Anyway, you didn't come here to listen to me moan on. Tell me how you met Paul."

"I didn't know him at all until I got here. I got divorced and I was looking for a relatively cheap break and a friend knew Paul."

"I'm surprised. The way he talked about you I thought you'd known one another for a while."

"Really? He talked about me?"

"Ah," said Fiona and put her fingers to her lips. "Perhaps I shouldn't have said that."

"That's fine," Jude said and it was. The thought of him talking about her made her feel good.

"He's a good man and he's single." Fiona leaned forward conspiratorially. "Could there be some kind of holiday romance on the cards?"

"I hadn't planned for one."

"Well, it'd be better for you than your boy."

"Why do you say that?"

Fiona's brow pinched into a quick frown. "Charlie's very capable and self-contained but I sometimes get a similar vibe from her to the one I get from Mia."

"Do you?" Did Fiona really believe Charlie was chasing Andy? "She seemed nice enough to me."

"And I'm sure she is," Fiona said quickly. "It's just little things Andy has said."

Jude didn't want to get drawn into this discussion so she nodded then changed the subject. "Both Paul and Charlie were telling me about the lido. I'm keen to see it."

"Oh you should. Perhaps Paul will give you a tour."

Chapter 11

Market Street crossed the top of Regent's Row and the shops looked old-fashioned but well-maintained. A narrow channel between two buildings was filled with rubble and a sign proclaimed Victoria Arcade would 'soon be restored to glory'.

"I've been taking a couple of pictures of that each week," Charlie said. "I saw someone do it in the London docks a year or two back because things get modernised and people quickly forget what was there before."

"Like at the lido?"

"Yep."

She steered into a cycle bay along from a small parade of shops. Patterson's Pharmacy was double-fronted with two leaded-pane windows. A Kodak sign hung over the door.

"I love it here," said Charlie as she slipped off the bike and walked to the shop.

The man behind the counter looked over his shoulder as a bell tinkled to announce their entrance. He smiled at Charlie but there was something sour in the expression. He didn't seem happy to see Dan.

"Well if it isn't Charlie."

"Hi, Malc. Is your dad about?"

"Just nipped out," Malc said.

Dan followed her to the counter. The shop was tidy and precise and all the price tags he could see were handwritten.

"I'm going to use the darkroom if that's okay?"

"Always," Malc said. "And if you need any help, just give me a shout."

"I think I'm on top of things," she said and beckoned for Dan to follow her to a door marked 'private'.

"I'm not sure my father would want you to take your little friend in there."

"I'm sure he won't mind," Charlie said. "Dan's very interested in photography too."

Malc looked Dan up and down and his attention felt uncomfortable. "Yeah, I'm sure he is."

"We shouldn't be long."

"Make sure you aren't," he said and looked at Dan. "You be careful in there. Don't touch anything you're not supposed to."

The insinuation was clear and Dan felt Charlie bristle at it.

"No problem," Dan said.

Charlie opened the door and Dan followed her into a brightly lit small room with a central worktop, cupboards around the walls and no windows. There were several pieces of equipment on the table that reminded him of items from the science lab at school. The shelves were filled with trays, bottles and racks and a line with pegs on it hung across the room. There was a sink against the far wall and the air smelled sweetly chemical.

"Malc can be a bit of a creep. A couple of times he's come in with me and always managed to get too close."

"There's not a lot of room."

"There's even less with him about." She shook her head. "Have you ever been in a darkroom before?"

"Nope."

"Okay. I'll talk you through stuff." She took a plastic film case out of her bag then put the bag on a shelf. She slid the film roll into her palm then put her hands into a large, padded box. "I need to open the film so can you switch the lights off when I tell you?" She jutted her chin over his shoulder and he turned to see two light switches on the wall. One was white and the other red. "Hit the white one," she said.

The darkness was so complete it seemed to press against him and he held the table for support. Something popped and he heard rustling.

"I've opened the film cassette."

"What's the box for?" he asked.

"Extra protection. The tiniest bit of light can destroy the negative and trust me, you only let that happen once."

He listened to her work. "How long did it take you to learn how to do this?"

"Quite a while. I started doing it at school when I worked on the student magazine in the fifth year and got fed up with older boys telling me what to do so I taught myself from library books. A couple of years back I wandered around Seagrave one day and asked in all the chemist's until Mr Patterson gave me a chance. He showed me the basics then let me get on with it providing I didn't touch any of the films his customers left. By the end of that week though, I was developing their photographs too."

She wound something and moved towards him. Her perfume had a clean fresh scent that was very pleasant. Something clicked loudly.

"Done," she said and then, in a surprisingly good impression of Sting, sang, "Roxanne! Can you just put on that red light switch?"

He felt along the wall until he found the two light switches. "What happens if I put on the normal light?"

"You and I will have a major falling out."

He flipped the switch and the room was bathed in a soft red glow. "That was lucky," he said.

"Good for you." She filled a pint container with some liquid. "This is developer fluid. Would you like to help?"

"So long as it doesn't make us fall out."

"It won't." She handed him a glass. "Fill this with cold water from the sink."

He did as she said and handed it to her. Charlie poured the developer fluid into a metal flask then topped it up with the tap water. She took off her watch and laid it face up on the table.

"Ten minutes until it's ready," she said.

"What shall we do until then?"

She looked at him through her eyelashes. "Are you flirting with me, Dan?"

He felt heat in his cheeks and hoped she didn't notice with the red lightbulb. "No."

She mumbled something that might have been "shame" but he wasn't sure.

"It makes a nice change to be in here and not have to be on guard." She shook her head. "I threatened Malc the last time that I'd tell his dad everything. He's like a bloody octopus when you switch off the lights." She checked her watch. "How about we ask each other a question? You go first. Ask me anything."

"Anything at all?"

She brushed some hair away from her face and gave the flask a shake. "Yes."

"How come you get to spend your entire summer on the coast?"

"It's the way things turned out." He thought that was all she was going to say but then she took a deep breath and exhaled so it blew her fringe up. "My dad's an accountant with a lot of clients in what he calls the entertainment industry which mostly means comedians, singers and dancers who do the club circuits. Louise was one of his clients and one thing led to another and they started to go out. She's a professional dancer and very good – she's been on the telly and cruise ships – but she grew up here and loves the pier so she does the summer season in Seagrave. If he wants to keep seeing her, he has to be here for the summer."

He frowned. She'd raised more questions than she'd answered there and she clearly knew it.

"But then…"

"Why do I live on my own in a caravan all summer while he's in a flat in town with his bit of stuff?"

"That wasn't quite how I was going to say it, but yes."

"Me and Louise don't get on. I was nine when we met and she didn't take to me at all." Charlie checked her watch again. "Once the summer season's over we head back to Sheffield and she calls in when she can."

"Couldn't you live with your mum during the summer?"

She quirked an eyebrow. "Hardly. She died when I was little."

Dan wanted the ground to swallow him even though Charlie's expression hadn't changed. "I'm sorry."

"It's not your fault."

"I should have asked your favourite band or something."

"Altered Images," she said without missing a beat. "I don't mind talking about this though. In fact it feels good to be telling you because I don't talk enough about her. I'd just started school and she got a part-time job to fit in with the hours. One day she was crossing near Castle Market and some drunk driver went by trying to light a cigarette.

He reckoned he didn't see her, or the other half-dozen people on the same crossing, and got put away. She died on the way to the hospital."

Dan felt as if all the air had been sucked from his lungs. "That's terrible."

"It really was," Charlie acknowledged. "My auntie Flo got me from school and all I remember about that day is how big and red her eyes were. I didn't realise at the time it was because she'd spent the day crying. Dad took it really badly, as you can imagine."

"How did you take it?"

"As hard as you'd expect even though everyone kept telling me kids bounce back. Dad did his best and we muddled along for a few years then he met Louise. That's why her rejection really hurt. I thought they'd get married and we'd be like a proper family again and when I found out we'd live at the coast for two months a year I was made up." She rubbed her hands together. "But life isn't a Disney story. Louise was in her early twenties and had ambitions that didn't include a little kid who was a bit broken. She wasn't a wicked stepmother or anything but it didn't work."

Dan watched the emotion flash through her eyes and felt like he wanted to comfort and protect her.

Charlie picked up her watch. "My turn then."

His thoughts were a jumble. "Okay."

"How come you're here at the arse-end of the season? It's unusual for people to start their holidays now and certainly on a Monday."

"It's all we could afford. I told you."

"That's part of it but there's something else."

"It's kind of complicated," he said but that was mainly because he was never really asked to tell the story from his perspective. As soon as people found out who his dad was, they knew the story and that was that. On the other hand, this was partly his mum's story and she knew Charlie so it didn't seem fair to say. "I don't want to hurt my mum."

"Shit. Is your dad dead?"

"Nothing like that."

"But it would hurt Jude if you told me?"

"Yes but I really do want to tell you."

"Well don't. I don't want you to hurt Jude." She checked her watch. "Anyway, we're ready."

She turned the flask over and over then emptied it into the sink. She took a plastic bottle off the shelf above her head.

"This is stop bath and stops the film from developing further." She filled the flask and counted to thirty then emptied it out. She picked up another bottle and refilled the flask. "This is stabiliser and after this we can expose the film to light. You might have to time it on your watch though, as it takes five minutes."

They didn't speak as she rocked the flask and he checked the time but they occasionally looked at one another. She stuck out her tongue at one point and laughed. He did the same back.

After the five minutes she poured out the stabiliser and opened the flask. She washed the film reel under cold water for a minute or so then pegged the negative strip to the line and pulled it taut with a bulldog clip attached to the edge of the table.

"It's got to dry so let's go and have crab cakes for lunch."

* * *

They rode down to Marine Drive and Dan watched glimpses of golden sand and the sea go by before they pulled into a car park behind a roller skating rink.

"Have you ever had crab before?" she asked.

"Isn't it expensive?"

"It can be but all I need from you is ten pence."

"Ten pence?" He followed her across the car park and over the road to the Fun Time arcade. "Are we just leaving the bike there?"

"Nobody will nick it."

"How do you know?"

"I don't," she admitted. "But if they do, we've got a long walk back."

"What will Ade say?"

"You're both into computers, I'll leave you two talking and sneak away."

"Nice," he said.

She held out her palm and he put a ten pence piece into it. "Thank you. Now we'll eat like kings."

"How are we going to do that?"

Charlie tapped her nose. "That's for me to know and you to find out. I have a secret method."

She changed the ten pence to twos then set to work on a tuppenny falls machine. Within a few minutes she'd filled a coin pot with winnings. Within ten minutes she had upwards of ten pounds and decided that was enough. She cashed it in for one-pound coins.

"Now we'll eat like royalty," she said.

Dan felt the heat of the sun on his arms as they queued at a seafood hut near the funfair. It took almost ten minutes to get served and Charlie assured him a queue for a fish place at the seaside was a good sign.

The owner was short with thick arms and jet-black hair and he greeted her like a long-lost friend. "Great catch in today, Charlie, if you're looking for crab."

"Always, George. Your crab cakes are the best."

He gave her two large portions and only charged for one. Even though she thanked him profusely and offered to pay more he wouldn't have it and shooed them away after making her promise she'd come back.

They sat on the edge of the promenade and Charlie slipped off her loafers and wiggled her toes in the sand as they ate. Dan took a tentative bite and found he liked crab a lot.

Chapter 12

By the time they got back to Patterson's, an older man in his sixties with white hair and half-moon glasses stood behind the counter.

"Charlie!" he exclaimed. "Malcolm said you'd been in."

"We just nipped out for some lunch while the film dried, Mr Patterson. This is my friend Dan."

"Well hello, Dan. Any friend of Charlie's is a friend of mine."

"Thank you," Dan said.

"Is it okay if I go and print up a contact sheet?" she asked.

"Of course," said Mr Patterson. "You do that better than me these days."

Charlie and Dan went back into the darkroom and she switched on the overhead light. He closed the door but Charlie hadn't moved far enough into the room and he bumped her.

She glanced over her shoulder and smiled. "Easy tiger."

"Hey, you stopped so I'd bump into you."

Her smile widened. "Oh yes, is that a fact?"

"Probably not," he said and she laughed.

Charlie unclipped the negative roll and took a plastic sheet out of one of the drawers. She cut the negative roll after every six frames and fed each one into little sleeves on the sheet.

"Do me a favour, Roxanne," she said and nodded over Dan's shoulder.

He put on the red light and switched off the overhead.

"I'm going to print up the negatives onto a contact sheet so we can look and see if any are worth printing up."

"You don't just print them all?" he asked.

"That's too expensive, especially if they're garbage shots."

"The kind you get with little stickers on from Truprint?"

"Exactly."

She lifted the lid of a narrow box on the table to reveal a glass base. "This is the printing frame," she said and laid a sheet of photo paper on the glass. She put the negative wallet on top of it.

Charlie moved with purpose and ease and Dan thought it was the first time he'd seen someone his age so locked into something that clearly fascinated them.

"You're very good at this," he said.

"I try."

"You know this stuff like it's your job."

"I wish it was."

She closed the printing frame lid and slid the box under a piece of equipment that looked like an overhead projector.

"This enlarges the image," she said and pressed a button that shined a light onto the printing frame.

She counted to twenty then opened the lid and took out the photo paper. She slipped it into the first of three trays then lifted it out with tongs to put into the second. Twenty seconds later she put it into the third. By now Dan could see images on the paper. After counting to thirty she picked it up with tongs.

"Almost done." She ran the paper under the tap then shook it off and pegged it up. "Now we wait for it to dry. It doesn't take long." She folded her arms. "So your dad's still about?"

Her curiosity from earlier had obviously got the better of her.

"He is."

"How would it hurt Jude if you told me?"

"It would hurt her if she knew you knew."

"Did he have an affair?"

"Uh-huh."

"How did she find out?"

It was one question too many. The honest answer was when the police turned up at the door, but if he left it there Charlie was just going to have more questions.

"I can't," Dan said. "It's not that I don't want to tell you but…"

She held out a hand. "I'm just being nosey." She unpegged the photo paper and laid it flat on the table. "You can put on the normal light now. This is now the contact sheet."

She put it into an oversized envelope while he switched the lights.

"I've got into the habit of checking my contact sheets at the caravan. Mr Patterson told me one of the older photography shops had shut down and were getting rid of stuff so I picked up a loupe from there."

"A loupe?"

"It's a gizmo to check the prints. I'll show you it."

"Why don't you check them here? Is it because of Malc?"

"He should be so lucky," she said with a sour laugh. "I just don't like people behind me when I'm working. I was fine until I was laying out some photographs at the lido."

"Why? What happened?" Was Paul some kind of pervert?

"There's a big display table in the main office and I'd spread some of my prints around to see them better. I heard Andy come in but didn't pay much attention until he was standing close enough behind me that if I'd moved back a centimetre I'd have had his knob pressing against my bum."

"Yuck."

"I know. That's what I thought. I mean Andy's ancient. He's in his fifties. It's grim."

"Did he say anything?"

"He didn't have a chance and that's what was worse. His wife came into the office and bloody freaked out. She shouted at him and glared at me as if I'd done something wrong. If she'd waited five seconds, she'd have seen me giving him a mouthful but no such luck. She hasn't said a civil word to me since."

"Bloody hell."

"I know and that's why I check everything at home so I can't get into trouble. Let's head back to the camp."

Chapter 13

Jude saw the Jaguar as she turned the corner and felt a nice tingle of surprise.

Paul got out as she got closer and the way he quickly looked her up and down was subtle but she still saw it. "Hope I'm not calling at a bad time."

"I'm on holiday. No time is bad and it's nice to see you."

He looked good in tailored suit trousers and an Oxford shirt with his tie loosened. He'd rolled up his sleeves and his heavy watch face was almost on the back of his hand. He looked successful and sexy and thoroughly at ease with himself.

"And after the day I've had, you really are a sight for sore eyes."

She looked down at herself. "You must have had a really bad day."

"You wouldn't believe me if I told you. As much as Andy keeps telling me we property developers are the playboys of the eighties, there are days when I feel like I'm trying to roll a rock up a hill with my nose."

"I'm sure we all feel like that at times."

"Absolutely. So I thought I'd come and blow off some steam and be incredibly forward and ask you to lunch."

"Oh," she said with real disappointment. "I've just had a sandwich with Fiona."

He quirked an eyebrow. "Lunch with Fiona, eh?"

"It wasn't planned. She saw me from the beach and we went to The Smugglers Rest."

"Nice pub. Okay then, so plan B. Would you like to come and see the lido?"

"I would love to."

They got into his car and he drove out of the camp carefully, wary of all the little kids.

"Nice car."

"Thanks. The leasing company will be very happy to hear that."

"Do you and Andy both lease?"

"Uh-huh, and we swap and change the cars depending on who's where. It's okay when he drives because we're roughly the same height but when Fiona uses it, I can barely get in." He turned left onto Marine Drive. "I live over there."

Jude widened her eyes as she looked where he pointed. "In one of those monsters? Wow. You property developers really are the playboys of the eighties."

He laughed. "It might look grander than it really is. I only have the first-floor corner apartment."

"It still looks very grand to me."

"I'd love to give you a guided tour."

She looked at him. "I wouldn't mind that at all."

"Then we'll make it happen."

He drove further and they passed the pier. Some of the stalls there were already shuttered.

"Tail end of the season," he said as if he'd known what she was looking at. "Some of the craft stalls don't open until the evening."

"Have you lived in the town long?"

"I came over from Worcester in the mid-seventies. I got fed up of the hills and grand views and decided I wanted to live somewhere completely flat." He laughed. "I like looking at the sea as well."

"Were you into property then?"

"Kind of. I was an estate agent and enjoyed meeting the sellers and trying to guide their thinking because most of them believed they were sitting on goldmines. I got out in 1979 when everything slowed down and I was able to buy properties up cheaply."

"How did you and Andy come to work together?"

"Seagrave isn't that big and people know one another. Sometimes we were bidding against each other on projects and other times we were in the pub laughing about colleagues who'd lost their shirts on bad deals we'd had the sense to step away from." He pointed towards a building a couple of hundred yards ahead of them. "That's the Winter Gardens."

Jude looked out to see a large building made of glass and white metal. It looked majestic and beautiful. "That's lovely."

"The council sold it off in 1981 and some idiot thought he could pick it up for pennies and turn it around. He lost a fortune. Eventually someone figured out how to make it a popular venue and it's thriving now and as lovely inside as out. I'm annoyed I missed the boat with it, to be honest. Andy and I were talking about it one day and discussed the idea that if something like it came up again we should throw in together. Which is what we did with the lido."

"What exactly are you planning to do with it?"

"We're bringing glamour to the east coast," he said with a knowing smile. "That's one of the taglines on our brochures Andy came up with because he's really got the gift of the gab."

"I do like a good salesman," she said with sarcasm.

He raised his eyebrows. "The lido is going to become a luxury apartment complex like you see in the USA with a series of units built around the existing pool. We're going to keep as much of the original building as we can and put in a tower too. We're talking big-time London-style apartments with all mod cons at every step of the way."

"That sounds like a big project."

"Oh it's very ambitious and we're sticking our necks out but if it comes off we're talking Monopoly money." He pulled a face. "Of course the opposite is also true. I've got a lot tied up with this so if it doesn't come off then I'll end up working in the arcades."

"That doesn't sound so positive."

He chuckled. "Nah, I'm just a Gloomy Gus. Look at everything happening in London right now. Property prices are booming, the docklands is exploding and people are looking to invest. I think we're riding the crest of that wave."

"I hope you are."

They lapsed into a comfortable silence and drove past Seagrave Funfair which was enclosed by a high wooden fence that hid all but the tops of the largest rides. At the far end was a tall wooden rollercoaster and as a series of cars roared through it, Jude could hear the riders screaming. Beyond the fair was a grassy track to the beach and Paul stopped just after it.

"Here we are," he said and Jude looked up at a blank red brick wall. "Imagine this with some neon and geometric shapes."

"I'll try. Perhaps you could get a Patrick Nagel print of a swimsuit model?"

"Now that's an idea," he said and pretended to write in a pad as he got out. "I've made a note."

Two metal gates were locked with a heavy chain to bar the entrance.

"Some parts aren't safe and Andy was worried about getting sued." He unlocked the padlock and pulled open one gate and gestured for Jude to go up the brick stairs to a landing where two broken turnstiles stood lonely guard.

"Wow," she said.

A wide walkway surrounded a fan-shaped pool whose concrete base was green with mould that looked worse against the white-tiled walls. Access ladders for swimmers had rusted blood-like trails. Three diving boards were set up at the far end and there was a large hole in the sea wall behind them.

To her right was a small concrete terrace that extended slightly over the pool and led to a two-storey building with plenty of windows. Dock cranes were just visible over the tiled ridge.

"Those were the old offices and we've converted one into a display room to show off to the investors in."

A terrace opened off the office block and was supported on this side by brick pillars. It ran the length of the pool and although the undercroft was deep in shadow, she could see two doors.

"Changing rooms and storage," he said.

It looked decrepit and in need of attention but she could still see the beauty in the place and the view was glorious.

"It might not look like much, but it will."

"I believe you," she said.

"Shit."

"What?"

"I think there's a door open," he said and pointed towards the undercroft. "I need to check because if someone gets in and gets hurt we're in trouble."

"Do you have security?"

"We share a guard who patrols between the funfair and the docks but he doesn't spend much time here. It's only going to take one teenager or tramp to get through the fencing and we've got problems."

"Couldn't they just climb over the sea wall? That's a big hole over there."

"Not really. The beach is a good drop down onto rocks and it's a rendered wall." He started down the steps. "I'll only be a minute."

"Can I come with you?"

"Sure," he said and held out his hand for her. "Just be careful."

They went down the steps and crossed the terrace and up into the shadow of the undercroft. The nearest door to them was slightly open.

"It's probably just the wind," he said and opened it wider.

The hinges squealed and echoed across the expanse of concrete. Jude peered into the darkness only broken by faint glows high up on the walls.

"These were the changing rooms," Paul said. "Those grills by the roof let in fresh air and some light. Hold on a second." He patted the wall and something rattled. "Mind your eyes," he said and clicked on a torch. "We keep this hanging up just to be safe."

The bright beam picked out a long wide corridor with tiled floor and walls that looked as if they hadn't been cleaned in years. The changing cubicles were against the sea wall and the doors were in primary colours. The air smelled damp and sour.

"Anyone here?" Paul called. His voice echoed lightly but nobody replied. "You stay here and I'll go down and check. I'm pretty sure it's empty though."

Jude stood by the door as he walked cautiously down the corridor. He opened a door and the light faded. He was gone for perhaps a minute then came back.

"The communal changing room and showers are through there so I had a good look around and there's steps leading down to the pump room but it all seemed empty. I think we're on our own this afternoon."

As he put the torch back the beam swept up the wall.

"Hold on," Jude said.

"What's up?"

The grill at the top of the wall was about two feet wide and she could see the sky through the mesh. Slightly above it and just below the ceiling was a deep crack that stretched as far as the torch beam allowed her to see. Plaster had come away so the gash looked like a ragged mouth.

"That doesn't look good," she said.

"I mentioned it to Andy because he's in charge of the construction side of things and it's apparently subsidence."

"That's what I'd have said."

"You know about this stuff?" he asked with surprise.

"Not much. My sister and her husband tried to buy an old terraced house when they got married and found a crack like this across their back bedroom. The survey report found it and they couldn't get the mortgage. Subsidence is not your friend."

"We've had surveys done," he said in a defensive tone. "The site manager said it's fixable."

It looked bad to her but maybe she was wrong. Andy and Paul were hardly likely to take on a project if the surveys said not to.

"I'm sure it's fine," she said. "I know nothing about construction."

He moved towards the door and she followed but her foot caught something. She stumbled and Paul caught her arm but dropped the torch. Her momentum pushed him into the wall and she fell against him. Her heart thudded and her toe throbbed.

Their faces were so close she could see the stubble on his chin and from this angle his lips looked good enough to kiss.

"Are you okay?" he asked and looked at her intently.

She looked into his blue eyes and her stomach seemed to flip-flop. He tilted his head forward and she matched the movement.

Their lips touched and it felt like someone had lit her up. The kiss was prolonged and their tongues tentatively explored. When it broke they were looking into each other's eyes.

"Sorry," he said. "I didn't plan for that to happen."

"I know, I fell onto you."

"Spontaneous," he said.

She kissed him quickly and stood up straight. "Always the best way."

"Always," he said and traced the line of her jaw with his fingertips.

"Is this one of your moves?" Jude asked as she enjoyed the sensation of his touch.

"Oh yes," he said with a lazy smile. "I often bring ladies out to my lair for our first kiss."

"If it works it works."

"Something like that," he said.

After he jammed the door shut, they walked across the terrace and he held her hand.

"Are you doing anything tonight?" he asked.

"Not unless The Sultans of Swing are back at Neptune's Palace because I can't miss that. Why?"

"Because I'm having a dinner party with Andy and Fiona and I'd love for you to come."

"Do you think they'd mind?"

"I don't care. Will you come?"

"I'd love to."

Chapter 14

Ade was out of his shed and shooing them off the bike before Charlie had braked to a halt.

"What's the rush?" she asked.

"Tommy's on the warpath and if he found out I'd let you use another bike he'd kill me."

"I won't tell him," she said. "And if he does kill you, I'll kill him."

"That isn't helpful," Ade said and wheeled the Surrey bike around behind the rack.

"Has Mia not turned up yet?" Dan asked.

"Nope. The reception has gone up the spout and made Old Man Mackintosh short on field staff so Tommy's letting everyone know."

"That's really not like her," said Charlie.

"That's what Becky says. I reckon Mia had enough and left."

* * *

They walked down the roadway towards the lawn and it was cool and pleasant in the shade of the conifers. Someone was emptying bottles into a bin behind the fence and whistling *Into the Groove*. It made Dan think of Mia and obviously had the same effect on Charlie.

"It doesn't make any sense," she said. "I've never known her to skive off and why would she risk losing her job before she'd done her auditions?"

"Perhaps the person in that car she got into was offering her a job."

"Do you think they offered it before or after saying 'do you want to see my puppies, little girl'?"

"Hey, I don't know," he said. "Perhaps she got some bad news from her family and had to leave."

"She'd have told someone, and anyway, her dad lives in Seagrave so she wouldn't be away for a day seeing him."

"Does she have a boyfriend?" In Dan's experience, girls as beautiful as Mia always had boyfriends.

"Not that I know of."

Becky walked onto the roadway and waved when she saw them. "Have you heard anything?"

"No," said Charlie. "We just got back onto camp."

"Nobody knows anything." Becky looked tired and frustrated. "I haven't had a moment to myself since roll call and Tommy's been an absolute shit because we're short-staffed and I'm worried sick. He keeps saying she's out of order and being deliberately obnoxious but everyone else is worried."

Someone shouted her name and they all turned to see Tommy coming towards them.

"What the fuck are you doing? You're supposed to be on the field supervising the rounders not gabbing up here with these…" He paused and glanced at the photograph envelope Charlie was carrying. "These grockles."

"She's not gabbing," Charlie said.

"My shift's finished," Becky said carefully as if she was trying to keep calm. "It's been a hot day and I feel like I'm melting so I'm going back to my chalet for a rest." She checked her watch. "I told Alison I'd help her out on the donkey derby at three so all the time you're talking is delaying me."

Tommy looked like he knew he was beaten but didn't want to lose face. "Well, just make sure you're there. I've had enough today with the whole world stopping for Mia bloody Garwood."

"Do you really think she's skiving?" Becky asked.

"Why not? Her head's full of dreams and she can't wait to get away. You know that. Something's come up and she's taken a chance and bugger to the rest of us."

"That's not true," Becky said sharply. "And if you didn't have such a downer on her you'd see that."

"All I see is that she's let the team down badly."

"You're an arse, Tommy Mackintosh," Becky said and pushed past him.

Charlie followed her.

"What're you looking at, grockle?" Tommy said to Dan.

He felt his stomach turn circles but knew he had to stand up for himself. "I don't know," he said after a moment. "The label's fallen off."

Tommy covered his surprise with a sneer. "Fucking kids," he muttered and walked away. "You're not as smart as you think you are."

"We're smarter than you," said Dan but Tommy either didn't hear him or chose to ignore it.

"Anyone would think he ran the place," Charlie said.

"He wishes," Becky said. "But when Mia comes back he's going to make her life hell."

"Might she have left you a message?" Charlie asked.

"If she did it would probably have been dropped off at the chalet. Do you want to come back with me to check?"

"Sure."

They'd almost reached the top of the hill when Charlie's dad intercepted them. He was wearing a suit and looked too hot.

"Where have you been?" he demanded, slightly out of breath.

Charlie held up the envelope. "To Patterson's to develop my film."

"I didn't know you were heading into town today."

Charlie tilted her head. "You didn't ask."

Simon glanced uncomfortably at Becky and Dan. "All the same, I'm glad I found you. Auntie Flo is in town and we're going to see her."

"Now?"

"Yes, now. She's waiting in the caravan. I said we could catch a show on the pier then meet up with Louise and get some dinner."

"But I was going to…"

"We don't see Auntie Flo often," Simon said, slowly and carefully like he was dealing with a reluctant toddler. "It won't kill you to spend a few hours with her or me and Louise."

Charlie shot him a look and Dan saw he had the good grace to look slightly abashed.

"Let me know," Charlie said to Becky.

"I will."

"Come on," said Simon. "Flo's waiting."

"Well that was awkward," said Becky as they watched them walk away.

"Yeah."

"Come on then, Dan. Let's go and see if there's a message."

The path to the staff chalets led down from behind Ade's shed and ended at a latched wooden gate that Becky pushed open.

"This was the original camp," she said. "It's a bit tatty now."

He saw four small chalets, each with a front door, picture window and a flat roof. One had been painted in bright colours but the others looked shabby. A slab path led between the two middle units and Becky walked down it to the next block of four. Two of these had deckchairs and clothes horses full of drying uniforms in front of the windows. Another had an ash-filled barbecue.

Becky pulled a key out of her pocket as she went into the third block and opened the door to number eleven. "Welcome to my home," she said and went in.

Dan followed her into a spartan living room with a kitchen area to his left and three doors in the back wall. A Live Aid poster hung over the television and Duran Duran smouldered from a poster between two of the doors.

Becky went through the middle door but didn't close it. He heard a spray of deodorant and a few moments later she came back into living room wearing cut-off jeans and a Joan Jett T-shirt. Her feet were bare.

"Did you go?" Dan asked, jutting his chin towards the Live Aid poster.

"I wanted to, but Old Man Mackintosh wouldn't let us, even though we were going to hire a minibus. On the day, everyone moved their televisions into the windows so whenever you got a moment you could run back here and watch a band or two before you had to head back. Did you go?"

"No." He'd watched most of it with his mum because her decree absolute came through that day and although she said she was happy, there were tears in her eyes. "Wish I could have done though."

Becky went into the kitchen. "She hasn't left a message. We leave notes to one another on the fridge, and if she'd rung the front office, they would have posted it through the door." She looked ill at ease. "This really isn't like her. We've been room-mates for three years and she's probably the most reliable person I've ever met in my life."

"Could she have gone home?"

"This was her home," Becky said. "Her dad threw her out a few years ago and she's had virtually nothing to do with him since." She tapped her teeth with a finger. "There is another way she might have left a message."

Becky went to the furthest door on the right and Dan followed her into a bedroom that looked like a bomb had gone off in it. The wardrobe doors were open but most of the clothes were either on the floor or the bed. A poster of Smurfette gazed at them from the wall.

"She's not the tidiest," said Becky and opened the top drawer of a chest. She took out a wooden jewellery box decorated with Smurfette stickers.

"Mia likes Smurfs, doesn't she?" Dan asked.

"She liked Smurfette," Becky corrected him.

She opened the jewellery box and took out a tray laden with thin chains and bracelets and a few rings. Underneath was a man's leather wallet and when Becky checked inside it, Dan saw a lot of notes.

"She's been saving," Becky said. "She was planning to go to London and this looks as full as I've ever seen it, so if she went anywhere she went without money."

"Which is unlikely.

"Unless she met up with her boyfriend."

"Charlie said she didn't have one."

"She kind of does," Becky said. "But it's a secret and if I tell you any more you have to promise me it won't go any further."

"Who do I know here to tell?"

"Charlie," she said as if it was obvious. "She idolises Mia and it would hurt her that she didn't know but I think Mia is a little embarrassed about it. He's more of a sugar daddy than a boyfriend."

Dan had never heard the term. "A sugar daddy?"

"An older man who's helping her out. It's her big secret and I found out by accident but she wouldn't tell me who he was so he's either married or involved elsewhere."

"Oh," said Dan and felt a little stab of sourness. After his dad's exploits he was short on sympathy for people having affairs.

"Don't be like that. I could hear you making a judgement in your tone."

"I'm not," he protested.

"Whoever it was, he made her happy and she was talking about moving away with him to London. She needed to get away because no one was going to appreciate her talent properly here. Just because he made her happy didn't mean she wasn't ashamed though. If the news got out, he'd be a hero for bonking a young woman and she'd be a slag for breaking up a marriage."

"I won't tell Charlie."

"Thanks." Becky sat on the threadbare sofa under the window. "The only other option is that whoever was in the car wasn't her boyfriend."

"Why would she get into the car if he wasn't?" Dan asked.

"We're assuming she had a choice. Perhaps she turned down the wrong bloke and he didn't take no for an answer. Mia's pretty and men hit on pretty women all the time. Mostly you can deal with it but if they've got a drink in them, they think they're Richard Gere."

"You think she's been kidnapped?" he asked.

"Not really," she said. "But it's the seaside. There are new people here every week and some very odd things happen from time to time." She shook her head. "Look at me jumping to conclusions. I'm going to sound really silly tomorrow when Mia turns up, aren't I?"

"Do you think we should go to the police?"

"And tell them what? I think people have to be missing for longer than a day before you report them."

"So what do we do now?"

She shrugged. "We wait. That's all we can do."

* * *

When Dan got back to the caravan the front door was open.

"Mum?"

"I'm in my room," she called through the closed door. "I'll be out in a minute."

He went into the lounge and switched on the portable. The *Anglia News* was almost over and a smiling blonde woman was standing on a beach eating some fish and chips.

His mum came out wearing a red and white dress that didn't reach her knees. "Hey," she said. "How was your afternoon?"

"It's been a bit odd."

She padded to the lounge in her bare feet and sat next to him. "What's up, tiger? Is everything okay with you and Charlie?"

"We're fine but Mia's gone missing."

"Missing's a strong word to use. Are you sure?"

"Nobody's seen her since last night and her friend Becky said the bloke who runs the camp is apparently going spare."

"Perhaps she just went out with friends and lost track of the time."

"Apparently it's not like her to let people down."

"Well, fingers crossed she comes back tomorrow."

"Yeah," he said. "You look very smart."

"I'm going out," she said and there was a twinkle in her eyes. "It's not a date but Paul's invited me to a dinner party and I'm looking forward to it."

"That's great," he said and meant it. She deserved some happiness. "Just remember though that I don't want you bringing random men back here late at night, young lady."

"I hardly think that's going to happen but I'll bear it in mind." She stood up and smoothed her dress against her thighs. "How do I look?"

"Great as always."

She dropped a kiss on his forehead. "Since I'm eating later did you want me to get you something now?"

"I can sort myself, Mum. You go and have a good time."

She walked back to her bedroom. "I have some structural work to finish before then," she said and closed the door behind her.

Chapter 15

Jude walked off camp with a bottle of wine she'd bought from the shop in one hand and her cardigan draped over the other arm.

To her horror she'd discovered the dress and her only pair of shoes clashed but decided she was okay with wearing flip-flops. She took them off to cross the pitch and putt green and the grass felt wonderfully cool under her feet.

She recognised Paul's building because his Jaguar was parked in bay five. An identical Jaguar was in the next bay. There was a buzzer plate by the front door and she pressed the one with his name against it.

"Is that the impossibly glamorous Jude Moore?"

"It might be," she said.

"Excellent. I'll buzz you in."

She pushed the door open onto a large hallway with black and white chequered marble tiles and wallpaper that looked heavy and expensive. A double-width staircase took her up to the first floor. Four doors opened off this and Paul's was at the front in the north corner.

He opened the door as soon as she pressed the bell.

"Good evening," he said with a big smile and she felt warmth in her belly. "You look wonderful," he said after looking her up and down quickly. His smile got broader when he noticed her flip-flops.

She wiggled her toes. "Couldn't find a damned pair of shoes to go with this dress."

"Nice toes work for me. Come on in. Andy and Fiona arrived about five minutes before you did."

He let her in and she saw a chair by the door. She slipped off her flip-flops and slid them underneath then draped her cardigan over the arm. The carpet was thick and felt nice against her soles.

The room was twice as long as her lounge at home. French doors opened onto a small terrace facing the sea. Two sofas faced each other over a coffee table by a chimney breast dominated by an iron fireplace. A television was in one alcove next to an expensive stack stereo system and a shelf filled with albums.

At the other end of the room was a wooden dinner table. Andy stood up as she walked towards him.

"Evening," he said. His pale floral-pattern shirt looked like he wanted to wear a Hawaiian shirt but had compromised. He kissed the back of her hand again.

Fiona had been looking at a picture on the wall. "Hi, Jude."

She suddenly felt on the spot as all three of them looked at her. Self-consciously she handed the wine to Paul and he held it up to squint at the label.

"Not the greatest vintage I'm afraid," she said, trying to pass off her embarrassment with a joke.

"It all goes down the same way," he said.

She stood beside Fiona to look at the picture. It showed the lido in all its glory with the image made up of a series of overlapped photographs.

"Charlie's handiwork," Paul said offhandedly.

"That's such a clever idea," Jude said.

"There's so much detail," Fiona agreed.

"Something smells lovely, Paul," Jude said.

"I always like it when people say that," Paul said.

"Do you cook often?"

"He loves to entertain," said Andy with a hint of innuendo.

Paul and Fiona pointedly ignored him so Jude did too.

Paul gestured for her to follow him and took her into a large and airy kitchen. Several pots were steaming on the hob and an island held empty serving dishes. Four plates were sitting on one of the worktops.

He put her wine into the fridge. Another bottle stood in a wine bucket next to the sink.

"I've just got to sort this," he said and leaned over a chopping board. Light bathed his face as he focussed on the task at hand.

A hand slapped her backside lightly and the fingers curled at the last moment to cup her buttock.

Jude cried out in surprise and twisted around to find Andy grinning at her.

"Nice arse," he said and licked his lips carefully.

She glared at him but he continued to smile.

"Are you joking?"

Paul was absorbed in whatever he was doing and hadn't apparently seen or heard anything. Jude wondered where Fiona was.

Andy had the gall to look affronted. "What do you mean?"

"You can't slap my bum."

"Even if it's just a friendly tap?"

"That wasn't a friendly tap. I've never had a friend smack my bum."

"Well all I can say is that you and they are missing out."

He seemed so calm and collected it would have been easy to assume she'd made a mistake but that absolutely wasn't the case and her anger grew. "What do you think you're doing?"

"Being friendly."

"Your wife" – she stressed the word – "is in the next room."

"Why are you so worried? It's a compliment."

"Not to me it's not."

"Ah," he said. "You're one of these women's libbers. I think you need to chill out a little, love."

Jude was about to retort when Fiona came into the kitchen. She smiled sweetly and Jude's brain froze. She knew she should say something about Andy's behaviour but how would Fiona take it? How would Paul? Was this something Andy did to every woman he came into contact with and everyone before her had let him get away with it?

He tilted his head and gave her a smile that dimpled his cheeks.

Fiona took her arm. "How are you?"

Jude glared at Andy. "I'm doing okay."

"That's the spirit," Andy said and went over to speak to Paul.

Chapter 16

Dan was watching *Carry On Cleo* when someone knocked at the door. He wasn't even halfway down the caravan when they knocked again. "I'm coming," he said.

"Good," Charlie said. "I haven't got all evening."

He opened the door and she looked up at him holding the film envelope and a small black case.

"How was your aunt?"

"She's very well like she always is. I love Auntie Flo and she always makes Dad feel guilty for prioritising Louise over me which is wonderful."

"I don't imagine Louise likes it very much."

"Louise and Auntie Flo don't get on well so it was only me and Dad and Flo who went for dinner."

"It seems Louise is the common denominator here."

She widened her eyes. "I know, right?" She grinned. "I need you to talk to Dad."

"I'm not sure he'd listen to me."

"Probably not. Especially when he finds out you left his only daughter standing outside the caravan when you could have asked her to come inside."

Bugger. Why hadn't he asked her that straight off? "I didn't think you'd need asking," he said, thinking on his feet.

"I wouldn't normally but I didn't want to come in if you and Jude were having some family time."

"Mum's gone to Paul's for a meal."

Charlie made an 'ooohing' sound that was both amusing and lurid.

"It's not like that," Dan said. It might have been, but he didn't really want to think about it.

"I'm just saying she's a good-looking lady…"

"Well, please don't. And come in, why don't you?"

"I thought you'd never ask," she said breathily then came into the caravan.

"Did you want a drink? We have some Panda Cola."

"You're spoiled," she said.

He got two cans from the fridge, gave her one and sat across the table from her.

"So what did I miss?" she asked.

"Not much. Becky checked Mia's money and it was there so she's not gone to London. She also says Mia's dad had thrown her out so she's unlikely to be there."

"It gets odder," she said. "And speaking of which, I decided to check the contact sheet and found something peculiar."

"Peculiar how?"

Charlie unzipped the case and took out a device with a curved metal rod on a dish base. An eyepiece attached to a small barrel at one end made it look like half a microscope.

"What's that?" Dan asked.

"A grain focuser but I like to call it my loupe. It's basically a magnifying glass to pull focus when you're blowing up negatives to print them on the enlarger. I like to use it to look at my contact sheets." She gave him a shy little smile. "It makes me feel more professional." She sounded almost embarrassed.

"I think you're very professional."

Her smile faded as her eyebrows raised in surprise. "Do you really?"

"Of course."

"Thank you," she said quietly. "That means a lot, Dan." A faint tinge of colour came into her cheeks and she swallowed. "Anyway," she said as if to move them on briskly. "Look what I found."

She took the contact sheet out of the envelope and positioned it so the overhead light made the photo paper shine. She put the loupe on the edge of the paper and then stood to look through the eyepiece.

"That's it," she said and gestured for him to have a look. "Look through here like it's a microscope."

He was looking at a brick column and an area of sky in pin-sharp clarity.

"What can you see?" she asked and he told her. "Okay, hold on a moment."

She moved the loupe gently and the brick column slipped out of sight leaving only the black and white sky until he saw the top of a head.

"Is that a person?"

"Yes," she said and moved the loupe down.

He now saw a woman who seemed to be trying to pull away from a hand that gripped her wrist. A brick column hid their identity.

"Is that Mia?"

"I think so."

"Who's she with?" he asked.

"No idea. Until I saw this, I wasn't even aware she was there. I was photographing the structure of the gatehouse and if you saw the whole picture, you'd see her section was a tiny bit."

"The other person's got a tight hold. And what's that on their wrist?"

"It looks like a loose bangle or something. I checked the other shots and there's nothing in them."

"When did you take these?"

"Yesterday morning. I like to go to the lido early because there's a bit of sea wall missing and if you catch the right angle the rising sun is cradled by it. I keep trying to get the perfect shot because I think it'll look excellent on the publicity material."

"So on the morning of the day she went missing Mia was grabbed by someone outside the lido?"

"It all seems a bit odd, don't you think?" she asked.

"But what would link an argument in the morning and then not being seen the next day?" he asked.

"You saw her get into a car. What if the person she argued with came back to apologise?"

"Or came back to continue the argument."

"That works too." She popped the ring pull on her cola and dropped it into the can. "Did you want to look at the other pictures?"

"Would you mind?"

"Of course not. I love people looking at my work."

He moved the loupe and it took a moment to gauge the right speed. "So what are the rest?"

"It's all at the lido. Because the place faces east the early morning light does terrific things to the rooms with windows."

The first line of images were all inside and too dark to make out much detail. "I can lighten them quite easily," she said.

The second line was all of the same room with a window and door and several mechanical devices that looked like boilers.

"That's the pump room. It looks like something out of a sci-fi film."

One image showed the upper edge of a window with a deep crack in the wall above it.

"It looks like it's falling apart," he said.

"There are cracks like that all along the south side. I told Andy and he reckons he's got a contractor in to sort it out but I've never seen them."

"So is it dangerous?"

"It could be, I suppose. That door opens onto a fire escape leading to the beach but it's a hell of a steep drop. And once the tide's in you'd be walking down into the sea."

The third row showed a large hole in the sea wall. The last line was of a brick building where Mia was trying to pull away from her mystery grabber.

"I'm going back to Patterson's tomorrow to print them up. I know it was probably as boring as hell for you today, but did you fancy coming along?"

It hadn't been boring and he'd enjoyed their closeness but wasn't sure if he should seem eager or reserved. The very fact she wanted to spend more time with him but assumed he might say no was astonishing.

"Yeah," he said with what he hoped was just the right hint of nonchalance. "I'll come along."

"Great. How about going to the lido early to try and get the sun? You might be my good luck charm and I get the perfect picture."

Her good luck charm? That sounded good too. "Sure. What time would we need to leave?"

"The sun's up for about six-ish but I need it to have cleared the horizon."

"Six-ish?" He was on holiday! "Ade won't be open then, will he?"

She gave him a sly grin. "I was hoping you'd say yes so I already got us a bike. It's at my caravan with strict instructions from Ade that if Tommy asks, I'm to tell him I stole it." She put the loupe back in its case. "I'd better get going. I don't want too late a night."

She slipped the contact sheet into its envelope then walked to the door. When he opened it, he could hear the strains of The Sultans of Swing who sounded like they were physically assaulting *I Want to Break Free.*

"I'll knock on your window," Charlie said. She kissed his cheek quickly then rushed off into the night.

Dan touched his cheek gently and watched her go.

Chapter 17

The roast beef dinner was superb and they ate mostly in silence. Paul was the perfect host and made sure their glasses were constantly topped up.

"That's probably the best thing I've eaten in a long time," Jude said when she finished.

"Thank you," he said and seemed particularly pleased.

Fiona was still eating but agreed. Andy had finished a while before, after eating like it was his first meal of the day, and simply nodded. He'd barely made eye contact with Jude since she'd flared up at him. She wondered if he'd tried the same thing with Mia and Charlie? If they objected and Fiona caught it then Jude wouldn't put it past Andy to lie.

Now he caught her eye. He put his elbows on the table and rested his chin in his hands. "So what's your son doing this evening?"

"Probably hooked up with Charlie," said Fiona dismissively.

Paul, who'd either not caught Fiona's tone or chosen to ignore it, swept his arm towards Charlie's composite picture on the wall. "The girl's a genius."

"We're lucky to have her," Andy said and Jude caught the daggers glance Fiona threw at him. It didn't seem to faze him at all.

"He and Charlie are enjoying themselves," said Jude. "They're both worried about Mia though."

"Why?" asked Paul.

"Well apparently nobody's seen her since last night."

"She's missing?" Fiona asked.

"Dan said she missed a photo session with Charlie this morning then didn't turn up for work and it caused some aggro from what I understand."

"That's odd," said Paul and he looked at Andy.

"Is it?" Fiona asked. "I imagine we'll find some bloke at the end of it. It's like I told you in The Smugglers Rest, Jude. Mia's a flirt. She can't help herself and she wants to get out of this town."

"That's a bit harsh," said Paul.

"And it's not necessarily true," said Andy.

Jude could almost feel the chill of the look Fiona shot him. "We'll have to agree to disagree on that," Fiona said tersely before adding a "dear" draped heavily with sarcasm.

Paul quickly got to his feet. "I hope everyone saved room for dessert."

"Of course," Jude said, happy to move the conversation on. "What've we got?"

"A slab of Vienetta."

Paul went into the kitchen and Jude thought it best to keep a neutral conversation going. "Paul showed me around the lido today. It's a big project."

Andy leaned back in his chair. "It could be excellent for us and also for the town. We've obviously got to pitch it right, but we're in Thatcher's Britain now and this is the kind of urban renewal she's looking for. Have you been down to London recently?"

"Not recently, no."

"Well next time you do, head out past Tower Bridge and look at the docks there. Those huge old warehouses are being done up and the yuppies love them so much they're moving in as fast as they can be renovated. The developers are making out like bandits and the money is astronomical. I tell you, if you watched a TV programme set in the docklands five years ago you wouldn't recognise the place now."

"And you think that could happen to Seagrave?" Jude asked.

"Obviously not to that extent," said Paul as he returned from the kitchen.

"Not quite but there's as much potential as we can generate, Jude, let's put it that way," said Andy. "All we have to do is find willing investors."

"To ease our burden," Fiona said.

"Indeed, darling." Andy patted her hand and she quickly pulled it away. "Our company is funding things to this point but some investors are starting to show an interest. The architect's plans do the job to a certain point but with Charlie Fraser's photographs I'm convinced the brochures will bring in the rest of the capital."

"We couldn't have chosen better," Paul said.

"She's very young," Andy said, "but she's got a great eye."

"As do you," Fiona said with an insincere smile.

"How did you find her?" Jude asked.

"Me and Andy were having a drink in the Neptune and her dad was in there. Didn't know him from Adam but he overheard us talking and suggested Charlie. We met up and she showed us some pictures – she's always got a camera with her – and that was it."

"You could have hired a professional from town," Fiona said.

"We could, my dear," said Andy. "But Charlie's doing it for experience and pin money so we all win."

"Yeah," said Fiona. "I'm sure."

Paul drained his glass and stood up. "I'll get us another bottle."

"Shall I clear up?" Jude didn't want to be left alone in the middle of this marital battle.

"You don't have to do that," he said. "You're my guest."

"I've had enough practice clearing up behind a teenager that this lot is no problem whatsoever." She stacked everyone's plates and followed him into the kitchen. "Well, that wasn't uncomfortable."

He uncorked her bottle of wine. "They have their moments, don't they?"

"Uh-huh. Where do you want the plates?"

"In there," he said and gestured with his foot towards a dishwasher.

"Bloody hell. Did you win big on *Bullseye* or something?"

He laughed. "Us successful and busy professionals need all the latest gadgets."

She loaded the dishwasher. "We're going to have to go back in, aren't we?"

"With any luck they might have killed one another."

* * *

"It's time for a smoke," said Andy and took a pack of Hamlet cigars from his breast pocket.

"Don't smoke those horrible things in here," said Fiona.

"I wasn't going to smoke alone," he said and held the pack up to Paul. "Did you fancy one?"

"I could be tempted," Paul said and opened the French doors. "Are you interested, Jude? It's a lovely evening out here."

She went out onto the terrace. A bistro table sat in one corner with four chairs tucked underneath it. Paul set them out against the railing to face the sea.

The men lit their cigars and were soon standing in one corner clouded with smoke. Jude and Fiona stood in the other corner. Fiona didn't smoke so Jude blew hers to the sky. The sea was calm and a line of lights on the horizon moved towards the docks.

"We stood on this terrace when Andy first suggested the lido project and Paul got on board," Fiona said. "He told us he wanted to see the lido even from here."

"He's certainly got ambition," Jude said.

"You're not the first to comment on it. But he needs it. If everything goes how these two have predicted, we could be sitting on a small fortune."

"I've covered projects like this for school and most of them are very successful."

"I just hope they can transfer the London eagerness for urban renewal to an east coast seaside town."

"I'm sure they will."

"I like your confidence," Fiona said.

* * *

It was a little before eleven when Andy and Fiona decided to leave.

The four of them stood by the door to say goodbye. Fiona hugged Jude tight. When Andy moved in, she quickly stepped out of range and he kissed her cheek instead.

Paul shut the door. "And then there were two," he said.

"Not for long. I'm going to head back too."

"Did you want me to walk you?"

It was tempting but walking back to the caravan on her own might help her to decompress after the evening. "I'll be fine," she said and picked up her cardigan. She slipped her feet into her flip-flops.

"That's a shame," he said and cupped her cheek as he leaned forward.

Heat rose through her when their lips connected. She closed her eyes and lost herself to the enjoyment of the kiss.

"Are you sure you have to go?" he asked when they broke off.

"Yes." She didn't open her eyes. "No. I don't know."

"Then maybe you do," he said. "We'll do it again."

"I'll hold you to that."

Chapter 18

Seagrave came awake as Dan and Charlie pedalled along Marine Drive and the rising sun cast a reddish tint upon the sea and clouds.

Charlie seemed happy and alert. Dan tried hard not to yawn. His alarm had woken him to darkness and even washing his face in cold water had failed to perk him up.

"You're really not an early bird, are you?"

"Nope," he said. A mist clung to the beaches. The air smelled fresh but it was cold and he wished he'd put a jacket on. "I don't like early mornings. I struggle to get up for school."

"I love them, especially the mist and the light. It's glorious. I'm not sure how I'd feel if I wasn't up taking photographs though."

"You'd do what normal people do and roll over and go back to sleep. Are you in bed for nine o'clock every night?"

She shook her head. "It's usually midnight for me. I don't need a lot of sleep."

"It must be nice living on your own."

"You'd think so, wouldn't you?"

"Don't you then?" he asked with surprise.

"Making all my own decisions was nice at first but then I see the life you have with your mum and the way you chat and I miss that."

She said it matter-of-factly but Dan still felt sorry for her.

The townhouses converted into hotels had their restaurant doors open and the smell of cooked breakfasts made his stomach rumble. His rushed bowl of cornflakes didn't seem to have helped much.

They rode by Seagrave Funfair and at the back of it was a grassy track. Dan caught a glimpse of a jam sandwich police Rover at the end of it, almost on the beach. The other side of the track was hemmed in by a high wall.

"There she is," Charlie said.

The entrance was a square structure with sturdy columns forming the entry posts. Two fence panels were padlocked together to block access.

Charlie slid out of the bike and grabbed the camera case she'd carefully put on the seat between her and Dan. It had 'Leica' printed on it.

"How long has this place been closed?"

She shrugged and put the Leica case over her shoulder as she walked to the fence. "For years, I think. It's a real shame because it was built in the thirties and looks gorgeous. There's literally something interesting to capture wherever you point the camera."

"Do you have a key for the padlock?"

"Not quite."

"Are we allowed to break in? I saw a police car down that little track there."

"They're probably having an early breakfast." She put a hand on her hip. "They won't worry if we break in." She gave him a teasing smile.

"Even so, I'd rather not get arrested."

"Where's your spirit of adventure? I'm allowed in because I'm kind of an employee. We'll be fine." She pointed to the corner of one fence panel. "Pull on that bit there."

He did and the metal creaked as it shifted towards him. Charlie kicked at the lower corner and metal scraped on concrete.

"Open sesame," she said and crouched low to duck-walk through the gap.

Once through, she pushed where Dan had been pulling and he clambered through the gap.

"That didn't feel very much like you're allowed in."

"Be like Frankie," she said. "Relax."

They went up the wide steps to a landing with two broken turnstiles and Charlie held her hands wide. "Behold," she said. "Isn't it glorious?"

Dan took in the empty pool with its mouldy green bottom and the big hole in the sea wall that looked like a mouth with a missing tooth. It all looked old and knackered to him.

"I take it that's the hole you mentioned? How did it get there?"

"There was a big storm a few years back and the lido got battered. The waves apparently pounded the sea wall hard enough to break that bit off."

"There's nothing between the wall and sea?"

"A beach and rocks at the base of the wall but the tide comes right up. The whole thing bows out in a semi-circle." She pointed to his right and he looked up at the two-storey building over which he could see dock cranes. "Those are the offices and under the terrace to the side of them are the changing rooms. The pump room you saw in the pictures yesterday is at the far end."

Her enthusiasm was starting to work on him and he could imagine the place in its heyday filled with people swimming and hanging around with their mates. It must have been something back then.

He followed her down the steps to a terrace that extended over the pool. "They're going to have to do a lot of work to make this place into luxury flats."

"So long as they keep wanting me to document the process they can take as long as they like."

"Why will people pay for a flat that looks over at the docks?"

"Who knows?" She turned in a circle with her arms outstretched. "But look at all this space. You could dance out here."

"I don't think I'm going to."

"I promise not to laugh at your moves, Dan. I'm not that cruel."

"You wouldn't be laughing, you'd be in awe."

"Oh really?"

"Uh-huh. Did you ever see the video for *Uptown Girl?* I taught Billy Joel everything he knows."

"He doesn't dance in that video, he just sidesteps."

"I didn't say it was a complicated move. I just said I'd taught him it."

Charlie laughed and shrugged the camera case off her shoulder. Her handbag slipped and she let that drop as she gently put the Leica case down.

"Expensive camera?" Dan asked.

"It really is." She put her handbag over her head so it didn't slip off again. "I told Dad I needed something decent for my A level and got it for my sixteenth. It's second-hand but really good."

Charlie knelt and opened the case. She took out what looked like a folded Meccano construction and in quick movement assembled it into a rudimentary homemade tripod. She fitted the camera to the tripod then slipped off the lens cap.

"Impressive," he said.

She looked up at him and closed her eye against the light. "Thanks. I made it all myself."

"I like it."

"It does the job and cost virtually nothing. I'm getting into practice for the student life." She leaned down to peer through the viewfinder and moved the tripod slightly. "There. Did you want to have a look?"

She jumped to her feet and brushed her hands together as Dan knelt behind the camera. The concrete slab felt chilly against his knee. He looked through the viewfinder and understood exactly what Charlie was trying to do.

From this angle the hole looked almost like a cup containing the red haze in the sky. The glowing ball of the sun just peeked over the base.

"That looks cool," he said and stood up.

"Thanks, but it's looked cool every other day too and those pictures never turned out." She flicked a couple of small switches then leaned down to look through the viewfinder. She twisted the focus. "We've got a few minutes before the sun's in the right position."

Dan heard a heavy vehicle brake then someone shouting. It sounded like it came from the grassy track.

Charlie smiled apologetically. "Sorry. This bit's a little boring."

Then a woman started screaming.

Chapter 19

The scream startled Dan and gooseflesh marched up his arm.

"That came from the beach," Charlie said and ran towards the sea wall.

Dan sprinted after her and they skirted around the pool.

"We'll check through the hole," she shouted over her shoulder. "Be careful of the drop."

The damage around the hole was immense. Bricks had sheared away and there were big dents in the remaining mortar. The gap was perhaps four feet at the widest point and Charlie leaned against one side. All Dan could see beyond was wet sand when he leaned over the wall.

"I told you," she said.

The sand was at least two storeys below and the tide was freshly out leaving little pools of water in the rocks to reflect the sunlight.

A woman was rushing towards the lido and apparently chasing a small black dog. "Bowler!" she shrieked and Dan realised it hadn't been screams they'd heard but this owner trying to get her dog back.

Charlie laughed. "I hope she catches him."

A policeman came into view and spread his arms as if he intended to catch the dog. Dan leaned further over and saw a handful of police milling around the mouth of the grassy track. A couple of paramedics were talking to another officer.

"What the hell's going on?" he asked.

Charlie leaned forward and then gripped his arm so tightly it hurt. "Shit," she said. "I think there's a body down there."

Dan rested his chest on the wall so he could see down to the rocks. There was something under a white sheet ten feet or so around from the track and two policemen were standing next to it.

"You'd better stop that dog!" one of them shouted to the officer who was on the beach. He didn't turn around.

"Bowler!" the woman shrieked again.

Another man came off the grassy track wearing jeans and a Le Shark sweatshirt. His hair was mussed up and he carried a big camera with another slung around his neck. He waved to one of the policemen. "Hey, Johnny!"

Johnny was the policeman who'd just shouted to his colleague on the beach and he waved to the newcomer. "Hey, Pat. You got here quick."

"That's Pat Davis," said Charlie. "He's a photographer for the *Seagrave Telegraph*."

The woman shrieked "Bowler!" again.

The policeman crouched low as if he expected the dog to jump into his arms. As it went around him instead, he dived like the world's greatest goalkeeper and somehow got his finger snagged in the animal's collar. Bowler's run came to an abrupt end and he licked the officer's face.

The owner shouted "Thank you" as she ran.

Pat Davis looked up and waved to Charlie. "Hey you! I hope you didn't scoop me, Charlie Fraser. How long have you been up there?"

"Not long," she said.

"How old are you?"

"We're both sixteen."

"Great stuff," said Pat.

"What's going on?" she asked.

He jerked his head towards the sheet. "Body on the beach. I heard it on the scanner and zipped over. My reporter hasn't arrived yet."

"Surely you're not going to take a picture of the body," Dan said. That seemed like a horrible thing to do.

"I might," said Pat. "But I need another angle for the paper. Could I take a picture of you?"

"We didn't see anything," said Dan.

"I didn't think you did." Pat took a slim notepad out of his pocket and wrote Charlie's name down. "What's your boyfriend called?"

"Dan Moore," she said without correcting him.

Pat wrote his name down then put the pad away and lifted his camera. He took a handful of pictures, crouching to get different angles that made Dan think he wasn't going to appear in many of them.

"Bowler!"

The dog had got free again and raced towards the rocks. It bounded through one puddle then jumped up and onto the sheet.

"Bowler!" shrieked the woman.

The dog had the corner of the sheet in its mouth. Seemingly pleased with this new aspect of the game, Bowler jumped off the rock and dragged the sheet to expose the left side of the body.

Charlie let out a gasp. Dan felt uneasy at the sight but couldn't look away.

The body was female. She wore a red bra and white knickers and her skin looked horribly pale. Her hair was a damp straggle over one shoulder.

Pat took some photographs as Johnny ran up to him waving his hand. "For fuck's sake, Pat!"

The dog turned and ran at another angle and pulled the sheet away altogether.

Dan realised it was Mia a moment before Charlie screamed.

Chapter 20

A seagull pecking on the roof woke Jude up.

She checked her watch on the bedside cabinet, groaned and rolled over. It was a little after seven and that felt cruelly early for a holiday morning. The seagull wasn't giving up though, so Jude dragged herself out of bed and went into the kitchen. The caravan felt very quiet and then she saw his note on the counter.

Although Jude was happy he'd gone out with his friend she felt his absence like a weight against her chest. Or was she feeling her loneliness? Is this how she could expect to feel more and more?

No, this wasn't going to get her anywhere. She didn't want to cry now or for the rest of the holiday so she made a strong cup of coffee and had a cool shower. Both served to wake her up properly.

She got dressed and sat on the step to have a cigarette. The sun was climbing and the day was already warm and she decided a walk would clear her head further. She put her book in her handbag, locked the caravan and set off for Seagrave.

Paul's car wasn't in its bay but she still checked his terrace as she passed. It would have been nice to bump into him.

It was almost eight thirty when Jude passed the pier and Fiona called her name. She came along Regent's Row waving. She was wearing a dark skirt suit and carrying a small document case.

"Hello," she said once she'd crossed the road. "I hope you don't think I'm stalking you."

"Not at all," Jude said. "It's nice to see you. Are you working today?"

"I'm delivering paperwork to the council," Fiona said and held up the case. "Even though we bought the lido from them they're having us jump through so many hoops you'd think we were trying to blow the place up. How about you?"

"An easy day – a walk then a coffee and some reading."

"Lucky you. It's glorious today and I'm working, yet the weather forecast said we're due a massive storm on Friday. I could be sitting in the garden topping up my tan."

Fiona took a deep breath as if steeling herself to ask a favour. "If I suggested a decent cafe would you mind if I joined you for a cuppa?"

Deciding she'd have plenty of time to read later, Jude realised she would welcome adult company. "Of course not. But what about the papers?"

"The council can wait," Fiona said and linked her arm through Jude's then guided her across the road. "What book are you reading?"

"*Lace* by Shirley Conran. I missed the miniseries last year."

"Have you got to the bit with the goldfish yet?"

"No."

Fiona smiled. "You're in for a treat then."

* * *

Lesley's was a small cafe one street back from Marine Drive. It had old teapots on shelves all around the room and behind the counter were posters for events happening in Seagrave. When Jude looked at them, she saw none were for anything earlier than 1980.

They took a table by the window and Fiona bought them two coffees.

"When Andy and Paul are trying to charm the investors," she said, "they take them out to fancy restaurants or the exotic dancing club in Great Yarmouth. I said they should bring them here."

Jude sipped her coffee. It was very hot and very strong and tasted lovely. "I agree."

"Is Dan having a good time?"

"I think so. He and Charlie went to the lido this morning to take some photographs."

"I hope he's not getting too involved with her in case he gets hurt," Fiona said.

"Why would he get hurt?"

"Because Charlie seems to pick up with a new lad every week."

"Does she?" Jude asked. She couldn't quite believe that. "I'm sure he'll be fine and so will she. I mean, she doesn't hurt anyone, does she?"

"Only her reputation."

Fiona said it with such a straight face Jude felt instantly sorry for laughing.

"You're joking, surely?"

"She uses people, Jude."

Jude took another sip without saying anything. Fiona's issue with Charlie was deeper-rooted than she'd originally thought.

"She knows what she's doing. It's like the lido project and her working with two men old enough to be her father. I don't like to cast aspersions…"

"But you're going to?"

"I'll tell you this. A few weeks back I went into the lido office and Charlie was at the big table looking at some prints. Andy's standing right behind her and she's pressing her backside into his groin."

"What?"

"I swear she only stopped when she noticed me."

"What did you do?"

"I hit the bloody roof of course and laid into him once we were out of that room."

"What did he say?"

"That Charlie was feeling down and he'd been trying to give her a bit of comfort but she misunderstood what he was trying to do."

Having witnessed Andy's behaviour at close quarters last night Jude was prepared to give Charlie the benefit of the doubt.

"Did you speak to her?"

"Hardly. The little minx would only deny she'd done anything wrong." Fiona stirred her coffee listlessly. "Can I be honest with you, Jude?"

"I'd hope so."

"You seem straightforward and kind, and I like you."

"I try," Jude said.

"I know we only met on Monday night, but I could really do with a friend to talk to."

"That's lovely," Jude said with a twinge of embarrassment. "But surely you have friends here?"

"None I'm particularly close with and it's a small town. Gossip fuels lunches and that kind of thing, plus I'm not exactly a member of the First Wives Club."

Jude finished her coffee as she waited.

"I'm worried Andy's having an affair," Fiona said quietly, with a sure-eyed confidence that suggested she didn't want to hear platitudes. "He's different and distracted. At first, I thought it was because of all the problems with the lido, but now I'm not so sure. He's always had girls chasing him around because successful men of a certain age are like catnip to them, and I should know."

"Surely you don't think Charlie…?" Jude felt her stomach twist. "He must be more than thirty years older than her."

Fiona shook her head firmly. "I think my problem is Mia. She and Andy have always got on well and he's been funding her recordings, and I don't trust her as far as I could throw her."

"But his life's here and if she's gone off to the bright lights of London he's hardly likely to chase her there, is he?"

"Why not? She's younger and prettier than me. He's good at what he does and with a bit of ready capital behind him he could properly set himself up."

"I don't want to say you're wrong, but it doesn't make a lot of sense to me. If all his money is tied up in the lido and he stands to make a massive profit, why would he throw that away? If she's so mercenary why would she accept someone with no money? Maybe it is the stress of the project and once you get some investors on board, he'll give you his full focus again."

Fiona looked relieved. "I'm being selfish, aren't I?" She shook her head with annoyance. "I'm always seeing the worst of everything and now I've ruined your day whittling about something that's probably never going to happen."

"You're not being selfish and you haven't ruined my day. I don't mind listening. And don't forget you're involved with the lido too so perhaps you're processing the stress by having a particularly bleak take on Andy. We always hit out at those closest to us."

"It'd be nice to think so." Fiona looked at her watch. "Bugger, I need to get these papers delivered. I'm sorry for taking over your morning and talking through my own woes."

"Don't worry about it," Jude said but hoped they didn't have any more conversations like it.

"You're an angel," Fiona said and rushed out of the cafe.

Jude got herself a fresh coffee and settled down to read, glad of the peace.

Chapter 21

Charlie had managed to calm herself down by the time the first police officer came into the lido. Neither of them had looked over the wall again. Dan felt giddy and his heart seemed to be thumping way too fast.

WPC Townsend introduced herself and took them down the grassy track to sit in the back seat of one of the police Rovers.

Another officer got them both cups of sugary tea. "Drink this," he said. "I promise it'll make you feel better."

It stopped him feeling so giddy but his heart still hammered.

The policeman from the beach called Johnny sat in the passenger seat in front of Dan. "I'm PC Kent," he said and asked Dan his name and how he'd come to be at the lido that morning.

PC Kent dutifully wrote down everything Dan told him. WPC Townsend asked Charlie similar questions.

It seemed to take a long time and when PC Kent went to speak to the officer standing with the dog owner, Dan leaned his head against the seat and closed his eyes.

"Are you okay, Dan?" WPC Townsend asked.

"Not really."

"Still feeling sick?"

"I just feel weird."

"I'm not surprised. You two have had a busy day."

Charlie held his hand and offered him a wounded smile as she squeezed his fingers. He squeezed back.

"How are you?" he asked.

"Been better."

"What happens now?" he asked WPC Townsend.

"A forensics team are coming down from Lowestoft to set up their investigation and then the body will be taken away for identification."

"I've told you," said Charlie with a remarkably steady voice. "Her name's Mia Garwood."

"Neither of you are her next of kin though. PC Kent knows her father so he'll identify her at the hospital."

"He's not the most pleasant of men," said PC Kent as he got back into the car.

"What do you think happened to her?" Charlie asked.

"We couldn't really say," WPC Townsend said. "That'd be for the medical examiner to decide."

"Do you think she'd been swimming?" Dan asked. "She was only wearing her underwear."

"Like Shirley says" – PC Kent gestured to his colleague – "we won't know for sure yet. But it looks like that to me. This kind of thing gives me the chills. There's something about suicides that–"

"She didn't commit suicide," said Charlie brusquely.

"That's just my opinion," PC Kent said and held up his hands. "I've patrolled Seagrave for a few years now and jumping off Julia's Point is a route some people take when they can't see a way forward."

"We're a long way from Julia's Point," said WPC Townsend.

"I know. I probably shouldn't have said anything."

"She didn't kill herself," said Charlie defiantly. "There was no reason for her to."

"Sometimes people have things going on in their lives we don't know about," said PC Kent.

His radio squawked and he walked away. "AM12," he said. "Go ahead."

The response sounded like a badly tuned radio station to Dan but PC Kent nodded. "Confirmed," he said and walked over to the group of officers.

They separated the crowd as a plain white van came down the grassy track. He said something to the driver before the van drove onto the beach then he came back to the car.

"Forensics are here now so we're clear to take you both home. Are you feeling okay to go or would you rather we took you to the hospital?"

Charlie and Dan looked at one another. She seemed as disorientated as he felt. "I'm okay," she said and he agreed with her.

PC Kent reversed up the grassy track and some of the onlookers peered closely into the windows. Dan tried to ignore them and Charlie didn't even look. She sat with her hands in her lap and her thumbs wrestled each other.

"Something's been on my mind since the sheet came off and I've just figured it out," she said.

"What's that?" Dan asked.

"Mia wasn't wearing her necklace. It was apparently the only thing she has that belonged to her mum and that's why she never takes it off. She used to stroke it when she got stressed."

Dan didn't want to point out that if Mia had thrown herself off Julia's Point – whatever that might be – then the necklace could have slipped off then or after.

Nobody else spoke until they pulled into the camp driveway and stopped. WPC Townsend turned in her seat.

"How are you both feeling?"

"I'm okay," said Charlie.

"You don't really sound it."

"I don't know what you want me to say," she said. "I just want to go home."

"You've had a shock. It's normal to feel disorientated."

Charlie forced a smile that actually looked quite scary. "I feel like shit but I'm not in shock. I've been there before and I didn't feel like this."

"Her mum died," Dan said helpfully.

The WPC nodded. "How about you, Dan?"

"Better now," he said and he knew it was because they were away from the body.

"Will someone be at home for you both?"

"Yes," Dan said.

"No," Charlie said.

"Oh," said WPC Townsend.

"You can come to mine," Dan said to Charlie.

"Thanks," she said.

"You need to be aware Seagrave is small and the jungle drums are loud," said PC Kent. "People here might already know about the body and you too, but you mustn't tell anyone it was Mia Garwood until she's been positively identified."

"But we know it was her," Charlie said.

"We understand that," WPC Townsend said. "But it's the law, Charlie."

She got out and opened both their doors. "Take care," she said and handed them each a card. "If you need anything then get in touch with us at the station."

"Thank you," said Charlie. "Sorry if I've been a cow."

"You've both been very brave." WPC Townsend got back into the car and drove away.

"Shit." Charlie shook her hands out. "What a morning."

"How're you feeling?"

"Not good." She gave him a look that quickly softened. "I'm sorry. I feel like shit because I saw her and she was my friend, but we weren't sisters and it's not like losing my mum. It did hurt to hear them say she killed herself too because I guarantee you that didn't happen."

"How can you be so sure?"

"I just am." Charlie shrugged. "Maybe I didn't know her well and there are things I didn't understand but she was too positive and had too many plans."

There were things she didn't know, he thought. Like the sugar daddy boyfriend. He also knew from bitter experience that sometimes you don't know everything about people you're very close to.

"People hide stuff sometimes," he said.

"But what about her necklace, Dan? She never took it off so where was it?"

"Perhaps it got pulled away by the tide."

"Nope," she said. "I thought of that, but it wasn't loose enough to slide straight over her head. Do you think I should tell Becky?"

"The copper told us not to."

"Do you do everything the police tell you to do?"

"No but…"

"We both saw her and one of those gawkers might have recognised her too. Becky will never forgive me if she finds out from someone else but knows I was there and didn't tell her. I wouldn't forgive myself."

She had a good point. "Maybe you should."

"Why do you keep changing your mind?"

"Because I'm trying to help you."

"I know." She scratched the corner of her mouth. "I'm being a cow again."

"You're not."

"I am because I need to say something to Becky before the shit hits the fan, so she doesn't think I'm a horrible friend."

"Nobody would ever think you're a horrible friend."

"You're sweet," she said and smiled the saddest smile he'd ever seen. "I think I need a bit of time on my own." She stroked the back of his hand and then walked away.

Ade came out of his shed and shrugged as if to ask where the bike was. She waved at him and kept walking.

Chapter 22

When Jude got back to the caravan, she found a note stuck to the door with Blu Tack.

> *You'll probably read this and roll your eyes and wish I'd leave you alone but I'm working at home today and couldn't stop thinking about you and wondered if you wanted to have lunch? I called by but you weren't in – and why should you be when you're on holiday? – but on the off chance you'd be back soon, I thought I'd leave you this note.*
> *If you can, I'd love to see you.*
> *Px*

Knowing he'd been thinking about her sent a pleasurable tingle down her spine. That was the kind of lift she needed from this holiday.

The cool air inside the caravan was a welcome relief and she went into her bedroom to check her shoulders. As she'd feared, they'd burned slightly, and her white bra strap looked ridiculously bright against the red skin.

Dan came through the front door as she was gently rubbing in some after sun.

"Hi, love," she said. "Did you have a nice morning at the lido?"

"Not in the slightest," he said in such a resigned tone she rushed out of the bedroom.

"Are you okay?" He was about to go into his room and there was something in his eyes she didn't like. Charlie wasn't with him and she wondered if Fiona had been right. "Where's Charlie?"

"She wanted some time on her own. We've had a bit of a tough morning."

Jude was starting to worry now. What had Charlie done to him? "What happened?"

"While we were at the lido they found Mia on the beach."

"Well that's good, surely. Was she okay?"

He shook his head. "She was dead."

His words seemed to suck the air out of the room and it took her a moment to properly process what he'd said. "Oh no."

Dan told her everything and when he finished, she pulled him into a fierce hug. He and Charlie were too young to see death.

"She screamed and I tried to support her but I wasn't enough."

"I'm sure you were, Dan. I wish it hadn't happened to either of you though."

"I think I'm okay. It just scared me. It's worse for Charlie because they were friends. The police told us not to tell anyone because Mia hasn't been formally identified but Charlie wants to tell Mia's room-mate Becky."

"Is that where Charlie is now?"

"I don't know." He extricated himself from her hug. "The police annoyed her because they think Mia killed herself but Charlie doesn't. She says Mia wouldn't have hurt herself."

"Do you mean she thinks someone hurt her?"

"I don't know."

"I feel like I should be doing something to help. Is her dad at the caravan?"

"No, he lives in town with his girlfriend. I should try and find her, shouldn't I?"

"You need to do what you think is right, Danny."

He got himself a glass of water from the kitchen and drank it down. "I'll go and find her."

"Do you want me to come with you?"

"It's okay," he said and sounded like an adult taking charge. "I'll go."

"If you want me, I'll be here."

"I know, Mum," he said and gave her a quick, awkward hug then went out.

She felt a little empty but as much as she wanted to go with him to help comfort Charlie, she couldn't overrule him. It wouldn't make him feel any better, and who was to say Charlie would open up to her?

Jude sat on the step and had a cigarette, inhaling deeply and blowing the smoke at the clear blue sky.

Chapter 23

By the time Dan found Charlie sitting on the clifftop by the steps he still hadn't quite figured out what to say to her. He called her name before he reached the footpath so he didn't startle her. The last thing he wanted was to make her jump and fall.

"I know you said you wanted to be on your own but…"

"But…"

"I told Mum what happened this morning and she was very worried about you."

"That's lovely of her," Charlie said softly. She rubbed her cheeks with the palm of her hand.

"Can I sit with you?"

"It's a free country."

He sat next to her. "How're you feeling?"

"I've been better." She looked at him and closed one eye against the sun. "My mind just keeps going back to whether I could have done something to stop this."

"You couldn't have and you know that."

"She was always good to me." She ran a hand through her hair. "I thought I'd never make any friends the first summer Dad left me here. Somehow Mia realised what was happening and made a point of speaking to me and soon the other workers joined in. When she found out I was into photography she asked me to take her headshots and seeing them in town gave me a real boost. We were never best buddies and she didn't tell me everything but she was finally getting somewhere with her singing and I know she wouldn't kill herself."

"What if it was an accident?"

"She was in her underwear. Do you think she was shagging and fell into the sea?"

"No…" He had to be careful.

"She didn't tell me everything but I overheard her talking to Becky about a secret boyfriend. But even if this was a bonking accident, don't you think he'd have come forward when she went missing?"

"What if he couldn't?"

"Like he was married or something?"

"That would explain why he was secret," he said and thought of something his dad had told him. "You can't choose who you fall in love with."

"Now you sound like you're reading Love Hearts sweets. Do you know who her boyfriend was?"

"How could I?"

"So what's with…" He saw it in her eyes as she put two and two together. "Oh," she said. "Was this you?"

"No," he said indignantly.

"I don't mean you falling in love with the wrong person, I meant your mum or dad."

"Mum didn't do anything wrong," he said and she raised her eyebrows at his vehemence.

"I wouldn't suggest otherwise. I like Jude."

"It was all him," Dan said and realised he was going to tell her everything. "He hurt Mum even more than he hurt me."

"You don't have to tell me, you know."

"I know," he said. It might do him some good to get this off his chest. "They were both teachers at my school so you can imagine how thrilling that was for me."

"He had an affair?"

"Uh-huh."

"With someone your mum knew?"

"Yes, unfortunately."

"Well that's really shitty."

"It was. Mum taught her a couple of years before."

"Oh." Charlie's look of surprise would have been amusing under other circumstances. "That's even shittier than I thought."

"The girl's mother found some love letters Dad wrote and recognised his name." Dan took a couple of breaths. Charlie put her hand next to his so their little fingers were close enough it wouldn't take any effort to touch them together. "She caused a real scene at school and the police turned up."

"The girl was underage?"

"Thankfully not. She was in the upper sixth so almost eighteen but that doesn't make it any better."

"So what happened?"

"By the time the police arrived, one of the secretaries had found my mum and told her in private. I found out at first break when someone threatened to beat me up in the corridor."

"Bloody hell."

"The week went by in a blur. I got sent work from my teachers so I didn't have to go back into school and Mum stayed home too but spent most of her time crying. I didn't see Dad again for a few weeks."

"When was this?"

"Last year."

"I don't know what to say except 'poor you'. And I feel so sorry for your poor mum."

"She's just starting to pull herself together and it's been hard because she had to go back to work."

"You had to go back to school too."

"Yes and the first few weeks were terrible; notes and whispers and people calling me and my mum horrible names. I was lucky because most of my mates stuck by me, but a lot of her friends stopped ringing and that really hurt her. But she kept her head down and got on with teaching and things moved on eventually."

"Now I understand why you didn't want to talk about it before. I hope she kicked the bastard in the balls?"

Her comment surprised a laugh out of him. "She wanted to but the police got to him first. They got divorced, obviously, but it wiped them both out in terms of money. The only reason we're here is because she got a special deal on the caravan."

Charlie put her hand over her mouth. "I made that crack about people coming down for less than a week. I'm so sorry."

"You didn't know and I've heard a lot worse. You wouldn't believe how many people thought my mum was somehow responsible for my dad wanting to fuck a schoolgirl."

"And yet she picked herself up."

"Every time."

"Then that's it," Charlie said. "Jude's my new hero and I'm going to be as strong as her."

"What do you mean?"

"Me sitting here feeling sorry for myself isn't going to help anybody and I owe it to Mia to try and find out what happened to her."

"And how are you going to do that?"

"I don't know," she said. "The thing about being in her underwear and the missing necklace means something, I'm sure of it, but I don't understand yet. I know it sounds mad but please help me, Dan."

"Of course I'll help you," he said, although at that moment he wasn't sure how.

"You believe me?"

"I agree that it doesn't make sense," he said.

"That's close enough for me."

"So what do we do first?"

"Did you never read *Nancy Drew*?"

"I watched the television show and read *The Three Investigators*."

"That's good enough. We need to investigate."

"How? We're hardly Dempsey and Makepeace."

She smiled. "I'm as pretty as her and you're quite rugged, I suppose."

"Thanks," he said, mock offended.

"You're welcome."

"So where do we start?"

"We know that on Monday morning she was at the lido where someone wearing a bangle grabbed her arm and then on Monday night she got into a mystery car. All we have to do is work out if those two events are connected and then what happened between Monday night and this morning."

"How do we do all that?"

Charlie got to her feet and brushed the sand off her backside. "I don't know, Sherlock. I'm making this up as I go along."

"What if you develop that photograph and we take it to the police?"

"That's a great idea," she said.

"They won't be able to identify the other person," he said, carried along by her enthusiasm. "But they'll surely think it looks suspicious that she had an argument in the same place where she was found."

"You're a genius. Come on, get on your feet and we'll go and develop the print."

* * *

Charlie stopped outside a caravan with no car parked beside it. "So now you know where I live."

He made a show of checking the caravan out. "Looks like a nice place."

"You're a real Prince Charming," she said and unlocked the door and went in.

She was back a few moments later with a white envelope. "The negative strip," she said and locked the door behind her.

Becky was crossing the lawn with a net full of footballs over one shoulder when they reached the road.

"Hey, you two. How's it going?"

Charlie looked at Dan. "Well we had a bit of a weird morning. Did you hear about the lido?"

"Someone found a body there." She looked from one to the other. "Shit! Did you find it?"

"We didn't but..." Charlie started. "Have you got a moment?"

Becky pulled a face. "Not really. Mia's still missing and Tommy's angrier than he was yesterday trying to cover all her shifts. If I don't get these footballs down to the south field soon I'm in trouble."

"It's important," Dan said.

"I know but..."

"It's Mia they found," Charlie said as gently as she could. "It looks like she drowned."

"No." Becky let go of the net and the footballs scattered across the ground. Her eyes glistened.

"I'm so sorry," Charlie said and touched Becky's shoulder. "I wanted to tell you rather than you hear it from a stranger."

"How did it happen?"

"They don't know," Dan said.

"Did she look…?"

"No," said Charlie. "She looked like she was asleep."

Becky pulled her into a hug. "That's awful. Poor Mia. And poor you for seeing her. I don't know what else to say. I feel winded."

"For fuck's sake, Becky."

Tommy was behind her and looked hot and bothered. The menace in his glare was terrifying. "What're you doing? Pick those fucking balls up."

"Yes," Becky said and let go of Charlie. "Sorry."

"You haven't got time to mess about." He fixed first Charlie then Dan in his glare. "And I might have bloody guessed it'd be you pair."

"Tommy," Becky said wearily. "Leave it."

"What?" he demanded then seemed to see her properly for the first time. "Have you been crying? What's been going on?"

"They found Mia," she said.

Dan saw a flash of panic in Tommy's face. "Good. That fucking bitch has caused me nothing but upset since she buggered off."

"She's dead, Tommy," said Becky and tears streamed down her cheeks. "Have a bit of respect."

"What're you talking about?" He looked bewildered. "How can she be dead?"

"We were at the lido this morning," said Charlie. "We saw her but she's not been formally identified yet so you can't say anything."

He looked like he was weighing up whether to believe her. "Fuck," he muttered. He turned his attention to

Becky. "Get those balls together. And if I find out you're lying to me, Charlie, I'll fucking have you."

"I'm not but you mustn't say anything."

"Yeah and fuck you too," Tommy muttered and stalked away across the lawn.

"That went well," said Dan.

"I'd better get going," Becky said. "He's going to go mental."

Dan and Charlie helped her gather the footballs. Becky hugged Charlie and then pulled Dan into a quick but tight embrace. He didn't know where to put his hands.

"Thank you for telling me," she said.

"You're welcome," Charlie said. "Are you going to be alright?"

Becky shook her head. "Nope but the show must go on."

Chapter 24

"I didn't know if you'd get my note," Paul said as she walked up the stairs in his building.

"I could hardly miss it Blu-Tacked to the door."

"As I've got older," he said, "I've realised it doesn't always pay to be subtle."

The cuffs of his dress shirt were undone and he'd opened several buttons at the neck. She thought he looked fantastic.

"I couldn't agree more."

He leaned in and she felt the crackle of energy as they kissed.

"Hello," he said and ushered her into the flat.

She nudged her flip-flops under the chair. The French doors were open and a breeze whispered through the nets covering them. A soul compilation album played softly on the stereo.

"I've been working in the study so haven't got much in but I'd planned to have a chicken salad sandwich for lunch."

"That sounds good to me."

"I might also be able to rustle up a bottle of wine and some cheese."

"Sounds even better." She followed him into the kitchen and leaned against the door frame as he got chicken and lettuce from the fridge and bread from a bin on the counter. "Can I help?"

"You can sort the wine."

Paul made the sandwiches and she took a bottle of wine from the fridge and some glasses from a cupboard. He carried the plates to the table in the lounge and she sat across from him facing the French doors.

"You have a wonderful view from here," she said.

"I really do."

"Very smooth, Mr Reid."

"Please take note because it doesn't happen very often." He bit into his sandwich. "How's your morning been?"

"It's been odd. I saw Dan before I came out. He and Charlie were at the lido when a body was discovered there."

He looked panicked for a moment. "In the lido?"

"No, on the rocks outside," she said and told him what she knew. "He said it was Mia."

Paul looked shocked and upset and opened his mouth then closed it again. He shook his head with dismay. "That's awful, just awful. I thought she'd just had enough of Seagrave and decided to move on. Shit. If it's true then Andy's really going to be cut up."

"He liked her, didn't he?"

Paul rubbed his face. "He and Mia had a…" He seemed to search for the right word. "An understanding, I suppose."

"Was he seeing her?"

"He wanted to but I don't think they had that kind of relationship. It was more that he helped her out with financial support."

"Fiona thinks they were having an affair."

Paul smiled grimly. "Once Fiona gets a bee in her bonnet about something she's like a dog with a bone."

"She's not Charlie's biggest fan either."

"Just between us," he said and leaned forward as if someone were eavesdropping, "she has issues with all younger women where Andy is concerned."

"She apparently saw Charlie and Andy getting close in the office."

That clearly surprised him. "I've never heard that before and I think Charlie would have more sense. I mean, he's the best part of three times her age."

"It can happen," she said carefully.

"I doubt it would with Charlie." He glanced at the clock. "The news'll be on in a minute. Come through to the study and we can listen."

They finished their sandwiches and she followed him past the kitchen and down a hallway to the study. The room was large enough for two medium-sized desks and several bookcases. One window was open and the sounds of birdsong and someone mowing their lawn drifted in. The radio stood on a desk under the windowsill that was cluttered with files and brochures.

"This is mine," he said as he switched on Seagrave Sound.

"Do you work here often?"

"More often than not. The lido office is just for show really and Andy closed his place in town just before we started the partnership, so he moved his stuff here." He pointed to the other desk. It was very neat with a pile of box folders in one corner and a blotter. It looked like nobody had worked there for a while. "I leave it well alone because he gets very touchy if anything's moved."

She put her hands up. "I won't touch a thing."

Love of the Common People segued into a run of adverts before the news came on. They both listened intently but the report didn't add much to what Dan had already told Jude. Neither Mia nor the lido were identified.

Paul switched the radio off. "I wonder how long it'll be before they start referring to the lido."

"Not long," she said and wondered what kind of economic fallout they could expect.

"My entire life seems to be wrapped up in that place at the moment." He gestured to the wall behind her. "Behold my future."

The large display was centred around an oversized poster for Lido Towers that had an Art-Deco look to it. The artist's impression showed a tower block of apartments with balconies and smaller bungalow-type buildings around the pool. Photographs formed a ring around the poster.

"That's an aerial shot of the place as it is now."

The lido pushed out onto the beach in a bow shape and there were rocks against the wall at certain points. The docks seemed further away than she'd thought and there was another beach between them and the lido itself.

"I wonder where they found the body?" she asked.

He pointed at a spot on the apex of the bow. "If Charlie was looking through the hole, then it would be here." Paul tapped the next photograph down. "That's an aerial from the early fifties when the lido was in its heyday."

The pool was filled with shimmering water and the shapes of people enjoying it. More people were on the walkways and the tide was coming in over sand that looked as glorious as some exotic foreign beach.

The next few photographs were from the same era. A group of lads played water polo and a line of beauty contestants — shy-looking girls wearing swimsuits — stood beside the pool while older women enjoyed a picnic.

Below the circle was a floorplan for one of the apartments and six current photographs.

"Charlie took those for a kind of before and after project."

Jude leaned in close. The pictures were beautifully clear and well composed and she recognised the changing rooms from the brief tour Paul had given her. Another photograph showed a bright room with machinery in it. A window took up a large portion of the wall and above it was a long, wide crack in the plaster.

"Where's that?"

"The pump room," he said and moved closer to her. "It's on the floor below the changing rooms and we're planning to house all the utility points there since it has separate access where a fire escape goes to the beach."

"That's another big crack in the wall," she said, conscious of how close he was to her. His aftershave smelt very pleasant.

"I'm sure Andy's on top of it."

Their faces were very close now. If he dipped his head and kissed her now, she would absolutely respond.

"I love it," he said. "Older buildings like this are tough and resilient. They have a lot of charm."

She watched his lips as he spoke. "You should pay attention to charm."

"That's what they say."

He slipped his arm around her waist and she felt a rush of heat.

The front door clattered open and someone called, "Paul?"

Paul let go of her and stepped back. He adjusted his trousers. "It's Andy." He gave her a guilty smile and went out into the hallway. "I thought you were in meetings all day."

Jude took a couple of deep breaths to calm herself then walked along the hallway behind him. Andy was clearly unhappy about something. He paced from the door to the mantelpiece and back waving what looked like a folded newspaper.

When he saw Jude he stopped and glared at Paul. "You didn't say you had company."

"Hi, Andy," she said. "Everything okay?"

"You wouldn't ask that if you'd seen the front page of the local rag," he said and slapped the paper down on the dining table.

The story took up most of the front page under the gaudy headline 'Body Found on Beach'. Next to the text was a large picture of Charlie on the lido wall with 'D' and 'O' clearly visible. Much more visible was Charlie's left leg which the photographer had clearly made his focus.

"She's flashing a lot of leg," muttered Paul.

"She looks cheap," said Andy.

"That's unfair," Jude said. "The poor kid's wearing shorts and leaning against a wall."

"I don't care that she's showing a bit of leg," said Andy. "Sex sells but you can see she's standing on the lido wall. What if people link us with the body? How the fuck are we going to shift units when people associate the project with someone dying."

Jude skim-read the article but couldn't see mention of Mia. "It doesn't say who she is."

"I know that," said Andy, "I already read it."

"Dan told me it's Mia," she said.

Andy couldn't have looked more winded if she'd punched him in the stomach. "What?" He leaned against the back of the chair.

"He and Charlie were at the lido earlier and he saw her body."

"Fuck." Andy sat down heavily. "Are they sure?"

"The body hasn't been formally identified yet," said Jude. "But Charlie's convinced."

"Sorry, mate," said Paul and squeezed his shoulder. "I know you were friendly with her."

"Who wouldn't be?" Andy traced something on the tabletop with his thumbnail. "Shit." He rubbed his face then looked at Paul. "This might not be as bad as I originally thought," he said. "I know some of the attention will be ghouls wanting to see where the body was, but we couldn't buy this much publicity. A pretty girl is always guaranteed to draw attention so Charlie's leg and the lido sign could buoy us up."

Jude understood that the economy of business often meant you had to look at something objectively but his change of attitude was almost breathtaking. Or maybe he was in a state of shock? Paul certainly looked like he was struggling to comprehend the shift.

"I'll get going," she said. "Let you two talk business without me being in the way."

"Thank you," Andy said. "I'm sorry I interrupted your lunch date."

"It's not a problem," she said.

Paul followed her to the door and waited while she slipped her flip-flops on.

"We three had planned to go for a meal tonight. Why don't you come with us?" he asked.

"Do you think that's a good idea?"

"I think it's a great idea. You know what Fiona thought of Mia and Andy's clearly suffering. At best you'll be someone to talk to and at worst you can help me referee."

"How could I refuse when you paint such an enticing picture?"

"I knew I could charm you. We're going to a friendly Italian in town so no need for a ball gown. I'll come and get you for seven."

Chapter 25

The west side of Market Street was mostly in shadow as Dan waited for Charlie.

He'd picked up a pristine copy of *Christine* by Stephen King for twenty pence from a second-hand bookshop called Vinny's while she developed the photograph. Now he sat on a bench across the road from the chemist's and read.

She didn't spot him when she came out and he watched her sling the shoulder bag over her head so the strap crossed her chest. She held an A4 envelope and was looking towards Vinny's before she finally saw him and waved. He waved and crossed the road to her.

"Did you get anything?" she asked and shuddered when he held the book up. "Yuck. I can't stand the ideas of cars that move on their own. Have you ever seen that old horror movie *The Car*? I couldn't sleep for a week after that."

"I like being scared," he said. "Did you get the print done?"

"Yes and I blew it up as much as I could without losing to the grain. We'll head back to camp to have a good look."

As they got into the Surrey bike a moped went by and did a wide U-turn before coming back towards them. The rider tooted the ridiculously high-pitched horn and stopped at the kerb. He pulled the bike onto its stand then took off his helmet and shook out his hair.

"Hey, Charlie," Malc said and gave her a big wink. He glanced at Dan. "And her little friend."

"We're the same height," Dan muttered.

"I'm so glad I caught you," Malc said.

"I'm thrilled," Charlie said and sounded anything but.

Malc opened the pillion box and took out a copy of the *Seagrave Telegraph*. "Can I get your autograph, Legs Eleven?"

"What are you talking about, you mental case?"

Malc made a show of looking her up and down before he handed the paper to her. "Your moment of fame," he said. "I'm going to stick this on my bedroom wall."

Dan leaned in close to see what the fuss was about. The headline wasn't good but he assumed it was the picture that made Charlie gasp.

"Nice, isn't it?" Malc said.

By shooting at such an angle the photographer had made it look as if she was posing like some trainee page-three girl, all thigh and extended leg, her hair tousled with the breeze. All that was missing was a pout. The photograph was real but didn't contain any truth.

"That's terrible," she mumbled.

"I disagree. Your thigh looks fantastic."

"I'm wearing exactly the same clothes I've got on now, Malc."

He grinned. "I know."

Charlie pushed him away. "What's wrong with you, you pervert?"

"Hey," he protested. "What are you pushing me around for? You're the one going round flashing your thighs."

Dan saw how wounded she looked and got out. The older man squared his shoulders as Dan walked around the front of the bike.

"Yeah? Come on then, little friend. Take your best shot."

"Nope," said Dan. "I'm not hitting you first but I am going to stop you being horrible to Charlie."

"Horrible?" He made a 'ha' sound in Dan's face. "You don't know the half of it. But you'd better be ready to fight."

Dan felt adrenaline race through him and that's what kept him in Malc's face even though he'd never had a proper fight in his life and Malc still had the helmet in his hand. But he couldn't step away from this. "I am."

Doubt flickered in Malc's eyes.

Charlie held Dan's arm. "Leave him. He's not worth it."

"Listen to your girlfriend. She knows what's best for you."

The shop door opened. "What's going on here?" Mr Patterson asked sternly.

Malc looked sheepishly at his father. "Nothing, Dad, we're just messing about."

"If you want to square up for a fight, do it on your own time and not outside the bloody shop. Now get inside, I need you to do some more deliveries."

Malc gave Charlie a look then went into the shop.

"We're sorry, Mr Patterson," Charlie said.

He looked at the front page and shook his head. "I'd ask what the problem was but I think I can see. That paper gets tackier by the minute. If I were you, I'd write to the editor and complain."

"Do you think so?"

"You're a very smart and gifted young woman, Charlie. You don't need dopes like Malc seeing pictures of you like that and making the wrong assumption about you."

Her face crumbled into a sad smile. "Thank you, Mr Patterson."

"You're welcome, love, and I apologise for Malc. I'll set him straight." Mr Patterson looked at Dan. "Good for you for stepping up there, lad," he said and went back into his shop.

"Shit," said Dan and felt jittery as the adrenaline wore off.

"Yeah," said Charlie.

She got onto the bike and steered as Dan pushed it out into the road before getting on.

"Just so as you know," she said as they began to pedal, "you didn't need to stand up for me back there. I'm perfectly capable of looking after myself."

It felt like she'd just told him off and he tried to hide the hurt in his voice. "I didn't say you couldn't."

"I know but thank you. It's been a long time since anyone stood up for me like that and even though I could have dealt with Malc on my own I do appreciate it." She squeezed his hand. "Just don't let it go to your head."

Chapter 26

Charlie slid the photograph out of the envelope. It was about the size of a sheet of paper and she'd composed it so the brickwork of the arch formed a frame around the central image. The focus and detail were remarkably sharp.

"This is the last picture I ever took of her," she said quietly.

Dan wondered if this was the shock WPC Townsend had warned them about. "Are you okay?"

"Who knows?"

He didn't know how to respond to that so he looked at the picture. Mia looked worried and the person's bangle must have been metal because there was a small flare where light had caught it.

"What do you think?" she asked.

"She doesn't look scared."

"You're right."

"I wonder if the person's grabbing her or trying to stop her lashing out."

"I wish I'd caught more of the other person."

"You did a good job, Makepeace," he said and thought back to the mysteries he'd read. What would be their next move? "Is it a man's arm or a woman's?"

"Judging by the bracelet or bangle or whatever it is, I'd say it was a woman."

He leaned in closer. "That makes sense but I think it might be a man. Look at the shade on the upper side of the arm. It looks like hair."

"Women have hair on their arms."

"I know but not usually that much."

"If a man wore a bangle like that," she said, "he'd certainly stand out."

His mum came into the caravan and said hello then came up to the table. She touched the back of Dan's head then sat next to Charlie. "How're you doing, love?"

Charlie smiled at her. "I'm okay, Jude."

"Dan told me what happened and it must have been awful. I know you don't really know me from Adam, but I'm here if you want to talk."

Charlie looked like she might start crying.

"And a top tip. Try and avoid the local paper."

"We've seen it," said Dan. "Some bloke at the chemist's got all leery and showed us."

"Oh that's disgusting."

"I know the photographer too," Charlie complained. "I thought we were friends. We talked to him on the beach."

"It's out of order," his mum said. "I'd be happy to complain to the paper on your behalf. And on mine too. It's demeaning."

"Thank you." Charlie tapped the photograph. Actually would you mind looking at something for us, Jude? You might be able to help." She moved the picture so his mum could see it better. "I took this on Monday morning when I was getting some random views of the lido. I didn't realise Mia was there."

"Who's grabbing her?"

"We don't know," said Dan. "Do you think it looks like a male or female arm?"

His mum pushed her bottom lip over her top one as she peered intently at the photograph. "A man," she said. "Don't you think that looks like a watch strap?"

"I think it looks more like one of those big bracelets you used to wear years ago, Mum."

"I hardly wore anything that big."

"I think it looks like a bangle," Charlie said. "Whoever it is, it doesn't look like they're getting on too well with Mia, does it?"

"No."

"I'm glad you said that," Charlie said. "I think the police have got the wrong end of the stick saying she took her own life."

"What makes you think that?"

"Because this picture feels wrong and I know a lot of things were coming up for Mia that she'd worked hard for. And she wasn't wearing her necklace."

"Her necklace?"

"It belonged to her mother and she treasured it like it was gold. I never saw her without it, yet she wasn't wearing it when we saw her on the beach and something doesn't feel right to me. So we're going to investigate and find out what happened."

"How're you going to do that? You're a bit short of staff to be the Famous Five."

"I suggested we take the picture to the police," said Dan.

"That's a good idea. It's not going to tell them a great deal but it might be enough to make them pause."

"There's certainly something off about it, isn't there?" Charlie asked.

"Yes," Jude said. "But why not sleep on it? Nothing is going to happen today and it'll give you a chance to process everything."

"The picture won't be different."

"I didn't mean that. I meant for you to process what you've been through today. You've had a shock and it's knocked you about a bit even if you don't think it has."

"That's not a bad idea," said Dan.

"Thank you," Charlie said and stood up. "I think I'm going to get a paper to read what the article says."

Chapter 27

"Well, look who it isn't," said Tommy as he walked off the Neptune's patio. "How's it going, Legs & Co?"

"Don't call her that," said Dan.

Tommy glared at him. "What else am I supposed to call her? She's either getting under people's feet here and causing trouble or flashing her legs in the paper."

"She's wearing the same shorts now, you idiot. Why don't you grow up and leave her alone?"

"It's got her some attention though, hasn't it?"

"Only from creeps like you leering at her," said Dan.

"I'd do anything not to have seen her," Charlie said. "And I'm going to prove it wasn't her fault."

"Oh yeah?" Tommy said. "How're you going to do that?"

"I have a picture of her arguing with someone and I'm taking it to the police."

"You have a picture?" Tommy asked and Dan saw a little tic rattle above his eye. "You're lying."

"She's not," Dan said. He looked at Tommy's wrist but he wasn't wearing anything there.

"And why the fuck would I listen to you? I checked you out, grockle. You're in the rental section and got your caravan from that kiddie fiddler."

Dan wasn't sure he'd heard correctly and even Charlie pulled a face.

"What are you talking about?" Dan asked.

"That bloke Paul and his mate Andy whatsisname. It was bloody disgusting them sniffing around Mia. They're both old enough to be her dad."

The thought Paul might be the secret boyfriend made Dan feel cold. If it was true, then his mum would get hurt all over again.

"You're disgusting," said Charlie hotly. "You were the one sniffing around Mia. She turned you down and you didn't like it and then did everything in your power to make her life miserable."

"You vicious lying little cow," snarled Tommy and came towards her.

"Excuse me," said a voice from behind Dan.

Tommy glanced over and his face brightened. "Yes, my love," he said calmly. "What can I do for you?"

Dan was confused until he turned to a pensioner couple. Tommy had snapped back into work mode.

"We don't mean to interrupt," said the old man, "but we can't find the mini golf course."

As Tommy gave them directions Dan took Charlie's hand.

"We'll see you around, Tommy," he said. "Thank you so much for your unwanted advice."

"Yes," said Charlie. "You were so incredibly unhelpful."

Dan led Charlie towards the general store. "Did you notice that little twitch in his eye when you said about the photograph?"

"Do you think the grabber could be him?"

"He wasn't wearing a bangle or a watch but it might be he's not allowed to when he's in uniform?"

"Well if it is him then he now knows that we know his secret."

"That's not going to be fun," Dan said.

Charlie went straight to the counter in the general store where the newspapers were laid out next to the cash register.

"Afternoon, love," said the woman behind the counter. "Saw your picture and for what it's worth I think it was a shitty thing to do to you."

"Thanks, Marge, I appreciate that." Charlie scanned the various editions. "Do you have a copy? I can't see one here."

"I was so disgusted I hid the pile on the floor." Marge bent down to get a copy. "You take it, I'll pay."

"Are you sure?"

"Absolutely. You take care, love, and look after those legs. They're great."

"Thank you, Marge."

Chapter 28

"It's awful news," said Fiona.

The Italian Market restaurant was as good as Paul had promised, with simple wooden tables and a picture window that looked onto Regent's Row. The chef, with his toque perched at a jaunty angle over a thick tumble of curls, greeted Paul like a long-lost brother when they arrived.

Conversation started light but the situation with the body at the beach clearly wasn't far from any of their minds.

"Did anyone hear if she's been officially identified yet?" Paul asked.

Andy shook his head and forked some linguine into his mouth.

"That poor girl," Fiona said. "I mean whatever else she was, nobody deserves to drown."

"Charming," said Andy. He looked troubled.

"All I'm saying is that she didn't deserve it."

"I was thinking more of the 'whatever else she was'," Andy said.

"You were hardly her biggest fan, Fiona," said Paul.

"I could say the same thing about you," she said sweetly with a bland smile.

"What does that mean?" Jude asked.

"Nothing," said Paul as he wound spaghetti on his fork.

Fiona leaned in conspiratorially to Jude. "It means Paul wasn't as taken with Mia as some others on this table were." She seemed to be playing a game Jude couldn't quite follow.

"Can we just leave it?" asked Andy and sounded exasperated.

"You haven't been her biggest fan, Fiona," Jude pointed out.

"No," she said, "but you shouldn't speak ill of the dead."

"Something we finally agree on," said Andy and drained his glass of red wine. "Let's change the subject."

Paul refilled the glasses. It was a good bottle of wine and Jude could feel her two glasses already going to her head.

"I was only saying it's awful news," said Fiona with a shrug. "But I suppose these things pass. It'll be old news next week."

"That's awful," Jude said.

"It really is," Andy agreed. "Come on, Fiona. Be nice."

"You're drunk," Fiona told him with disdain. "Though at least the lido features in the paper alongside Charlie's leg."

"Andy seems to think all publicity is good publicity," Paul said.

"Until it's not," said Jude.

"That's right," said Fiona. "I mean, what if Mia fell off the lido?"

"Oh come on," Andy scoffed. "How the hell would that happen? People are saying she went off Julia's Point."

"Why would you think she fell off the lido?" Paul asked.

"I don't but that might be the link people make," Fiona said.

"They won't," said Paul. "They'll think a young woman made a mistake and the tide washed her around to the beach."

"What if she didn't make a mistake?" Jude asked and everyone's attention snapped to her. "Charlie seems to think there's something more to it. She reckons Mia had big plans and wouldn't do something like this."

"People take their own lives all the time," said Paul. "Most of the time, nobody knows they were planning to do it."

"Charlie thinks there might be someone else involved."

"Of course she does," said Fiona. "If she pipes up now it'll keep the attention on her. Wasn't she happy enough with her picture in the paper?"

"Hardly," said Jude sourly. "Charlie's got a picture from the morning Mia disappeared that shows someone grabbing her wrist."

"Can you see who it is?" Paul asked.

"No. All you can see is their arm and a bangle." She looked at her fellow diners' wrists. Paul wore his heavy watch and Fiona's bracelet was delicate and silver. Andy wore his watch on the other wrist. "It doesn't mean that person was involved but it's curious. She's taking the picture to the police tomorrow."

"She's such a bloody busybody," Fiona muttered.

Jude took a deep breath and held it a moment. She couldn't tell if Fiona was tipsy or obnoxious but the woman was really starting to get on her nerves. "She thinks it might be important and I agree with her."

"Load of nonsense," said Andy and held up his glass. "Any of that plonk left?"

Chapter 29

Dan knocked on the door of Charlie's caravan. The evening air was mild and there was a lovely golden light that made everything feel somehow right.

She opened the door and looked a vision in a white blouse with pastel culottes and white ankle socks that set off her tan.

"You look terrific," he said.

"You're not so bad yourself." He was pleased she thought so. He was wearing shorts and a checked short-sleeve Oxford shirt his mum had convinced him to pack "just in case".

She put on a pair of boat shoes then unclipped the Instamatic from her bag strap. "Do you mind if I take a picture of us?"

"Sure."

Charlie leaned her head against his and held the camera in front of them. "Smile," she said and took the picture then wound the film on. "I'm starving. What did you fancy?"

He resisted the temptation to say "you" because he didn't know if he had enough cool in his entire body to carry that off. "Did you want to go into Seagrave?"

"No, let's stay on camp then we can go for a walk on the beach. How about chips?"

"Sounds good to me."

She took his hand as they walked and he hoped it
didn't feel as clammy to her as it did to him. Her skin felt
wonderfully smooth and warm.

The chip shop was busy and the man behind the
counter greeted Charlie cheerily as they joined the end of
the queue.

"Is there anybody on camp you don't know?" Dan
asked.

"Not if they sell food. And Ivor's chips are lovely."

"Hey, Charlie," said Ivor when they reached the front
of the queue. "Who's your friend?"

"This is Dan."

"Hello, Ivor."

"Hello, Dan. Any friend of Charlie's and all that," Ivor
said. "What'll you have?"

"Cod and chips please," Charlie said.

Dan checked the prices and was relieved the fiver in his
wallet would cover them. "Make that two."

"Two coming up," said Ivor and worked quickly.

He wrapped their meals in paper after liberally applying
salt and vinegar and put them on the counter.

"I saw your picture in the paper," he said. "Just
remember that today's headlines are tomorrow's chip
papers. And I'll make sure every front page I come across
tomorrow is back to front and illegible with vinegar, how
about that?"

"That would be lovely, Ivor. You're a star," she said.

"So are you." He handed one portion to her and the
other to Dan. "That'll be a pound please."

Dan frowned but handed over the fiver. Ivor gave him
four pounds in change and two cans of Coke.

"Go on, you two. Enjoy your meals."

* * *

They sat on the beach to eat their dinner. Charlie had
picked up a few sachets of tomato ketchup and applied
hers liberally to the chips. Dan put a splodge on one side

of his paper. Once unwrapped the portions were even bigger than a normal adult size. The fish was lovely and Charlie was right about the chips. They ate in a contented silence and looked out over the water as the horizon got darker.

"I'm sorry I dragged you into all this," she said and ate a chip.

"It was hardly your fault."

"If it wasn't for me, you'd never have been at the lido."

"True but if it wasn't for you, I wouldn't be enjoying this holiday so much."

"You're enjoying being in Seagrave?"

"Sort of, but I'm enjoying being with this person I met."

Charlie finished her cod and licked her fingers clean. "Is that so? Is there anything I should know about this person?"

"Well, they're smart and funny and very pretty."

"Very pretty, eh?"

"I did use other words," he said and she laughed. "But yes, very pretty."

"She sounds like a great girl."

"I think she is."

"Cool." She finished her chips and crumpled the paper into a ball. "Have you ever had a holiday romance?"

"Not really. Have you?"

"Well, if you count the fact I live here for four months a year as a holiday then yes. A couple of boys this year."

"A couple?"

"Well, I snogged them but..." She stopped, as if suddenly realising what she was about to say.

"But what?"

She opened her can and took a long drink. "But they didn't make me feel the way you do."

It felt like someone had let a firework off in his chest.

"I'm not messing you about," she continued. "You make me laugh and you're brave."

"I'm hardly as brave as you."

The sunset coloured her face amber and he didn't think he'd ever seen anyone look so pretty in real life.

She smiled and he leaned forward because what was the point of being called brave if you didn't actually do anything to prove it?

She leaned forward too and they kissed.

* * *

The sun had gone down by the time they reached her caravan and looked at one another slightly awkwardly. She opened the door and yawned.

"Sorry," she said and giggled. "Early mornings do that to me."

"It's been a long day. Thank you for asking me to come out with you."

"Thank you for dinner," she said and kissed him quickly on the lips. "I'll see you tomorrow."

After a last kiss she went into the caravan and locked the door behind her. She waved through the glass panel and he waved back then walked home feeling like the happiest person in the world.

Chapter 30

The sky was tinged with dark reds blending into darkness by the time they left the Italian Market. The wine had given Jude a pleasant buzz and she felt quite merry.

Andy swayed slightly at the kerb. "Has anyone ever told you you're pretty, Jude?"

"Jesus, Andy," said Fiona. "I'm right here."

"I know," he said and patted her arm like she was a dog being rewarded. "I'm just telling Jude."

"You really don't need to," Jude said.

"I mean, you could probably do with gaining a few pounds if you don't mind me saying…"

"You already did," she said tartly. "And maybe you shouldn't have."

"I think you've had more than enough fun for tonight," said Paul quickly.

"He doesn't hold his red wine well," Fiona said and hit Andy's arm. "Let's find a taxi. You've embarrassed me enough."

"How?" he said.

Fiona gave Jude a quick hug then pushed Andy away. "Thanks for a great evening. Sorry about this dickhead, Jude."

"Well," Jude said after the couple had disappeared around a corner. "That was interesting."

"No it wasn't. Andy was proper out of order."

"Well, they've gone now so let's change the subject before my merriment is completely washed away."

He looked surprised. "Are you merry?"

"Just a little bit tipsy," she said.

"Well that's good, since we're on a date."

She fluttered her eyelashes at him and made him laugh. "Is that what this is?"

"It's what I was hoping before Andy started."

They walked down Regent's Row and he took her hand as they turned into Marine Drive.

"It's quiet," she said as they passed a crazy golf course where a lanky teenager in a bright yellow jacket was brushing litter into a pile.

"The season's almost over for the year," he said. "I'm looking forward to the town being a bit more peaceful but it's sad watching people go home." He squeezed her hand lightly.

As if he'd verbalised her own thoughts she felt a twinge in her stomach. "People have to though, even if they're enjoying themselves here."

"And sometimes you know you're going to miss them when they leave."

The conversation felt like a live wire leading them into an area they didn't have time to properly explore. "Will you miss me?"

"Yes. I'll miss lots about you."

It had been so long since anyone had said anything like that to her, she felt as though she was experiencing the emotions for the first time. "I'll miss you too."

"It might sound like I'm feeding you a line but I've never had a romance with someone here on holiday but I felt a connection as soon as I saw you on Monday." They'd reached his flat. "Would you like to stay?"

His words ignited a jolt of desire. She missed the simple pleasure of waking up beside someone and intimacy on all its levels. The warmth of his words and the wine were combining to make her feel horny and she'd almost forgotten how good that sensation felt. But – and wasn't there always a but? – was it the right thing to do? Leave aside the walk of shame in the morning and facing Dan, was this the right thing for her?

He pulled her close and she didn't resist. "What do you think?"

His warm breath on her neck sent a ripple of pleasure down her back and she had to resist the urge to shudder.

"I'm very, very interested."

"So am I. Have you had too much to drink?"

"Just enough to make me think tomorrow might be better," she said.

He looked so deeply into her eyes it made her feel giddy. When he kissed her, he slipped his arms around her waist and pulled her against him so she could feel his excitement. That fed into hers and the kiss got hungrier. She felt her resolve weaken with the taste of different lips, a new tongue to explore and hands she wasn't familiar with stroking oh-so-close to her breasts.

The kiss seemed to last forever but was over far too soon. They gazed at each other with slightly unfocussed eyes and neither spoke.

A car went by and honked its horn. "Get a room," someone from inside the car called.

"I should go," she said.

"Are you sure?"

"Only if you promise we can pick this up tomorrow."

"I'm writing it into my Filofax even as we speak."

"So you're asking me out on a date tomorrow night?"

"I am. Are you free tomorrow night, Jude?"

"I could be."

He laughed and kissed her again but broke it off before it became something else. "Did you want me to walk you back?"

"Thanks but I'm a big girl now. I'll see you tomorrow."

She instigated another goodnight kiss and made it deeper than his had been.

Chapter 31

The noisy seagulls on the roof woke Jude from a restless night filled with vivid erotic dreams.

She was onto her second cup of coffee in an attempt to kill her wine headache when Dan surfaced. He'd been in his room when she got back last night and, for a moment, she wished she'd taken Paul up on his offer. She might have regretted that this morning even more than she regretted the wine but it would have been good to know if the heat they'd clearly generated between them was going anywhere.

"Morning, Danny."

"Morning, Mum," he muttered and went into the bathroom. His hair was corkscrewed on one side.

She made them both toast and handed him his plate as he sat at the table.

"You're a wonderful mother. Don't let anyone ever tell you any different."

"I promise."

He seemed distracted as if he almost wanted to say something to her but didn't quite know how. She wondered how he and Charlie got on last night and if that was behind his reticence. Jude prided herself on them having a good relationship but she was aware that there were things she didn't want to discuss with her parents when she was Dan's age.

She made them both a drink and they talked as they ate. Dan was keen to try the Italian and Jude was keen to visit the chippy if the portions really were that substantial.

"You'd probably have to take Charlie with you though," he said.

"She seems like a popular girl."

There was a knock at the door.

"Bugger," he said and raced into his bedroom.

"You could have answered the door," she said and got up to do it as he came out pulling a T-shirt over his head and wearing shorts over his boxers.

"I've got it," he said and opened the door. He said "hi" a lot more quietly.

"Hey," she heard Charlie say. "You okay?"

"Yeah," he replied quietly. "My mum's here."

Jude smiled as she listened to them and wondered if Dan was worried Charlie might say something he didn't want to be overheard. "You can let her come in, Danny."

"I was just about to," he said and shot her a quick glare.

Charlie gave Jude a little wave. She was wearing a pair of denim cut-offs that ran to mid-thigh and Jude wondered how much damage that photo had done – and hoped the effects wore off quickly. Charlie's T-shirt had a colourful Keith Haring print on it.

"Would you like some toast, love?" she asked.

"I'd love some, Jude, if you don't mind."

"Of course not."

Jude made the toast and Charlie ate it like she hadn't been fed in a long time.

"So did you think any more about the photograph and going to the police?"

"I did," Charlie said between mouthfuls. "There's been a new development this morning."

"What's that?" Dan asked.

Charlie took a postcard out of her bag and put it on the table. The picture showed a buxom woman and an older man who was clearly besotted with her.

"I like mysteries," Jude said, "but you've got me here."

Charlie turned the postcard over with a flourish. On the back was a handwritten message in block capitals.

ACCEPT SHE'S GONE. IT WILL ONLY MAKE LIFE HARDER FOR YOU IF YOU KEEP PRESSING FOR ANSWERS.

"It was pushed under my door sometime during the night."

It might have been sent to the wrong caravan but Jude still felt an uncomfortable chill across her shoulders. She turned the card over. It hadn't been posted.

"I'm definitely going to the police now," Charlie said. "I knew there was something about that photograph and this confirms it. And even better, I know exactly who sent it."

"How?" asked Jude.

"Because I only told Tommy I was planning to take the picture to the police."

Jude must have looked confused because Dan said, "You've probably seen him about. Blonde bloke and he's not very nice. He runs the workers on the camp."

"And had some kind of problem with Mia," Charlie said. "He didn't seem happy when I told him about taking the picture to the police and the next morning I get a threatening postcard. It's only us three and him that know about it."

Jude couldn't fault Charlie's logic but she was wrong. "I'm sorry," she said, "but I told Paul, Andy and Fiona about it last night."

"Oh, Mum," grumbled Dan as if she'd confessed to selling state secrets. "Why did you do that?"

Jude felt terrible. "I didn't know."

"How could you have known?" Charlie asked. "Please don't worry about it. It just widens the field of suspects a little."

Jude was relieved that she hadn't upset Charlie but concerned she seemed to be brushing over the most troubling aspect. For one of them to send the note about a picture they hadn't seen must mean they were panicking about being exposed for having a physical argument with Mia before she died.

"This is dangerous," Jude said. "Why don't you let me drive you to the police station?"

"It's okay," Charlie said brightly, "me and Dan will go. If we have rattled someone's cage, they're not going to do anything silly, are they? I'll be safe. And once the police are aware they can do something and try to find out what really happened to Mia."

"But what if they misread it?" Dan said. "We think it's threatening but it doesn't say anything specific."

"Only one way to find out," Charlie said. She sounded excited.

Chapter 32

"Sorry, Charlie, but I can't let you have a bike." Ade didn't look happy to be passing on this news. "Tommy said I couldn't give any freebies to grockles."

"Well that's nice of him," Dan said.

"Do you give freebies to any grockles other than me?" she said.

"No." Ade fiddled with the corner of a page of his computer magazine. "But he didn't mention you specifically."

Her face softened into a smile that lit up her eyes. "I'm sorry I got you into trouble. I seem to do that a lot."

"You have your moments."

"And I shouldn't. But that's okay. Me and Dan will figure out some other way into town."

"You could always try the cliff path. It's only half the distance."

"I know," said Charlie and gestured at her tennis shoes. "But these don't have very thick soles and there are rocks and stuff."

Ade nodded. "It'd be a lot easier if you had wheels."

"I'll manage," Charlie said with an air of resignation.

"Well…" said Ade.

* * *

Ade had obeyed Tommy by giving them a Surrey bike that had obviously been out of commission for a long time. The paintwork was badly chipped and one of the front wheels had a kink in it so when they braked it sounded like there was a brass band on board with them.

The handlebars had partially rusted and Charlie was finding it difficult to steer.

Dan admired his ingenuity even if it made for a very uncomfortable ride.

"Do you think this was a way to stop us going to the police?"

"Who knows?" she said.

* * *

"I can't believe he wasn't interested."

Charlie's voice dripped with indignation as she stormed down the front steps of Seagrave police station. Dan rushed to keep up and when she turned abruptly on her heel, they almost collided.

"He's an idiot," she said.

Dan looked over his shoulder. The desk sergeant stood at the door watching them. "Be careful," Dan said.

"Why? Is he going to arrest me for disagreeing with him?"

"Probably."

"Don't be so silly." She started to walk along Howard Street towards the bike. "How can he say there's nothing suspicious?"

The desk sergeant had told them PC Kent and WPC Townsend were on patrol but offered to look over the evidence himself. He considered the photograph thoroughly but seemed unaffected and suggested the postcard had been delivered to the wrong caravan. When Charlie railed against him, he'd tried to calm her down by calling her "young lady" and that was like adding fuel to a fire. He then asked her to leave.

"I'm sure they're investigating every angle, Charlie."

"I seriously doubt it. And what are you eating?"

"A lollipop."

"What the fuck, Dan?"

147

"Well the copper offered it." The sergeant had clearly been taking the piss when he offered her a jar of lollies and she'd refused to take anything. "I got one for you too."

"You're a sell-out. You were supposed to be on my side."

"I am on your side. Did you want this lolly or not?"

"Of course I do," she said and snatched it from him. "There's a cafe around the corner. Buy me a ginger beer float and we can sort out what we're going to do next."

* * *

Horner's Corner Cafe was situated between a second-hand dress shop and a tobacconist and all three looked like they'd been in business since the end of the war. There were half a dozen people in the cafe and the smell of cooking made Dan's stomach rumble.

He bought their drinks and they sat at a table by the window. The floats were in large sundae glasses with straws and lumps of vanilla ice cream floating in ginger beer.

"Cheers," she said and sucked up some of her drink. "I can't believe he treated us like kids."

Dan shrugged and sucked on his straw. "Maybe he thought we were joking." The ginger beer was strong and burned the back of his throat. "What do we do now?"

"This is where we become Dempsey and Makepeace." She shrugged expansively. "I was kind of hoping you might have some ideas."

The problem was they were only characters and he'd never done anything like this before but Charlie was waiting for an answer.

"Let's take it one step at a time. What do we have so far?"

"A photograph and a postcard," she said and put both on the table. "And we'll assume the postcard wasn't wrongly delivered."

"And we know only four people could have sent it."

"I took the picture on Monday morning and that night you saw her get into a car. She wasn't seen again until Wednesday morning and the police think she jumped off Julia's Point."

"What is Julia's Point?"

"When you came into Seagrave did you drive through a town called Radnor?"

"Yes. There was a big hill after it."

"Right, so that's Duncan Hill and the crest of it is called Julia's Point because there's a little observation place there. It's also a suicide hotspot."

"So where is it in relation to the lido?"

She took a little jotter and a stubby blue pen she'd obviously stolen from Argos out of her bag then drew a quick outline of the coast. She marked where the lido was, and it didn't take a genius at geography to see why WPC Townsend hadn't been convinced yesterday.

"If Mia went into the water at Julia's Point," Dan said, "why wouldn't she get snagged at a beach nearer the docks?"

"Don't say snagged…" Charlie said and stuck out her tongue in a yuck motion. "But I thought the same thing. It's not impossible for her to have come all the way around to the lido but…"

"It doesn't make a lot of sense when you look at the diagram."

"No." She took a long draw on her ginger beer. "How about this for a theory? What if she fell off the lido?"

"Why?"

"Because it fits. She met the mystery person there on Monday which gives us her link to the place. What if the same person picked her up from the camp that night and took her straight back."

It felt like a huge leap in logic. "Why would she go back with them?"

"I don't know but given where her body was, it would make sense she was there. It can't be a random person because only four people knew about the photo so one of them must have sent the postcard. And if Tommy or whoever locked her in the lido, who would know she was there? She could scream and shout forever and nobody would hear her."

"So how did she fall off the lido?"

"Perhaps she tried to escape? Perhaps they killed her?" She scooped some ice cream with her straw and ate it carefully. "Then there's her necklace. She honestly never took it off but she didn't have it on when we saw her. If she chose to jump then she'd have still been wearing it."

"Might she have left it at home for some reason?"

"Why would she? We could ask Becky if we can check her room and also look for anything that might prove she wasn't suicidal, like letters from agencies or audition appointments. It might not sway the police but if we find enough stuff, they can't just dismiss us out offhand."

"We'll get Mum to go in next time. If they didn't take you seriously because of your age then she might have a bit more luck."

"Good thinking, Batman."

"Dempsey," he corrected her.

"Finish your float," she said. "We've got stuff to do."

Chapter 33

Jude was annoyed with herself for telling Paul and the Sykeses about the photograph although it seemed impossible one of them might have sent the postcard.

What if it was Paul? The thought of him, after their snog, coming onto the camp to slip the card through Charlie's door turned her stomach. Could he be capable of something like that?

Why would he have sent the postcard? Did he know something about what happened to Mia? Was he trying to help or hide someone else because he was involved in her death?

Jude shuddered and felt goosebumps. No, she couldn't have been that wrong and needed to refocus her thoughts before this drove her mad.

Since Charlie was determined to get to the truth and wouldn't give up, then maybe Jude could assist. Granted, she wasn't Miss Marple, but she could nose around and try to find something out, even if she only succeeded in eliminating the three suspects she'd inadvertently included.

That was it. Fiona had so far managed to intercept Jude every day as if hiding in plain sight waiting for the opportunity, so today Jude would make sure she had one too.

* * *

Jude walked into Seagrave but didn't see Fiona at all. Lesley's was so busy there weren't any seats left so she got a coffee to take away and walked down to the promenade with it. An old man was sitting on the sand winding rope onto a core. She sat on the edge of the concrete, kicked off her shoes and wiggled her toes. She took her book out of her handbag and lit a cigarette.

The man seemed to notice her then and turned around. He wore a ratty old cardigan over a dress shirt and his skin had the look of old leather.

"Morning," he said gruffly.

"Morning."

"Nice day for it," he said, without explaining what "it" might be.

"It really is."

"What're you reading?"

"*Lace*," she said and held the book up.

He nodded. "The wife read it. Said there's something weird about goldfish in it."

"Is that right?"

"So she says."

"What're you doing, if you don't mind me asking?"

"Sorting some rigging out for the crazy golf course," he said and jerked a thumb over his shoulder. "Bunch of noisy buggers in there at the mo so I thought I'd come out to get some peace. I need to do it now because the weather's on the turn."

"Is it?" The sun felt very hot and there was barely a cloud in the sky.

"Ayup, it's supposed to storm tomorrow so if you want to go for a paddle, I'd do it today if I were you."

"That bad?"

He grinned. His teeth were very white. "I'm old but I'm not old enough to be God so I couldn't really tell you. But we're due a bugger." He tied off the rope and got to his feet with remarkable grace. "Lovely to meet you, my duck. Enjoy your book."

"And you."

She read for the next hour but didn't see Fiona. By then her skin felt very warm so she brushed off the seat of her shorts and decided to walk back by way of Paul's flat. His car wasn't in its usual place and she pressed his buzzer for more than a minute to no response so she left a note.

She crossed the pitch and putt green and saw a man in his early twenties with a thick black beard sitting in a little shed by a bike hire. He looked up to squint against the sun as he slipped a computer magazine behind him.

"Good afternoon," he said. "Did you want to hire a bike? Reasonable rates and great exercise."

"I'm sure but not at the moment, thanks. I think my son Dan and his friend Charlie get their bikes from you."

"Are you Dan's mother?"

When she nodded, he smiled and even with the beard it made him look younger.

"I'm Ade. Charlie can be very persuasive and uses my bikes like some kind of free taxi service."

"I think they were hiring one this morning."

"Kind of but my manager collared me and said I wasn't to give them out for free."

"They paid?"

"Hardly." He grinned sheepishly. "I gave them an old bike that's due for the scrap heap."

"Are they in trouble with your manager then?"

"No idea. He's never done anything like this before and it seems odd but sometimes Tommy does things that don't make a lot of sense to me."

She felt a quick jolt at the name. "Perhaps I should settle their account. Where would I find him?"

"If you turn around now you'll see him."

Ade pointed over Jude's left shoulder and she turned to see a man about Paul's height and in his early twenties coming out of reception. He wore dark shorts and a white vest top that showed off his physique. Jude guessed he was a rugby player and carried himself with the air of someone who doesn't get messed with very often. His blonde hair was almost white and he had nothing on either wrist.

"Thanks," she said.

"Don't mention it," said Ade.

She intercepted Tommy at the mouth of a narrow roadway that ran down the side of reception. He offered her a polite smile.

"Can I help you?" he asked.

"I hope so," she said but her mind went blank. This didn't happen to Shoestring.

He inclined his head as if to prompt her then looked past her shoulder.

"I'm sorry to hold you up," she said.

"No need to apologise but I'm off shift and was leaving camp."

That was her opening. "Are you going somewhere nice?"

"Into Seagrave to see friends."

"That should be fun. My son and his friend are in town today too."

"Is that right?" He looked like he was itching to get away.

"Yes. I don't expect you'll know them but they found the body of the girl on the beach."

His whole demeanour changed. "Charlie Fraser?"

"That's right and you're Tommy, aren't you? My name's Jude Moore. Dan said you weren't happy with him or Charlie about finding Mia."

Tommy's expression didn't shift. "I said they shouldn't make her name public until it was confirmed."

"I agree with you," she said, utilising her teacher training. Back up the suspect, make him think you're on his side and then zap him into detention when he drops himself in it. "But why would they lie?"

Tommy grinned and showed off his teeth. It made him look good and she wondered how often he deployed this killer smile to get out of situations. "I don't understand this, Mrs Moore. It sounds like you're about to arrest me."

Jude forced out what she hoped was an amused-sounding laugh. "Of course not. I just wanted to ask if you'd sent any postcards recently?"

"Postcards?" he asked, and she couldn't tell if it was panic or confusion in his eyes.

"Yes. I was just curious."

"I can't remember any," he said. They looked at one another. "I'm sorry, Mrs Moore but is there anything else? It's just I…"

"Have to go? Yes, I understand. It was good to meet you, Tommy."

"Likewise," he said and walked briskly away to disappear behind some conifers.

A few moments later she heard a car door slam and an engine cough into life.

Chapter 34

Charlie braked the Surrey bike to a halt in front of Ade's shed and he winced at the sound.

"Has Tommy given you any trouble?" she asked.

"No but he's gone off camp now." Ade looked at Dan. "He was talking to your mum earlier."

"Are you sure?" he said.

"That's what she told me. A pretty lady about medium height with dark curly hair."

"That's her," said Charlie.

"Did you hear what they were talking about?" Dan asked but Ade shook his head.

"Not to worry," said Charlie. "We'll be back in a bit so can we leave the bike here?"

"Sure," Ade said.

"We'll be back," she said and got off the bike. Dan followed her down the path to the gate. "I wonder if Jude asked Tommy whether he'd sent the postcard?"

"I wouldn't put it past her. Mum does tend to speak her mind."

"Good for her. If she investigates a bit and we investigate a bit, we might be able to put the whole picture together."

* * *

Becky was sitting in a deckchair outside the chalet catching the sun. "Hey," she said and raised a hand to shield her eyes.

"How are you feeling?" Charlie asked.

"Not too bad but I've been better. How about you?"

"We're doing okay," said Charlie. "Can I ask you a favour?" She told Becky everything from discovering the photograph to the warning postcard and the police reaction. "So it looks like we've stirred something up."

Becky looked worried. "You need to be careful, Charlie."

"I know," she said and for the first time Dan saw the truth of the admission in her face. With the sun shining on her he could see the worry in her eyes and the tenseness of her expression. "So we need to gather more evidence to prove Mia didn't take her own life."

"And how do you propose to do that?"

"Dan and I can't remember seeing Mia's necklace on her."

Becky sat forward. "Really? It's unlikely it would have slipped off."

"I know. So I wondered if she'd taken it off for some reason on Monday night and left it here and we didn't notice. And we could also look to see if there are letters or anything from the auditions she was going to in London."

"We can try," Becky said and they followed her into the chalet and Mia's room.

"How are we going to find anything in this?" Dan asked.

"By doing it logically, Dempsey," Charlie said. "You go through that pile of paperwork on her dressing table and look for anything from booking agencies or a letter that looks positive about her singing. Becky and I will go through her drawers and wardrobe."

They set to their tasks and Dan sat on the corner of the bed to work through the unwieldy pile of papers carefully. There were some handwritten letters, Holidaze payslips and an official-looking form that made no sense to him called a P60. There were several type-written letters from one agency or another and after the fifth or sixth 'you're really very good but unfortunately not what we're looking for at the moment' he felt sorry for Mia and her dreams.

Half a dozen postcards from friends had been sent from what seemed to be all over the world.

The next letter came from a talent agency in Norwich who were interested in meeting Mia following one of their A&R people visiting Holidaze. Dan had no idea what an A&R person did but the letter seemed positive. The audition date was two weeks ago. He put it on the bed behind him. The next letter was another positive, this time from a London-based company who wanted to see her in early September at a rehearsal studio in Denmark Street. The signature was barely a line of black ink. Handwritten along the bottom of the letter was the word 'yes!' followed by a couple of train times. Dan assumed Mia had written those herself.

The Norwich agency wrote the next letter too. Mia had apparently aced the audition and they wanted to see her again. He checked the date on his watch – the return audition was for next Wednesday.

"I think I have something," he said and showed them the letters.

"She was excited about the Norwich agency but I didn't realise they'd called her back," said Becky.

Charlie was fiddling with a hairgrip that had a plastic Smurfette attached to it. "So she was getting noticed?"

"Sounds like it," said Dan.

"I checked her jewellery box and there's no sign of her necklace," said Becky. "It's not here."

"So where is it?" Charlie asked. "Maybe it could be at the lido."

"What's the lido got to do with it?" Becky asked.

"Probably nothing," said Charlie. "It's my photograph I think. I have a feeling about the place but can't properly explain it."

"Well let's go and have a look," said Dan. "What can it hurt?"

Chapter 35

"It feels odd being back," Charlie said when they got to the top of the stairs.

Dan knew what she meant and looked across the lido towards the sea wall. He had no intention of going over there and looking through the hole. "It does. So where did you want to look?"

"I'm not sure but let's pretend my theory is right and she knew the person who brought her here. At some point there must have been a problem and Mia didn't want to be in the lido anymore so the person who brought her panicked."

"And hurt her then?"

"Perhaps not. But if they were worried she'd cause a scene, maybe they tried to keep her here somehow?"

"Like locking her in, you mean?" It seemed like a ridiculous idea but Dan couldn't see any other way for it to make sense.

"Well there's no houses nearby to hear her screaming or shouting and you wouldn't hear that over the fair either." Charlie looked up to the office block. "If they locked her in there, she could just break a window and get out."

"What about the changing rooms?" Dan asked.

"That makes more sense but I don't think there's anything that locks in there. We'll try it though."

Dan followed her down the steps and across the small terrace up to the undercroft. Charlie pulled open the door and the hinges squealed. They went in and the darkness seemed to embrace him. The air smelled of must and neglect.

"These were the changing rooms," she said. "There's a torch here so close your eyes a moment."

He did but still saw the bright beam when she turned it on. He opened his eyes carefully and could now see he was in a long wide corridor. The changing cubicles with primary-coloured doors ended at a set of double doors.

They walked down the corridor to them. The floor was slippery in places and the green mould running down from the ceiling looked furry though he had no intention of touching it. In a couple of places there were big dark stains on the ceiling and one had water dripping through the centre of it.

"This place looks knackered," he said.

"I know."

Charlie pushed through the double doors which opened onto a wide area without windows that reminded him of the changing rooms at his school gymnasium. There were two benches with wire backs and hooks for coats and bags and behind them was an arch in a wall filled with shadows.

"Shower room," she said, gesturing towards it.

The door at the far end led onto a landing. Double doors marked 'To The Pool' were to his left and to his right was a single door marked 'Private'.

"That's us," she said and pushed it open.

The hinges protested and the base of the door scraped across the floor tiles. The sound made Dan's teeth ache.

The stairwell had brick walls and poured-concrete steps and the narrow windows near the ceiling gave the space some light. The stairs hugged the wall and Dan leaned over the top banister to look into the gap. He couldn't see the bottom and for a moment it felt like he was suspended over infinity.

"Scary, isn't it?" she asked. "I did exactly the same thing. There aren't any windows on the way down, so it just gets darker and darker."

She pointed the torch into the gap and he saw four flights of stairs.

"This is the way to the pump room that I showed you those pictures of. If I was trying to hide someone this is where I'd put them. This is the main way in and there's a fire escape leading down to the beach."

She started down the stairs and played the beam around. The steps were gritty with sand and there were bits of plaster scattered around. He looked up and saw the gaps where they'd come away from the ceiling.

A dark narrow corridor at the bottom of the stairs led to a sliding metal door he only saw when she shined the torch in that direction. There were a couple of electrical junction boxes on the wall above it and a mass of pipework looked like spaghetti running into the ceiling.

A big sign on the door read 'Pump Room: Absolutely No Admittance Unless Authorised'. A couple of health and safety plaques below it seemed to suggest there was imminent danger of death for anyone who entered the room.

She unhooked a big latch and slid the door open.

The room was large and bright. The machinery he'd seen in the photograph – pipes and tubes, cylinders and what looked like boilers – were all clustered on the left-hand side along with two panels filled with switches. On the right side were two wide cupboards flanking a sink unit. The floor looked dusty under the machinery but there were tracks of footprints to the fire escape door. The crack above the window looked even wider than it had seemed in Charlie's picture. In a couple of places, he could see daylight through it.

Charlie put the torch on one of the cupboards and Dan walked over to the fire escape door. One sign warned it was alarmed, another that it shouldn't be opened. Charlie stood beside him.

"Don't worry," she said. "The electric's off."

She pushed at the safety bar and the door swung open. Dan thought Charlie was going to step out into nothing and felt his stomach lurch when he realised the fire escape was missing. He grabbed the waistband of her shorts and yanked her back. She staggered into his arms and he held on until she regained her balance.

"Shit," she said and put a hand on her chest. "You saved my life." She embraced him tightly and he felt a glow of pride and something else. "Thank you." She kissed his lips quickly. "Thank you."

"Don't mention it," he said and reluctantly let go of her.

They leaned on either side of the door to look out. The fire escape ladder had broken away in sections and the lowest one was still attached to the wall but too far to reach safely. The other sections were in a crumpled heap against the rocks and on the sand.

"I wonder when that happened," she said.

"Who knows? You'd think someone would have reported seeing it by now."

"Not many people use this beach," she said and pointed towards the docks which were less than three hundred yards away. "I've never been able to open the door before because it was also too stiff." She shuddered. "Shit, that was close. Thank God you grabbed me."

"You'd have done the same for me."

She took her Instamatic out of its pouch on her bag strap. "Give me a smile, my hero."

He grinned and she took the picture then wound the film on. She got to her knees and put her hand out into space and took another photograph. "Not sure how that'll turn out," she said and stood up. One of her knees was dusty and she brushed it off.

"This place would be ideal to hold someone," Dan said and walked back to the door. "This locks from the outside and there's no way out the fire escape so they'd be properly trapped."

"It makes sense," Charlie said and shuddered. "Perhaps Mia thought she could get away and opened the door in the dark and then…" She stopped and swallowed. "Well, you know."

"Yeah." She didn't need to verbalise what they were both thinking; a frightened young woman who thought she was making her escape but instead was stepping out to her doom. "Poor Mia."

"Let's look around. There might be something that proves she was here."

Charlie used the torch to poke and pry below the boilers and cylinders while Dan checked the cupboards. One was empty apart from several stacks of plastic beakers while the other was filled with various bottles and containers whose warning symbols and long names were coated with dust and grime.

"I don't think anyone's been in here for a while," he said.

"Shit," said Charlie. She was kneeling in front of a small bench against the back wall and took three photographs of something he couldn't see. "Come and look at this."

She laid the item in her palm to present it to him. It was upside down and scuffed and it took a moment to realise what he was looking at. "Is that a Smurfette hairgrip?"

"Uh-huh," she said and seemed to shrink in on herself as if the weight of her discovery had pressed down on her shoulders. "I found one like it in her room. Do you think it could be hers?"

If it was, then the postcard message was even more dangerous than they'd thought. He picked up the hairgrip and saw it wasn't dusty or dirty. "This hasn't been here long because it's too clean."

"It can't just be a massive coincidence though, can it? Mia was the only adult I ever saw wear one because

Smurfs are kids' things. But how many little girls will have been down here recently?"

She played the torch beam under the bench and they saw the dust was badly disturbed. "Someone has been in here recently though," she said.

"I think we have to go back to the police," Dan said.

"Yes. I'll develop these pictures and we'll take the hairgrip."

"You should take a picture of the door lock too," he said and went out into the corridor.

She took her picture and wound on the film and in the silence afterwards he heard the crunch of grit from somewhere above them. The hairs on the back of his neck stood on end. It sounded like the door was being opened at the top of the stairs.

"Charlie," he hissed. His pulse raced. He tapped her shoulder and she jumped and turned.

"What?" she said and her voice sounded too loud in the corridor.

He put his fingers against her mouth in case the newcomer heard but she swatted his hand away.

"Shush," he whispered. "I think there's somebody else in here."

Chapter 36

"Someone opened that door up the stairs."

"It might be Paul or Andy."

He hadn't thought of that. "That's okay then."

"Maybe not. They might not like me bringing you here, especially after what happened."

"So shall we stay put?"

"Probably for the best since there's no reason for them to come down here. Perhaps they came out of the changing rooms and are going outside."

He wondered if their whispering had carried up the stairs though surely, if it was Paul or Andy, one of them would have said something.

Charlie tiptoed almost to the end of the corridor and he followed carefully.

The gritty noise came again and Dan realised it was the door to the stairwell closing. There was a few seconds' pause then the person took a step but the acoustics made it impossible to tell if they were moving toward the door or the stairs. Another step.

"Why are they moving so slowly?" Charlie whispered.

"I don't know. If it was Paul or Andy they'd have seen the bike and must have heard us talking."

"What do you mean?"

"I mean it's not them."

Her eyebrows rose and her eyes looked very wide and bright in the gloom. "Who else could it be?" The panic was clear to hear in her whisper.

Dan shrugged.

Another footstep and then there was a brief snatch of outdoor sounds – music from the funfair and a gull calling – before the door clicked shut.

Charlie let out a breath that seemed to almost deflate her. Dan breathed out as quietly as he could through his mouth.

"Bloody hell," she whispered. "That was scary."

"You're telling me. Let's get out while the going's good."

They tiptoed towards the staircase and he only just heard the footstep. He grabbed Charlie's arm and pulled her back against the wall.

A missile hit a flight further up and shattered. It sounded like an explosion and debris rained down. Dan pushed Charlie back towards the corridor as hard pellets peppered his legs.

There were more footsteps from above and then the door banged open and closed.

"They nearly killed us," Charlie cried with indignant rage. She flicked the torch on. The ground was littered with bits of mortar and concrete. Three bricks still attached to each other lay in the centre of the stairwell. She took a picture of it.

Dan shared her rage. Whoever dropped this had carried it from somewhere else and if they'd been hit the injuries could have been serious. He raced up the stairs and Charlie was right behind him shining the torch beam between his legs.

At the top of the stairs, he held Charlie back then pulled open the door and kept to one side. Nothing happened. He peered slowly around the frame to see the landing was empty.

Charlie rushed through the door and pulled open the double doors before he could stop her. She did have the sense to pause for a moment and then they both ran out into the warm brightness of the lido.

Dan shielded his eyes and it took a moment for them to adjust to the light. They were near the sea wall and he could see someone running towards the main entrance wearing a pale green coat and a cap. Charlie must have seen them too because she started to sprint. Dan kept pace with her around the pool and up over the terrace.

"Come back, you bastard!" Charlie called. "We've seen you."

The person ran past the turnstiles and out of sight down the staircase. Dan and Charlie had gained on them and ran up the stairs two at a time. He reached for her hand as they got to the top to slow her down in case the person was waiting for them with another brick to throw.

There was no projectile. They rushed down the steps and he yanked the fence open so Charlie could slip through then she pushed from the other side so he could.

Dan looked towards the town but saw no one even close to them.

"There," said Charlie.

A dark Vauxhall Viva was parked at the kerb a hundred yards or so up the road towards the docks. The person had just opened the driver's door and stopped to look back at Charlie and Dan. The brim of the cap was pulled low, and Dan couldn't see their face from this distance.

"Come back," Charlie yelled. "We're ready for you."

"Or are you too chicken?" Dan called.

The person got into the car and the engine started. Charlie started running towards it.

"No," he shouted but she didn't stop so he ran after her even though it seemed like a bad idea. The person had already proved they were willing to cause harm so what would stop them now from trying to run him or Charlie over?

"At least stay on the path," he said as he caught up with her.

The Viva backed away in an arc and bounced off the opposite kerb. With a lurch and a quick squeal of tyres it drove quickly towards the docks. They were never going to catch it.

"Get a picture of the number plate," he called.

She slowed to take the photograph and he ran for a bit further in case a lorry came out the docks and slowed the Viva but nothing did. He finally stopped running when it turned off Marine Drive.

Charlie caught up with him, breathing heavily.

"Who the hell was that?" he asked, leaning forward with his hands on his thighs.

"No idea but I got the picture." She arched her back and smiled. "It's all very curious, isn't it?"

She sounded almost pleased and he gaped at her.

"I can think of better words than curious."

"Don't you see?" she said. "Nobody has any reason to be in there other than Andy, Paul or the person who put Mia in there."

"We're not certain Mia was in there."

"Well, if she wasn't, why was someone trying to drop bricks on our heads?"

Chapter 37

Dan's stomach was in knots as they rode towards town and he kept glancing over his shoulder in case the Viva was behind them.

"Do you mind if we stop?" Charlie asked and they pulled into a lay-by in front of the Oceanview Hotel.

"What's up?"

She stood on the pavement with her hands on her hips and looked up at the sky as she took deep breaths.

"Wow," she said. "Sorry. I just feel a bit shaky."

"Me too. It was intense."

"I couldn't see who it was but I took a picture as we ran across the lido. I don't think we'll see much more than a blur though." She shook out her arms and checked her watch. "Shit. I forgot it's half-day closing on a Thursday. Mr Patterson will have closed up by now and I really wanted to get these pictures developed."

"We'll have to go tomorrow," he said.

It was a horrible feeling to know the holiday was almost over. The thought of going back to Hadlington and not seeing Charlie again made him feel bad. The thought they might not get to the bottom of this mystery by then and she'd be all alone to deal with it made him feel even worse.

"Uh-huh," she said then looked at him with an odd expression. "Are you okay?"

He wasn't. Thinking of her being alone made him realise how lucky they'd been to get out of the lido with nothing more than annoyance. "Not really," he admitted. "I got scared in the lido."

"So did I," she said and sounded relieved it hadn't just been her. "If we'd been up the stairs we really could have been hurt."

"It's fucking terrifying to think someone did it deliberately."

"And that we must know them because a random person wouldn't walk around the lido carrying bricks. It has to be one of the four and part of me is excited that we're on the right track and we're going to prove Mia didn't kill herself. The other part of me is scared to death because we seem to have disturbed a hornets' nest. I mean, how did they know we were going to be there?"

"The bike parked outside would be a dead giveaway if you were looking for it."

"True," she said. "Has this scared you away from looking further into it?"

"Not at all."

"Phew," she said with relief. "There is one thing we absolutely need to agree on though."

"What's that?"

"That we don't tell your mum. The postcard was bad enough but if we told her what just happened, she's not going to be happy. She'd either stop you from seeing me or go home today."

"She wouldn't."

Charlie quirked an eyebrow. "Really?"

"Okay," he said and conceded defeat. "We'll keep quiet about our adventures in the lido."

"Tomorrow we'll go to Mr Patterson's first thing and then the police. We'll show them the hairgrip and the photographs and they'll have the number plate to track down the person."

"Sounds good," he said. "Now we need to be careful for the rest of today."

* * *

Ade came out of his shed as Charlie steered into the camp and gestured for her to go the wrong way around the pitch and putt green.

"What's up?" she called.

"Tommy's just got back. He's in a foul mood and I don't want him to catch you."

Dan and Charlie exchanged a quick glance as she steered them around the back of the bike hire.

"You told us he wouldn't mind you giving out a knackered bike," she said.

"I might have told you a lie but he'll go ballistic. He's mad as a wasp."

"When did he get back?" Charlie asked.

"Just now I think."

"What car does he drive?" Dan asked.

"I don't pay much attention to cars," Ade said apologetically. "My mind's so full of programming ideas there's not much room for anything else."

They helped him park the bike then walked along to the roadway.

"This might be interesting," Charlie said. "If you follow the road past the docks it hooks around to the harbour by the old town. Tommy could have driven that loop and got back here without us seeing him." She clicked her fingers. "We could go into the staff car park and see if there's a Viva in there."

"We could but it's not exactly an unusual car and neither of us can remember the number plate."

"You're not helping," she said sourly.

"If it was Tommy and he catches us there then we're in big trouble. And he might have borrowed someone else's car."

"Good point," she said begrudgingly. "I hate it when you're right. Not that it happens very often."

"Thanks."

"So where are you going now?"

"I was thinking of heading back to the caravan," he said. "You know, we should lie low and that kind of thing?" She kept pace with him. "Would you like to come along?"

"I thought you'd never ask," she said.

Chapter 38

Jude spent most of the afternoon close to the caravan in case the kids called in after going to the police but they hadn't yet. Her one outing was to the shop to get some ham for her sandwich where she found a big revolving rack of postcards. Some were views of Seagrave and other Norfolk holiday destinations but the majority were the smutty kind Charlie had received.

She ate her sandwich sitting in the sun and got far enough into *Lace* that she now knew what the goldfish scene was all about. At first it seemed a bit disturbing, not least for the fish, but the more she thought about it the more she remembered the dreams she'd had about Paul and that led her mind down all kinds of paths. It was a very pleasant half hour and maddeningly hot.

The one downside was that he was in the limited pool of suspects but if she cancelled their date tonight she couldn't try to pick up any information that might help. It was a weak excuse but she had a shower and dried her hair without thinking of a better one.

The front door opened while she surveyed her limited choice of outfit for the evening. Jude put on her dressing gown and went into the hallway as Charlie came through the door.

"Hey, Jude."

"Hi. How did it go with the police?"

Charlie pulled a face. "Not so good."

Jude followed her into the lounge. Dan was in the kitchen making two glasses of squash.

"Did you want a coffee, Mum?"

"No thanks," she said and leaned against the countertop. "So what happened?"

In her experience teenagers often left key details out of the stories they told but Charlie was thorough as she went through what happened.

"How could they be so dismissive?" she asked.

"Perhaps they thought you were being a teenager and winding them up."

"I said we ought to have you go in next time," said Dan.

"I think that's a good idea. They're obviously going to need convincing before they do anything."

"They'll be convinced if one of us gets hurt," said Charlie hotly then immediately bit her lip.

Jude's teaching sixth sense kicked in. She glanced at Dan who looked back at her without expression. Alarm bells were ringing because she wasn't getting the whole story. "Did something happen?"

"No," Charlie said, too quickly. Another alarm bell.

"Have you had another postcard?"

"I don't know, I haven't been home yet."

It was clear Charlie wasn't going to say more and Jude didn't want to push her. "So what did you get up to all day?"

"Just wandering around," Dan said after a moment. "Nothing too exciting."

Jude squinted at him but he didn't crack. Whatever they were hiding wasn't going to be uncovered for a while but both of them seemed healthy and unharmed, which meant nothing major had happened.

"How was your day?" Dan asked.

"A bit frustrating," she said and told them she'd managed to not see either Fiona or Paul for the first time that week. "I did see Tommy though."

"Did he say much?" Charlie asked.

"No because once he knew who I was he thought I was questioning him and looked a bit panicky. Then he went into town."

"Did he drive?" Dan asked.

"He went behind that line of conifers near reception and then I heard an engine start."

"What did he drive?" Charlie asked. "Did you see?"

"No. Why are you interested in him driving?"

"I thought we saw him up by the funfair but Dan said it wasn't him."

That didn't sound right to Jude either. She rubbed her lower lip. "I was thinking about the postcard business this afternoon."

"I wouldn't," Charlie said. "If the police aren't worried why should we be?"

"I don't know. But I wondered if you wanted to stay here for the night? Dan can sleep on the sofa and you can have the spare bed in his room."

"Hang on a minute," Dan protested.

"Chill out," Charlie said. "Thank you, Jude, that's a lovely offer but I'll be okay."

"You're not going to change your mind, are you?" Jude asked.

Charlie shook her head.

"At least promise me you'll lock your door."

"I always do. And tonight I'll put a bear trap in front of it too."

"That's a good idea. So what're you two going to do while I'm out."

"You're out again?" Dan asked.

"I have another hot date," she said and Dan cringed. Charlie laughed at his reaction. "I'm going to use the opportunity to drill Paul for information."

Dan groaned. "We haven't made plans," he said.

"I wouldn't mind another chippy tea," said Charlie.

"At least let me pay for it," said Jude.

"Not when I can earn the money with my system," said Charlie. "Thanks for the offer though."

Jude looked at her watch and realised they'd been talking for longer than she'd thought. "I'd best get sorted. Whatever you do tonight, please look after one another and be careful."

"We won't go far, Mum, I promise."

"Thanks," she said and went into her room and closed the door.

"That was nice," she heard Charlie say quietly.

"What?" Dan whispered back.

"Your mum making sure I was okay. It's been a long while since someone did that for me."

"That's just Mum being Mum," he said but she heard pride in his tone.

Chapter 39

The Sultans of Swing were killing a song that might have been by Slade or perhaps Queen when Dan and Charlie went into the arcade. A few men were gambling on the big money fruit machines and some little kids were clustered around the Star Wars X-Wing cabinet.

Charlie went over to the nearest tuppenny falls machine where a little girl of about eight wearing a party dress was leaning against one of the glass panels.

"Excuse me," Charlie said and the kid rolled her head on the glass to look up. "Are you playing this or just looking?"

"Just looking," said the girl and pressed her finger to the glass.

Dan thought she was pointing to a small box on top of a pile of coins near the drop. Judging by the cheap artwork he assumed it wasn't a real Pound Puppy inside but that didn't seem to bother her.

"Do you mind if I play?" Charlie asked.

"Not if I can watch," said the girl.

"What's your name?"

"Milly."

Charlie began her system and Milly got very excited. She knelt and fished out the coins as they dropped and Charlie gave her at least one from each batch.

"Wow," said Milly. "Thanks."

Dan watched her play and liked that she poked out the tip of her tongue as she concentrated.

"What?" she asked. "I can see you smiling out the corner of my eye."

"I'm not."

"I think he is," said Milly and glared at him.

"I wasn't," Dan protested.

"Yeah," said Charlie but didn't sound convinced.

"Yeah," said Milly and went back to leaning her forehead against the glass.

He couldn't work out Charlie's system and settled for watching the machine lights play across her face. Her eyes were bright and he was fascinated by the tip of her tongue and felt the desire to lean over and kiss her.

The next coin got them a big win and she knelt down to help Milly take the coins out. The little girl got twenty pence for her trouble this time. Charlie gave the rest to

Dan and let her hand sit on his for a moment longer than necessary. He liked it.

"No mushy stuff," said Milly.

Charlie played on until Dan estimated they'd won four pounds. "One last go," she said and fed in a three-coin combo. The Pound Puppy box tottered. Dan thumped the frame and the box dropped and Milly let out a squeal of delight that hurt his ears.

"Thank you!" she shouted and rushed out of the arcade.

"That pleased her," Dan said.

* * *

They got generous portions of fish and chips and ate them at the caravan as they watched *Top of the Pops*. Charlie was disappointed Madonna had been knocked off the top spot but John Peel made them both laugh.

Dan packed away the rubbish and Charlie knelt in front of the television to switch channels. There was a Burt Reynolds film on Anglia and she left it on even though it just seemed like noisy rubbish.

They sat on the sofa without speaking. Their knees were touching. He wanted to say something but didn't quite know what.

"Did you want to listen to some music?" she asked after a while. She sounded a little annoyed as if she'd been waiting for him to speak and he felt like he'd missed an opportunity.

"That'd be good." He switched on the portable radio in the kitchen. "What's the local station?"

"Seagrave Sound," she said, imitating the jingle. "This should be their weekly indie hour."

He retuned the radio to find The Cure singing *Love Cats*. "Good choice," he said and sat back next to her.

"Where do you think Jude went on her date?"

"I'd rather not think about it to be honest."

Charlie sat up and grinned evilly. "Why? Do you think she and Paul are…"

"Yuck." He overexaggerated a shudder. "Please don't."

"Why not? She's young and very attractive. He'd be a fool not to try."

"She's my mum."

"No, she's a fun and independent woman who deserves some happiness."

"With Paul from the seaside?"

"Holiday romances can have their place."

"I know," he said and she met his gaze through her eyelashes.

"What time's she coming home?"

"I don't know."

Charlie bit her lip. "Maybe we shouldn't then."

"What?"

"You know."

Dan did. For once he was reading the signals and on absolutely the same page as Charlie.

He kissed her and she kissed him back hard. Her fingers reached into his hair and pulled him close and he ran a hand up her side. His fingers brushed the edge of her breast and she made a small moaning sound deep in her throat and it was the most exciting noise he'd ever heard in his life.

Charlie moved slightly and her hands slipped down his back. He risked putting a hand on her thigh.

"We can't," she said into his mouth.

"I know but…"

His hand slid up her thigh as hers slipped down his back. The kisses got stronger and harder. She moved her hand around his side and the sensation felt both ticklish and hot. Her fingers slipped under the hem of his T-shirt and he desperately wanted her hand to move down further.

Charlie shifted on the sofa slightly, turning towards him and his hand slipped down across her bum. She made that moaning sound again, her fingertips pressing into his stomach.

"Dan," she whispered. Her voice sounded hoarse and she cupped his cheek with her free hand.

Something knocked against the caravan and it felt like someone had tipped a bucket of water over Dan. He and Charlie scrambled away from each other as they both watched the door, waiting for it to open and his mum to come in.

But she didn't. The sound came again and then moved to the roof.

"A fucking seagull," he said and laughed sourly. "Shit."

Charlie looked at him and kissed him gently. "We could have been caught then," she said.

Would it have been so bad? he wanted to ask but yes, it probably would have been. They were on the sofa in the caravan and his mum could come back at any moment. "I know."

"This is so unfair," she said.

The Cure finished and Nena began singing *99 Red Balloons*.

Dan tried to think of a way around the situation but only one came to mind. "What about your place?"

She laughed sourly. "Not with my neighbours reporting any movement of eligible young men. I'd rather take my chances on Jude coming home and catching us."

"Are the neighbours really that bad?"

"You wouldn't believe what Dad knows about my week."

"Oh," he said and the sense of defeat felt almost absolute.

"I am sorry but it's not fair on us or on Jude if she comes back."

"I know."

She sat up and adjusted her T-shirt and shorts. "How about a board game?"

"You're kidding?"

"Nope. If I don't find something to fill my time I'll be all over you and then we're back to square one."

He groaned. How close had he come? "I saw Monopoly in the cupboard."

Chapter 40

Paul answered the buzzer immediately. "Is that the pretty lady from the Holidaze camp?"

"One of them," Jude said.

"I'll buzz you up."

"Don't you want to know which one of us ladies it is?"

"I think I recognise your voice," he said.

The door buzzed and she went into the hall and up the stairs with a slight bounce in her step. He was waiting for her on the landing outside his door in a dark blue shirt and pale trousers. He opened his arms and she gratefully accepted his hug. He smelled of soap and aftershave and his jawline was free of stubble. She dropped a little kiss on it.

"It's been a while," he said.

"I know. It'd be murder if we had to go longer than twenty-four hours, wouldn't it? I did call by earlier but you were out."

"I had a last-minute work thing to wine and dine some potential investors." He held her at arm's length and looked her up and down. "You look great."

"Are you sure?" She'd decided on a linen skirt and a sleeveless blue blouse which were the last of her clothes she would describe as "okay for going out". If Paul wanted to see her tomorrow, she'd either have to repeat an outfit or turn up in T-shirt and shorts. She'd decided on her flip-flops again too.

"Of course. I do like your flip-flops. You have such pretty toes."

He gave her a slow smile and she felt a melting sensation in her belly. "Thanks, they're my best feature. You look great too."

"Oh this old combo? I'll just grab my wallet then we'll go."

"Where are you taking me tonight?"

"Do you like curry?"

"I could be persuaded to have a curry."

"Then you're in luck because I've booked a table at the best Indian restaurant in all of Seagrave and the owner–"

"Happens to be a friend of yours?"

"However did you guess?"

* * *

The curry was as good as Paul had promised and she was full as they walked back through the evening streets of Seagrave with her arm linked through his.

"So how did our teen investigators get on at the police station?" he asked.

"Not so good. They didn't really take her seriously and Charlie was properly put out." She decided to push her luck. "They weren't even interested in the postcard."

"I don't remember you mentioning a postcard."

If he was lying he was very skilled at it. "They found it on the beach and didn't know if it was linked with Mia."

"How are they dealing with having seen her body?"

"Really well. They both seemed bright and chipper today." She decided not to share her worry that they'd kept something from her from this afternoon. "I wouldn't like to see a body on the beach."

"Or me and it's still weighing on Andy. You remember I said I spent the afternoon wining and dining? Well it wasn't supposed to be me but Andy buggered off somewhere without telling either me or Fiona where. She rang saying she couldn't find him and I'd have to step in."

"I can't imagine she was happy with that."

"Not at all. She sounded as pissed off as you'd imagine."

"Well it hardly reassures her nothing was going on between him and Mia."

By now they were almost outside his building. "Can I interest you in a nightcap, pretty lady?"

You only regret the things you don't do, she thought and rested her head against his shoulder. "I could be tempted."

"Excellent," he said.

He managed to unlock the front door and go upstairs without letting go of her hand but had to give in when he couldn't pick out his flat key from the keyring. She pouted and looked at her hand and made him laugh as he gestured broadly for her to go in. He opened the French doors and stepped onto the terrace and she leaned against the rail beside him as they looked out towards the sea.

"You're so lucky with this view."

"I know," he said in such a way she knew he was looking at her and not the water. It was corny but it made her smile.

He pulled her towards him and they kissed. It felt for a moment like everything else had dropped away except for him and her.

"Couldn't resist," he said when they broke. "Hope you don't mind."

She licked her lips. "You might ask first next time."

"I will," he said gravely. "And what would you like for that nightcap? I can offer you a cup of coffee or would you prefer wine?"

"A glass of white would be lovely."

"Come and make your choice," he said and led her through to the kitchen.

He took a bottle out of the wine rack for her consideration. She'd heard of it so nodded her approval and he opened the bottle. She remembered where the glasses were and got two down.

Paul stood very close as he poured and her body tingled with expectation. He dropped a quick kiss on her cheek and then another until the pecks became something much more and she worried he'd drop the bottle.

He didn't and finished pouring the drinks. They toasted and went back into the lounge. She sat close enough to him on the sofa that if things developed they wouldn't need to move but not so close she was throwing herself at him.

"What do you think of the wine?" he asked.

"I think it's very good."

"I think you look lovely."

He kissed the tip of her nose. She closed her eyes. He put his finger under her chin to tilt her head up and she kissed him then. Things became passionate quickly and the touch of his fingertips on her bare skin was electrifying. Her breathing quickened and her heart raced.

The telephone rang.

"Ignore it," he said into her mouth.

She was okay with that but the phone didn't stop ringing and it drilled through even her arousal.

"It might be something important," she murmured.

"No," he said. "This is important."

The telephone kept ringing.

"I could leave it," he said, kissing her between each word.

"You could." She kissed him. "But you probably won't."

"Buggeration," he said and sat back. "I'll get it."

He had to adjust his trousers before grabbing the cordless phone from a shelf. "Hello?" He listened for a moment. "Andy. So good of you to ring." He checked his watch. "Do you know what time it is?" He put his hand over the mouthpiece. "I'm sorry, Jude, but I need to take this."

"Don't worry," she said. "I'll look at the lido display again."

He stuck up his thumb, mouthed "sorry" then went back to the call.

She went into the office and, once out of sight, leaned against the wall to take a breath. That had been intense and she felt hornier now than she had in a long time. She fanned her face with both hands then switched the light on.

The window reflected her and she crossed the room to close the blinds. The string somehow got caught in a folder propped against the wall and fell onto a pile of box files on Paul's messy desk. Some of the papers inside slipped out and the edges were bright red. The folder was marked 'Andy to sign' with at least half a dozen exclamation marks. The last had been made so angrily it had ripped into the card.

Jude's curiosity flared even though she knew that she shouldn't be prying among the paperwork of a man who, less than five minutes ago, she was ready to sleep with. Even though she'd convinced herself Paul wasn't responsible for the postcard she wasn't sure about Andy and there might be a clue in the file.

The first invoice was from a solicitor, the second from an electrical contractor. Both were stamped 'Overdue' and there were at least half a dozen more invoices from other traders. A restricted cashflow wasn't new or unusual in this economy but it could point to problems.

Paul's voice got louder as if he was coming towards the office, so she moved towards the lido display on the wall. His voice ebbed and she imagined he was pacing back and forth in the lounge.

A copy of the *Seagrave Telegraph* was on Andy's blotter with Charlie's thigh disappearing into the fold. Jude looked back at the photography display and thought again about the crack in the walls. Something was nagging at the back of her mind but she couldn't quite put her finger on it.

"For fuck's sake," Paul said loudly. "Seriously, Andy, we've got to keep it together. You need to get a grip."

Jude knew she was listening to the conversation out of context but it didn't seem like something she should ignore. Andy had been missing for most of the day and now Paul was telling him to keep it together?

"Why the hell were you talking to Tommy bloody Mackintosh anyway?" Paul demanded. "That bloke's a major pain in the arse."

Why would Andy be talking to Tommy? Tommy said he was meeting friends but did he mean Andy?

"I can't do anything at the moment because Jude's here." A pause. "Yes they did go to the police." He sounded concerned and Jude felt a chill pull her shoulders tight. "I don't know exactly what happened."

Jude stepped back and caught her heel against something and almost fell. She put out an arm to steady herself and her backside hit the edge of Andy's desk. Her hand came down heavily on something smooth and even as she got her balance she heard something clatter onto the floor.

"Shit."

One of his box files had opened as it fell and papers had spilled out. There were overdue invoices and one carried a handwritten threat to break Andy's legs if payment wasn't forthcoming.

Jude picked them up as quickly as she could and stuffed them back into the file but stopped.

A pile of postcards were pushed into one corner. She suddenly felt sick and her throat went dry. She picked up a handful from the top and the first few were brand new smutty ones like she'd seen in the camp shop. Others had views of Seagrave and Cromer and the bulk were much older and second-hand. She turned one over and it had a handwritten message and a stamp she didn't recognise.

The chill ran down her back and she wanted to clear the items away before Paul came in. She stuffed the postcards back and disturbed a thick envelope with 'entertainment' written on it. As she picked it up a wad of photographs slid across the carpet.

"For fuck's sake," she said with a mounting sense of panic and tried to gather them up quickly.

The first picture showed the lido from the entryway. It was blurred and poorly composed, a snap rather than a proper photograph. The second was a blurred image of a person with longish blonde hair and a bare shoulder. The next picture was the same woman on the terrace with the sea wall behind her, and even though her face was in shadow Jude could see it was clearly Mia.

Jude felt a sickened sense of surprise. In the next picture Mia was inside an office and smiling widely for the camera. In the next she was wearing a high-legged bikini and pouting for the camera.

Jude's stomach turned.

The next photograph showed Mia from her belly button to the top of her head with the focus on her cleavage. The necklace Charlie had told her about was partially obscured by the flare of the flash.

Jude flicked quickly through the rest without looking at them specifically and saw a lot more flesh exposed. She felt ill at ease as she slipped them back into the envelope and put it into the box file.

People took photographs of each other, she knew that. She and Neil had done it when he bought a Polaroid in the mid-seventies. But whose photographs were these? They were on Andy's desk but in Paul's home office so they could belong to either man. What other acts were captured in those photographs she hadn't looked at – hadn't wanted to look at?

She felt her skin crawl as memories of Neil and that horrible meeting in the head teacher's office when she'd learned the awful truth about his affair. She didn't want to feel like this and knew she had to get out of the room, out of the flat.

"I've got to go," Paul said. "Are you working tomorrow or am I supposed to chase you around all day again?" A pause. "Fine. Get this sorted, Andy."

He slammed the phone down. Jude rushed across the room to get her glass from Paul's desk and he came into the office.

"Sorry about that," he said with a smile. "Andy wanted to bring me up to date with his day."

Each word hit her like it had weight. "You don't have to explain."

"I do." He leaned against Andy's desk and she thought he would notice the box file had moved but he frowned instead. "Are you okay?"

Her mind raced – she needed to get out. "No," she said. "I'm not feeling… It's my stomach. I'm sorry, I feel a bit sick." That, at least, wasn't a lie.

"That's not good," he said with a mixture of disappointment and concern. "Did you want me to run you back to the caravan?"

"No. A walk in the air might do me some good. I'm sorry, Paul, but I really should go."

He walked her to the door attentive and concerned. "I hate the thought of you walking back if you're not feeling right. Will I see you tomorrow? It's your last full day but you don't need to go on Saturday, you're more than welcome to stay the weekend. I won't charge you."

She smiled at his desperation and slipped on her flip-flops. "I'll see you, Paul. Okay?"

"Yes," he said and then she was walking down the stairs.

* * *

It was barely ten o'clock when she got back to the caravan and while the walk hadn't cleared her mind, it had allowed her to focus slightly more. The photographs were terrible, she knew that, but this wasn't the situation with Neil repeating itself. Mia was a young woman in her twenties, she was allowed to do what she wanted. Jude just felt weary at the thought of what Mia had found herself in and that weariness was tinged with sadness and frustration.

The lights were on and she knocked loudly in case Dan and Charlie were enjoying one another's company. "Am I okay to come in?"

"Of course," Dan called.

They were at the table midway through a game of Monopoly though both had colour in their cheeks and Dan's hair looked as if someone had run her fingers through it.

"Something smells nice and vinegary."

"The arcade funded us another chippy tea," said Charlie. "How was your evening?"

"It could have gone better," she said and told them what had happened and what she'd found. "There were also some photographs and postcards."

"Postcards?" Charlie said.

"What were the photographs?" Dan asked.

Jude sat on the edge of the sofa next to Charlie. "Did you ever take pictures of Mia at the lido?"

"No," she said. "It was mostly on the Neptune's stage for the background. Why?"

"The photos I found were of Mia in a bikini taken in the lido office."

Charlie made the connection quicker than Dan. "Oh. Were they bad?"

"The ones I saw were."

"Yuck," said Dan. "Is that why you came home so early?"

"Yes." Even talking about it made her feel grubby. "I feel like I need a shower."

"I'll get going too," Charlie said.

"The offer of a bed still stands," Jude said.

"I can't." Charlie put on her shoes. "I have a couple of ancient neighbours who report my every move back to my dad."

"I'm sure he'd understand if I explained the situation to him."

"I'm sure he would but, you know…"

"I understand." Jude touched the girl's shoulder. "Promise me though that if you hear anything or feel worried, you'll come here straight away."

"I promise," she said and looked genuinely touched.

Dan walked to the door and put his shoes on. "I'll walk you home," he said.

Chapter 41

Dan woke to the sound of rain hitting the roof. He rolled out of bed and opened the flimsy curtain. The window was smeared with water.

Last full day here and it was raining? Bloody marvellous.

He pulled on his dressing gown and left his bedroom.

"Morning, Danny." His mum was at the table with a coffee, listening to the radio. She'd marked her place in her book with her finger.

"Morning." He went into the bathroom and when he came out, she was in the kitchen and he smelled toast.

"Did the rain wake you?" she asked.

"I don't think so."

"You're lucky. I woke up at seven thinking someone was chucking marbles on the roof." The toaster popped so she buttered the slices and put his in front of him on a plate. "Raining on our penultimate day takes the biscuit. Did you have anything planned?"

"We were going to–" He managed to stop himself before he told her about developing the photographs from yesterday. "To Seagrave to play our way through the arcades."

"A grand way to say goodbye," she said and her smile carried a tinge of sadness.

He felt bad for deceiving her even if it was done through kindness – what she didn't know couldn't hurt her and she didn't need to know about their mystery attacker.

"Are you seeing Paul?"

"I don't know if that's a good idea, Danny."

She said it in such a measured tone he felt sorry for her. "Those photographs must have been Andy's, Mum."

"You can't know that."

"But you said everything on Andy's desk was in its place so if he found Paul's file there he'd move it."

"Probably but…" She took a bite of toast.

Seagrave Sound went into the news and if they'd still been talking Dan might not have heard the headline.

"The body found on Seagrave beach on Wednesday has been formally identified today as Mia Garwood, aged twenty-four from the town. Mia worked at the Holidaze resort and was pursuing a singing career."

* * *

They were reading when Charlie knocked. He opened the door and she stood on the step in a red and white cagoule with the hood pulled tight around her face. Her legs were bare and rain-slicked.

"Come in," he said and she did quickly.

She peeled off the cagoule and shook it outside then closed the door. "Phew." She blew her fringe off her forehead. "Nice weather for ducks."

His mum got her a towel to dry her legs. Dan saw her cut-off jeans were damp around the hem and stuck to her legs. He tried hard not to look but failed abysmally.

"Did you hear the news?" Dan asked.

"No, I got a bit distracted this morning and I listened to my tape on the way over. Why?"

"They've named Mia," he said.

"Well, that's something."

"What were you distracted by?" his mum asked.

Charlie pulled a postcard out of her pocket. The cartoon showed a woman with impossibly large breasts sitting on a beach. "I got another one," she said and put it face down on the table.

I SAW YOU YESTERDAY, YOU LITTLE BITCH. LEAVE WELL ALONE OR THERE'LL BE MORE THINGS DROPPING ON YOUR HEAD.

Goosebumps crawled up his arms and his scalp felt too tight.

"Leave what well alone?" his mum asked.

Charlie shot him a glance, as if to make sure he kept his mouth shut. "I don't know but I think I ought to take it to the police, don't you?"

"Yes," Dan said. He hoped her photograph of the number plate had come out.

"Absolutely," said his mum. She turned the postcard over so the joke was visible. "I can't help thinking this came out of that stash I saw last night."

"You can buy them anywhere, Jude. If I was going to be mean to someone, I'd definitely use a postcard," Charlie said. "Who could trace it?"

"Let me give you a lift. It'll be safer."

"We'll take a bike," said Charlie. "Honestly."

"I'm not sure…"

"We'll be fine," said Dan. "It'll save you going out in the rain."

"Are you mad?" His mum looked at him as if she thought he might be. "It's not a big deal to drive."

"The bikes have covers," Charlie said. "We'll be dry."

His mum looked from one to the other of them and he could see she knew something was being left unsaid. "At least put a cagoule on, Danny," she said.

"Can I ask you a favour?" said Charlie.

"Of course."

"Just in case we don't see each other before you leave, I wanted to give you this." She pulled her into a hug. "I'm going to miss you."

"I'm going to miss you too." She let Charlie go reluctantly. "Before you go though, I need you both to listen to this. I'm not saying Andy or Paul had anything to do with Mia going missing but something's off here and they only knew about you going to the police because I opened my big mouth."

Charlie went to say something and his mum gently squeezed her hand.

"Please be careful."

"We will, Jude, I promise."

* * *

They ran up the roadway through the rain. The bikes were out with covers over the seats and Ade was in his little shed. A puddle had gathered around his chair and he wore shorts, a rain mac in camp colours and a pair of wellies. His magazine sagged as if it had absorbed the damp.

"You want to go out in this?" he asked incredulously.

"If you'll let us borrow that old bike like yesterday," Charlie said.

"Hey!" The shout echoed around them.

Startled, Dan turned to see Tommy striding towards them. He wore a rain mac and his Adidas trainers kicked up a spray of water with every pace.

"Oh shit," muttered Ade. "I'm in trouble now."

"He looks pissed off," said Dan.

"He's going to kill me," muttered Ade.

"No he's not," said Charlie.

Tommy stopped in front of them and didn't look happy as he glared between Charlie and Dan. "I hoped I'd run into you two," he said. "What were you doing?"

"We were going to hire a bike from Ade," Charlie said in a loud and clear voice.

Tommy laughed. "As if. You haven't paid a day's hire since you got here." He looked over her shoulder at Ade. "What were you going to give them?"

"I, um, wasn't..." mumbled Ade.

"Yeah, like fuck you weren't." Tommy leaned in close to Charlie and Dan. "Follow me."

"Why should we?" she demanded.

"Because I asked you to."

"Are you planning to try and intimidate me some more?" she asked.

"What are you talking about?"

"The postcards didn't work so now you're going to threaten me in person?"

"What postcards?" Tommy looked at Dan. "Your girlfriend's a nutter."

"She's not..." started Dan.

"Maybe I am," Charlie said.

"I've never threatened you." Tommy shook his head in frustration. "This isn't getting us anywhere. I don't know what you're talking about but please come with me. I need to speak to you in private."

He walked down the gravel path towards the staff chalets and they followed after a moment or two.

"You told us not to go in here again," Charlie said.

"Are you always this fucking irritating?" Tommy asked over his shoulder. He pulled open the gate and stood to one side to let Charlie and Dan through then closed it behind them. "Stop here."

Fear chilled Dan's arms and his heart began to race. He put his hand close to Charlie's so he could grab and pull her if Tommy did something really stupid.

"Where are you going?" Tommy asked. He didn't make eye contact with either of them and that made Dan feel even more on edge.

"Into Seagrave," Charlie said.

"Something to do with Mia?"

"Yes," said Charlie. "If you must know."

"Tell me what you're doing."

"What's it got to do with you?" Dan asked.

Tommy rubbed his face and Dan saw his eyes were red. "I heard it on the radio this morning," he said and the muscles in his face seemed to pull together like a drawstring purse. "I thought you were a pair of idiots but you were telling the truth all along." He was crying.

"Why would we lie?" Charlie asked.

"I don't know." He took a deep shuddery breath and let it out slowly. "You piss me off, Charlie, and I think it's because you were close to Mia and it should have been me that helped her."

"Oh my God," she said. "You still love her."

"I do," Tommy said and his shoulders sagged. "I was a twat and I drove her away but I was starting to make amends. I think she'd started to trust me again too."

"Were you at the lido yesterday?" Charlie asked.

"No. I'm not a ghoul, why would I want to go and see where you found her?"

"So where have you been going the last couple of days?" she asked.

"Looking for Mia. I even went to see her manky old man. I felt bad because we had a big fight on Monday night. I heard the wife of the lido bloke knocking Mia and it drove me nuts. We had words when she came off stage and I was an arsehole. Then she got into that car when I saw you watching her."

"Did you see what kind of car it was?" Dan asked.

"No, it was too misty. Tell me what you've been doing so I can help."

Charlie told him everything and at one point he held up his arms so they could see his bare wrists.

"Let me drive you into town."

"No," she said. "We're going on the bike. I need to do this for me, Tommy. It broke my heart to see Mia on those rocks."

Tommy looked like a man struggling to keep his head above water and Dan felt sorry for him. "I understand." He bit his lip. "Tell Ade to give you whatever bike you want. But the minute you need anything, let me know."

"We will," said Charlie. "And I'm sorry you didn't have a chance to make things right with Mia."

"We all are," he said. "Now bugger off and speak to the police."

Chapter 42

Jude didn't want to see Paul. She still felt betrayed and hurt and knew seeing him wouldn't make things better but she'd promised to try and help Dan and Charlie so didn't have much choice.

The rain had stopped and the air was fresh enough with a strong breeze blowing in from the sea that she had to zip up her cagoule. She ran ideas through her mind about what to say to Paul but nothing seemed quite right.

A car horn startled her and a cherry-coloured Fiesta pulled up to the kerb. "Hello," said Fiona as she wound the window down. "I was just coming to see you."

"That's nice," said Jude and decided to roll with the opportunity. Paul could wait. "I walked into town yesterday hoping to catch up with you."

"I dropped by and you weren't in so we must have passed on the way. I missed you actually. I had a rare old day of it and thought you'd be a good sounding board."

Jude decided it would be intriguing to hear her side of the Andy story. "We could do it now if you wanted. I didn't have a destination in mind."

"And it's a bit grim for a walk too."

"It's only rain," said Jude as she got in.

Fiona executed a six-point turn in the wide road. "Sorry," she said, "but my car's getting fixed and the garage lent me this."

* * *

Lesley's was busy with people sheltering from the weather. A large dog was curled under one of the seats and smelled like it had been caught in the rain and was now drying out. Jude managed to nab them a table while Fiona got their drinks.

"I meant to ask you but how did Dan and Charlie get on with showing her photograph to the police?"

Jude had wondered how long it would take her to ask but hadn't expected it to be the first question. "They thanked her and took a copy of it," she said and watched Fiona's face for a reaction.

"Oh," she said blankly. "I heard on radio they've identified her now."

"That's why Danny and Charlie have gone back to the police today. She's had another warning."

"Another warning?" Fiona asked with a flicker of confusion that looked convincing. "What do you mean?"

"I don't think I told you but Charlie got a postcard yesterday warning her off going to the police."

"That's terrible."

"I agree. It was written on a smutty postcard."

"Lots of them about."

"That's what I thought," said Jude, "but then I found a pile in Paul's home office yesterday." Jude waited a moment and watched it sink in. "I did wonder whether one of them wrote it."

"Why would you think one of them sent it?"

"Because only four people knew about Charlie's picture. She told Tommy who works on the camp and I told you, Paul and Andy."

Fiona shook her head slowly. "So you think one of us felt so worried we sent her a threatening postcard?" The hurt in her voice had a sting to it.

"I'm trying to help her narrow the field of suspects."

"Well, this is charming," Fiona muttered.

"For what it's worth I don't think it was you, even though I haven't heard you saying anything nice about Mia or Charlie."

"But you do think it might be Andy or Paul?"

Jude sipped her coffee as she tried to figure out the best way to move forward. She was, after all, talking about men that Fiona had deep-rooted relationships with that stretched back years. "I also found some overdue bills and photographs."

"Every business has a red bill these days. You must know that because you teach economics."

"That's true."

"And what were the photographs?" Her tone turned sarcastic. "Were they of cracks in the brickwork?"

This was the tricky part. If Fiona kept up her blinkered approach she was either going to storm off or laugh in Jude's face. "They were of Mia and I'm pretty sure Charlie didn't take them."

"Really?" Fiona asked tersely.

"Uh-huh. From what I could tell she was in the office at the lido."

"So everything about this revolves around pictures of Mia at the lido? The bitch was clearly obsessed with the place."

"That's not—"

"I don't know where you're going with this, Jude."

"The first pictures were of Mia in a bikini. She seemed to be wearing less in the others."

Fiona's expression deflated like a tired balloon. She looked down at the table and they sat in a silence that quickly became uncomfortable.

"I don't know what you want me to say," Fiona said after a while.

"I'm trying to figure out what's going on," Jude said. "I know you don't like Charlie" – Fiona held her hand up and rocked it – "but *I* do. She's friendly with Dan and I find her refreshing. I don't like the idea of someone sending her threatening postcards and want to stop it."

"It's not me." Fiona sighed. "I know I haven't had a good word to say about Mia or Charlie but it's because they frighten me, okay? I drove Andy's marriage into the ground and know it takes two to tango, but I got involved knowing full well he was married. Now I live in fear that history repeats itself and I get cast off as the old wife. Have you ever had an affair?"

"No."

"He was my first and it felt fresh and exciting. Then one day you wake up to find you've wrecked a family and become the new wife and it's just a matter of time before Mia arrives to remind you of what you did."

"You said before you were worried he was seeing her."

"When they found the body his mind went somewhere and didn't come back. He rang me yesterday to say his meeting had overrun and he was booking into a hotel and I haven't seen or spoken to him since."

"He spoke to Paul when I was there last night."

"What did they talk about?"

"I have no idea except they were saying about sorting something out and mentioned Tommy Mackintosh."

Fiona pinched her lower lip. "If I tell you something, you must promise not to say a word to anyone."

"How can I promise that?"

Fiona acknowledged that with the slightest of nods. "Andy's partnership with Paul is going sour. The Mia issue hasn't helped but the surveyor reports weren't good and Paul's in well over his head so the cash is drying up."

Jude heard everything but her mind kept pulling her back to Fiona's turn of phrase. "What did you mean by the Mia issue?"

Fiona bit the inside of her cheek. "Nothing serious."

"Did Paul have something to do with her?"

"I never saw anything," she said categorically. "It was Andy that mentioned they were getting close but I don't know if that was his jealous viewpoint or real life."

Jude felt a shiver of revulsion at the sense of history repeating itself. How could she fall again for a man who wanted a partner young enough to be his daughter. "I hope it was jealousy."

Fiona shrugged and finished her drink. "I didn't expect to be discussing whether my husband was sending poison postcards when I got up this morning."

"I'm sorry to bring it up," said Jude.

"Don't be. I appreciate your friendship and you're trying to help Charlie."

"And Mia."

"Yes," said Fiona. "Even her."

Chapter 43

The rain hammered against the canvas roof of the Surrey bike as Charlie steered them into Market Street.

Dan glanced over his shoulder as he had done several times on the journey but he hadn't seen the Vauxhall Viva again.

"It's not there," she said. "I've been checking as well.

She parked in the bike space and they ran to Patterson's through the downpour. She clattered through the door and startled Malc who was behind the counter. His expression darkened when he saw Dan.

"Hey," she said. "Is your dad about?"

"Nah, he's gone to Lowestoft for some kind of official do."

"Oh. Do you mind if I develop another film?"

"Another one?"

"35mm Instamatic," she said and unzipped her cagoule. Her bag was dry inside it and she unclipped her camera from the strap. "Shouldn't take me long."

"I was going to do a batch later on if you want to leave it." He gestured out the window. "I can't see there's going to be much of a rush in this weather."

"Thanks," she said and leaned on the counter, "but you know I like to develop my own work."

"Go on then," he said and she moved towards the darkroom door quickly as if worried he'd change his mind. "And no funny business," he said as Dan walked by.

"There won't be," said Dan.

* * *

Dan found it fascinating to watch Charlie work.

"I won't bother with a contact sheet," she said and put her hands into the padded bag. "We only want two or three of the shots anyway."

"Malc really wanted to do it for you, didn't he?"

"He's not very efficient."

"Probably not but I think he's trying because he likes you."

"You think?"

"Oh yes. The only way he could make it more obvious would be if he wore a neon sign around his neck."

"I might notice that," she said and giggled. It took him by surprise and he laughed.

The door was yanked open and Malc glared at them almost in silhouette. "I told you not–" he started but Charlie cut him off.

"Shut the fucking door," she shrieked.

He came into the room and pulled the door shut behind him. "This isn't a knocking shop," he blustered and then finally seemed to see the table separated Charlie and Dan.

"No," she snapped. "It's a darkroom that's supposed to stay dark when the fucking light's on."

"You were giggling," Malc said weakly.

"Is that a crime now?" Dan asked.

"We were having a laugh while I worked and now you've probably ruined these images," Charlie said.

"What do you mean ruined them?" Dan asked.

"Precisely what I say," Charlie said. Anger made her voice rise. "Light fogs the film and you can't fix it. The first rule of a darkroom is that you never open the door if the light's on."

"So we've ruined the photographs from the lido?" If the images were fogged they wouldn't be able to see the number plate so they'd have nothing to show the police.

"We haven't," she said emphatically. "This dickhead has."

"I thought you were messing around in here." Malc sounded pathetic now.

"Well we weren't," Charlie said. She put the film into a bag and zipped it up. "Now clear off."

"Hold on," he said. "This is my bloody shop."

"No it's not," she said and glared at him. Even from across the room, Dan could feel the power of it. He hoped he never put himself into a situation where she glared at him like it.

They watched him slip out.

"Has he really ruined the pictures?"

"I don't know but it's likely. Let me check."

She unzipped the bag and worked with an expression of grim determination. Within ten minutes she was setting up the enlarger and looked through the eyepiece.

"Shit." She put some photo paper on the table and quickly made three prints. She checked them over and did it again. In the end, with a shake of her head, she laid out the prints and Dan walked around the table to stand beside her.

The first image showed what looked like a pale blur in the centre of a black background.

"I think that's the stairwell," she said. "I counted back from the end of the negative strip because I couldn't tell what that was otherwise."

The second photograph was brighter and he could see pale shadings of blue.

"Us running across the lido," she said helpfully.

"Oh."

The last photograph had a pale mess in its centre though a dock crane was clearly visible on the periphery.

"They're ruined," she said and her voice hitched.

"You okay?"

She snapped her head round to face him. "No, Dan, not really."

He felt like he was on very thin ice and kept his mouth shut. Something shifted in her eyes and she gave him an uneasy smile. "I'm sorry it's just…" She shook her head. "We haven't got anything to show the police." She gathered the photographs into an envelope and put it in her handbag then slipped the camera back into its pouch.

He opened the door for her and they left the shop without speaking to Malc. The rain was still coming down heavy so they rushed across the pavement to the Surrey bike.

Charlie slid into her side and said, "Yuck." She stood as best she could under the roof and pulled her cagoule up. The right leg of her shorts was dark with water. "That's all

I need," she said, as if it was the final straw on a terrible day.

"Don't worry. I'm sure lots of people wet themselves."

He thought for one awful moment that she hadn't got the joke and then she laughed. He got into his side and made sure the seat was dry before he sat down. She looked like she wished she'd parked the bike the other way around.

Chapter 44

Even though it had stopped raining, Fiona didn't believe Jude wanted to walk home from Lesley's and insisted she borrow a small foldaway umbrella.

Jude walked down Regent's Row enjoying the fresh sea breeze against her face. The rain began again when she reached the corner of Marine Drive and came down so heavily it sounded like pennies bouncing off the umbrella. She walked through the puddles glad she was wearing flip-flops rather than shoes.

A car pulled up at the kerb and the driver leaned over to wind down the passenger window.

"Jude!" Paul called.

"Hey." Her quick rush of pleasure was quickly tempered by the residual anger and disappointment of last night as well as Fiona's insinuations. Jude had to keep focus and not allow herself to be distracted by this handsome man she really shouldn't trust.

"What're you doing?" he asked.

"Trying to outrun the weather."

"How's that working for you?"

"Not so good. I don't think this brolly's going to cut it."

"I could give you a lift if you wanted?"

She was torn and from the way he smiled she knew he could see it. They looked at one another for a moment.

"Are we okay?" He had to raise his voice over the noise of the rain. "I dropped by earlier to see if I could find you but the caravan was all locked up."

"Were you after something specific?"

"I wanted to see you and make sure you were alright after last night. I felt bad about the curry."

"I felt a bit…" No, she couldn't say it now, not out here. "I can barely hear you."

"Why don't you get in and let me give you a lift?"

"Okay. I wanted to speak to you anyway."

"Good," he said and pushed the door open. "Damp out?"

"Not so as you'd notice," she said as he pulled away from the kerb.

"Are you sure everything's okay? I know you said you had a dickey tummy, but it felt like I'd done something wrong or overstepped a mark somehow. If I did, I'm really sorry."

Before she could say anything a kid on a BMX came racing across the road.

"Paul!" she shouted.

"Shit!"

He stamped on the brakes and the car skidded to a halt on the slick road. The kid on the BMX swerved, stuck up his fingers and then cycled away. The umbrella slipped out of Jude's grasp and clunked against the dashboard before falling into the footwell.

"That stupid little shit," Paul said angrily. "I nearly hit him." He put a hand on her arm. "Are you okay?"

"I think so," she said. The seatbelt was tight against her chest. "You?"

"No," he said sharply and held his hand out. It shook slightly. "I didn't see the little bastard. If you hadn't shouted, I'd have…"

"But you didn't."

"We were lucky nothing was right behind us." He drummed his hands on the steering wheel. "Bloody hell, my heart's pounding like nobody's business."

Hers was too. Jude unclipped the seatbelt and reached down for the umbrella. She couldn't feel it and swept her hand over the mat. Her fingertips caught against something cool and hard and she picked it up, surprised to see she was holding the thin chain of a necklace. The pendant was a thin slice of sea glass the size of a fifty-pence piece with a painted sunset on it. It was quite beautiful.

"Something of yours?" she asked.

Paul looked surprised. "Where did you find that?"

"On the floor. It might have slid out from under the seat when you braked."

"I've never seen it before."

"Have you had any ladies in the car recently?"

He looked at her askance. "No."

"I'm not checking up on you but it's clearly a woman's necklace and it's lovely. I can't believe someone would drop it and not want it back."

"It could be Fiona's," he said. "She borrowed the car the other night and might have lost it."

"Why would she borrow your car rather than Andy's?"

"Because mine and his are leased through Lido Holdings."

"You would think she'd notice it missing after a few days."

"I don't know," he said.

Jude turned the sea glass in her fingers and something nagged at the back of her mind but she couldn't pull it into focus. She wrapped the chain around the pendant and slipped it into the pocket of her shorts for safekeeping.

Chapter 45

They biked back to camp without saying much. Charlie seemed deep in thought and Dan knew there was nothing he could say to make the situation better. Ade directed them where to park and Dan looked at his wellies with envy. His own shoes were so waterlogged it wouldn't surprise him if he contracted trench foot

"I feel such a failure," she said as they trudged down the roadway.

"You're not. We did everything we could."

At the corner of Neptune's she pointed him towards the patio and they took shelter under the club portico. Charlie peeled off her hood and ran her fingers through her hair. Dan wiped a hand down his face.

"Do you think we did?" she asked.

"There was nothing else we could have done."

"I can't believe Malc opened the door," she seethed.

Now they couldn't go to the police Dan was more worried about the postcards and he couldn't tell if Charlie had either forgotten or didn't want to mention them.

"We could take the postcards to the police with Mum and see if she does make any difference."

Charlie smiled. "As much as I love Jude and know she'd do it I would rather not embarrass her. We haven't got any evidence. We can't even find her necklace."

He didn't want to press the idea of her still being under threat but he was going home tomorrow while Andy, Paul and Fiona would still be here. She was tough enough to look after herself but was it safe? And what could he do? He couldn't just move here.

"I've got some bits I need to do at the caravan," she said. "Is it okay if I call round later?"

"Yes," he said selfishly. He wanted to spend as much time with her as he could. "If you want to."

"Of course I do, you nitwit." She swatted his arm. "I told you before that once I latch on, I never let go." She rubbed his arm awkwardly. "I'll see you later. If you're not doing anything with Jude, we can always have chips again and then try to dance the night away to The Sultans of Swing."

He laughed and she joined in.

"Whatever else happens, Dan, I hope you know I'm really pleased we met up."

Her words warmed him. "Same here. I'm so glad you knocked because I wouldn't have dared speak to you."

"I kind of got that idea but you know what, Dan Moore? You're alright."

"Thanks. So are you."

"Oh, I know that," she said with a smile. "Later, gator." She pulled on her hood and went out into the rain with a little wave.

Chapter 46

Jude took off her flip-flops and peeled off her cagoule.

Paul handed her a towel. "Just hang your coat over a chair," he said.

"It's sodden."

"So am I. Did you want a coffee?"

"That'd be lovely," she said and followed him into the kitchen, drying her hair as she went.

He put the kettle on and leaned against the counter. "So what's up?"

"Am I that obvious?"

"No." He gave her a lopsided smile. "But something's changed and the thought of you going home and us not parting on good company would be awful."

The emotion in his voice connected with her but there was too much she didn't know, not only from what she saw last night but what Fiona had said. She'd been hurt so badly this year that she wasn't going to allow Paul to catch her in another web of lies.

"Who said that would happen?" she asked.

The kettle boiled and he made two mugs of coffee and carried them through to the lounge. She sat across the coffee table from him facing the French doors.

"I'm helping Dan and Charlie out," she said and leaned forward with her elbows on her knees. "How friendly were you with Mia?"

"Blimey." He sat back. "Where did that come from?"

"Fiona took me for a coffee this morning and told me you and Mia were getting close. She said Andy had told her."

He shook his head but she saw the pinched expression he tried to hide. "Andy was just trying to throw her off the scent. I barely knew Mia. I told you that."

"You did."

"I haven't lied to you, Jude."

"I want to believe that."

"Which means you don't." He stood abruptly and leaned on the mantelpiece. "I don't know what happened to you in the past, Jude, but I'm not them. I'm not going to hurt you."

"I would never allow you to. I've got enough scar tissue already and it's slowly healing. I don't want to tear it open."

"I didn't do anything to Mia," he said softly.

"That's not what I asked you."

"I know but I want to tell you that right from the start. I didn't do anything to her."

"So you were friendly?"

He twisted his mouth. "I wouldn't say friendly, but we talked."

It felt like he was playing with the words and saying a lot about nothing. "Charlie's convinced Mia didn't kill herself but the police weren't interested. I'd have left it at that except I saw the postcard."

"What is this about a postcard? You mentioned it last night."

"Someone posted one through her door on Wednesday night warning her off going to the police. She got another this morning."

"I don't even know where Charlie lives."

"Charlie only told one person she was going to the police about Mia. I told three people on the Wednesday evening and that was you, Andy and Fiona. Do you see my dilemma?"

"You really think I sent it?" He sounded wounded.

"I don't know what to think, Paul. I found some postcards in your office last night."

"I'm sure you'd find postcards everywhere. I live on the coast, Jude. Every single shop in this town has a rack of postcards because it's easy money. You can even buy them in the butchers."

"I saw the photographs too."

He threw his arms up in exasperation. "You'll have to be more specific. There are a lot of photographs in my home."

"Do you mind if we go into your office?" she asked and stood up.

"Why?"

She walked through and he followed her. The sky was so dark she could see their reflections in the window. "I knocked that box file over last night. It had the postcards and pictures in."

"Shit," he said and she knew right then he was aware of them.

Jude opened the file and pulled out the photograph wallet.

"Don't!" He grabbed for the wallet but missed and his fingers wrapped easily around her wrist.

Angry and scared, she twisted to one side and pulled him around in front of her. She tried to shake off his hand but he had too good a grip. He reached for the packet with his free hand and she tried to block him but missed and caught his watch instead. The impact knocked the clasp and it opened. The bracelet flopped away from his wrist and he let go of her instantly to do it up.

Jude felt as if the wind was knocked out of her and she gasped for breath.

She'd thought Charlie's photograph showed someone wearing a bangle but that hadn't been the case at all. It was an unclasped and heavy watchstrap.

Chapter 47

The caravan was empty when Dan got back to it.

He kicked off his shoes and took off his sodden socks and wet shorts and dropped them in the shower along with his cagoule. His hair was plastered to his head so he dried it with a towel.

What a shitty day for so many reasons.

He changed into fresh clothes and made himself a drink then flopped onto the sofa. He switched on the television but there wasn't much on Anglia and the BBC was showing the cricket so he turned it off.

What a properly shit day.

He got his Walkman and *Christine* from the bedroom then settled on the sofa. He put on his headphones but soon found his attention wandering.

Why couldn't today have been different? He hadn't planned to spend his last full day here separated from Charlie and now she was gone he missed her smile and her laugh and her pretty face. Their relationship might develop or fade away after he went home but he wanted to find out for himself. He wanted to stay as the new version of himself.

Charlie obviously liked him but was she waiting for him to say something?

What if he didn't get a chance to do that and missed this opportunity? That would be the absolute topper to the shit he'd already had to endure this year.

A hand thumped against the window and he nearly jumped off the sofa. Charlie pressed her face to the glass and cupped her hands around her eyes. When she saw him, she shouted, "Open up."

Dan pulled off his headphones and raced down the caravan to let her in.

Charlie raced down to the steps and gave him a big smile. "How are you? You must have that music loud because I've been knocking."

"Shit, I'm sorry. I wasn't expecting to see you."

"Or invite me in, clearly."

He'd left her standing out in the rain like an idiot.

"Whoops," he said and moved so she could come in.

She gave her body a thorough wiggle and giggled while she did it. "Still chucking it down," she said.

"It's not the best day."

"Well, rather than stay in the doldrums, why don't we do something exciting for your last day?"

"Like what?"

"I got a note."

"Oh," he said and felt his joy fade like a punctured balloon.

"No." She grinned. "It's a good note. Andy must have put it in while we were out." She took a folded sheet of paper from the pocket on her shorts and handed it to him.

"Shall we go?" she asked eagerly.

The idea of going back out into the rain wouldn't normally have appealed but if it meant he could spend time with Charlie then he was okay with it. "Go on then."

"I was hoping you might say yes." She whooped and unzipped her cagoule to show him the Leica bag which was over the opposite shoulder to her handbag.

Dan left the note on the counter and got his cagoule out of the shower. It wasn't a pleasant sensation to put it back on, but it felt much better than when he slipped on his soggy shoes.

Chapter 48

"It's not what you think," Paul insisted but looked like a man who knew he'd been caught out.

She shook his hand off. "What the fuck am I supposed to think?" Anger burned through her veins and she welcomed it. The alternative was to be fearful and she wasn't going to let him have that hold over her. "What did you do?"

"Nothing, I swear to you. I didn't do anything." He seemed to crumble. "I met her at the lido to warn her."

"About what? That if she wasn't careful she was going to end up in the sea?"

"No." He flinched as if she'd slapped him. "You have no idea how bad I felt when she went missing."

"My heart bleeds for you."

"It was eating me up, Jude. Then when you said Charlie had a picture of Mia and me at the lido that morning, I felt physically sick."

"I'm sure it was horrible." Betrayal left a bad taste in her mouth.

They'd only become close after Mia went missing which meant all the time her attraction for him was growing, he was keeping this secret. She felt grubby.

"I mean it was your choice to intimidate a young woman," Jude said, "and then the teenaged girl who photographed you doing it."

"You've got it all wrong. I didn't do anything to Mia and I certainly didn't do anything to Charlie. You have to believe me. Mia was perfectly fine when I left her that morning."

"She didn't look fine in the picture. What were you saying to her?"

Paul took a deep breath and let it out slowly. "I was trying to warn her off Andy."

"Were you jealous he was making a move on her?"

"You can't believe everything Fiona told you. There was never anything between me and Mia. I mean I liked her and she was very pretty but she's twenty years younger than me."

"Doesn't stop some people," Jude said bitterly.

"You're right but it stopped me."

"And yet there you were. Why did you grab her arm?" Her anger was still growing. "Did it make you feel like a big strong man to be manhandling her?"

"You're on the wrong track, Jude."

"Then why don't you explain it to me? A girl goes missing and turns up dead and I find out by chance that a man I've spent a week getting close to was photographed grabbing her."

"I promise I didn't hurt her, Jude."

She waved her hand dismissively at him. "And I'm supposed to believe your promise?"

His shoulders sagged. "I was telling her to keep away from Andy for her own good."

"Because if she didn't Fiona was going to give her a good hiding?"

Paul stood by the window and stared out at the rain for a moment before leaning on the sill. "Andy Sykes uses people, okay? You need to understand that. I'd heard it from other people and they were absolutely right. He told me it himself. 'Everyone has an angle,' he'd say, 'that you can exploit for your own ends.'"

"So what was yours?"

"Enthusiasm and drive? Some ready capital? I don't know. It happens in business all the time. I used him too – I wanted his contacts, knowledge and the kudos being involved with him would bring me."

"How does that make you different?"

"Because I know where the line is. If Andy thought seducing someone could give him an edge, he'd seduce them."

"Like slapping my arse in the kitchen at your dinner party."

He raised his eyebrows. "What?"

"I told him to bugger off."

Paul considered for a moment. "He knew I liked you so maybe he thought it would give him something over me."

"Or he's just a dirty old man," Jude said. "Like I assume he was with Mia."

"I thought so at first, but he did like her and Mia was smart. She liked the attention and what he was prepared to do for her career. Unfortunately he knew her game and outplayed her."

"So why were you warning her?"

"It was the money."

"He was taking money from Mia?"

Paul barked out a quick laugh. "She didn't have two pennies to rub together but, by then…" He let the sentence fade.

"He didn't have two pennies to rub together either, did he?"

"How did you know?" he asked with surprise.

"I saw the bills and the letters."

"Oh. He invested everything in the lido and got me to do the same."

"But you were so keen to pick it up for a steal from the council you didn't check it out properly. Those cracks in the wall are serious, aren't they?"

"Uh-huh." He looked defeated. "He kept telling me they were under control but he got burned. We" – he emphasised the word – "got burned. The place is about to fall into the fucking sea and both of us will lose everything."

"Why not cut your losses and get out of it? It's prime real estate on the coast."

"Because we're up to our eyeballs already and to make the site work, you'd literally have to knock everything down and clear the land and start all over again." He cleared his throat. "Andy kept up a good front and I wanted to believe everything he told me. The idea was sound and judging by what's going on in London we should've been sitting on a goldmine."

"Isn't the bank interested?"

"No. They're planning to call in their loans."

"Oh, Paul…" she said. "But this is just bad business practice. I don't see what it has to do with Mia."

"She was his ticket out of this mess. His plan was to go to London with her when she left to audition and leave me and Fiona with all the shit here. He and Mia could set up somewhere and she'd support him while he set himself up again. Bankruptcy would kill him but he was an entrepreneur and could start earning money in an empty room."

"Were they having an affair?"

"I assume so. I saw the same pictures you did."

"So what happened?"

"Mia got cold feet and I think her friend Tommy at the camp tried to warn her. I only put it all together as he was schmoozing her."

"Because if they'd taken off, he would have saddled her with debt too?"

"Of course. If his plan went ahead then everyone lost out but him. Me and Fiona would've gone bankrupt and Mia would end up working for peanuts while Andy got to start again. I knew if she turned him down, he'd have to focus on getting the lido out of the shit."

"Except he couldn't because it was unsafe. So what happened to Mia? Did she jump?"

"I didn't know her well enough to answer that. She seemed bright and lively to me but maybe there were issues in her past. From what I understand, she had a rough childhood and her father isn't pleasant. Maybe me saying Andy had taken her for a fool was too much." He scratched the corner of his mouth. "That's what I've been torturing myself with since they found her."

"So why didn't you go to the police?"

"And say what? I think my business partner is forcing a girl to do something she doesn't want to?"

"You think Andy pushed her?"

"I never said that. He can be a shit if he doesn't think you have anything left to offer him, but I don't think he'd kill anyone."

"What if he was worried Mia would tell Fiona?"

"That might be a problem if his escape route was shut down."

The door buzzer rang and made them both jump. He walked out of the office.

"Hello? Oh hi, Andy, we were just talking about you."

Chapter 49

"Hi," said Andy and seemed surprised to see Jude. "How are you?"

"I've been better. I got caught in the rain."

"Me too." He leaned closer to Paul. "I wanted to have a quick word," he said and tilted his head in Jude's direction. "I didn't realise you'd have company. I can come back."

"You can talk in front of Jude."

"It's work-related so I'd better not."

"She knows," Paul said softly. "I told her everything."

Andy looked startled. "What do you mean?"

"She'd figured it out," Paul said. "I just confirmed what she thought."

"I found the photographs of Mia," Jude said. "I found the overdue bills and saw the cracks in the lido walls."

"For fuck's sake." Andy glared at Paul. "Brilliant. Absolutely fucking brilliant. I thought she was some single mother holiday fling of yours and now you're trying to blackmail me?"

"I'm not trying to blackmail you," Jude said. It was a struggle to keep her voice calm. "I'm trying to find out what happened to Mia Garwood and why Charlie is getting anonymous postcards telling her not to go to the police."

"What're you talking about?" asked Andy.

"Which bit didn't you get?"

"Are you saying I threatened Charlie?"

"Someone did and I found your collection of postcards."

"Hold up," Andy said and held out his hands in what he obviously hoped was a calming gesture. "You're putting two and two together here and making five."

"How so? Paul told me you'd been lining Mia up for your new life."

"For fuck's sake, mate, can you literally not keep anything to yourself? What else did you tell Miss Marple here?"

"I'm not interested in you losing money," Jude said. "I want to find out what happened to Mia and make sure Charlie's safe. We're going home tomorrow but she's not. I can't leave her with this hanging over her head."

"I have no idea what you're talking about," Andy said flatly.

Jude's anger was being diluted by her fear. If either of them were involved in Mia's death or the threats against Charlie then she'd just dropped herself into the middle of a wasps' nest because nobody knew she was here. Paul was by the mantelpiece and Andy at the French doors so she took a step towards the front door. If one of them turned on her she might just be able to get out.

"I want to know what you did to Mia," she said and took another step towards the door.

"Nothing," he said and she could see he was struggling to keep his emotions in check. "She broke up with me. She rang me in tears to say she thought our situation wasn't good for either of us." He glared at Paul. "I assume someone helped her come to that realisation."

"So when was this?"

"Monday morning. When I found out she was missing after the concert that night I thought she'd run away to London like she'd promised to do."

"What did you say to her?"

"That I was gutted."

"Were you angry?"

"I wasn't happy she'd fucked up my plans." He gestured to Paul. "Like Blabbermouth here has probably told you."

"You weren't unhappy because she'd broken up with you?"

He shrugged. "There are a lot of Mias in the world, but it would take me time to find the next one."

His arrogance rankled. "You clearly thought she was worth more than that."

Andy laughed mockingly. "How long have you been divorced?"

"None of your business.

He came towards her casually and she put her hand on the door latch. "Was it your first marriage?" he asked.

"Yes." She wasn't particularly scared of him but he was getting too close.

"Andy," Paul said. "What're you doing?"

"Just asking questions," he said without looking away. "Like she's been doing." He smiled easily. "I'm curious that you think I did something silly because a girl turned me down."

Her panic rose and she didn't like it. "I want to know the truth."

Andy spread his hands wide. "I didn't hurt Mia, Jude, and I didn't lead her on. It hurt when she broke up with me but shit happens. You know about hurt, don't you? Did you want to hurt your ex-husband when you got divorced?"

"Yes, I absolutely did."

Andy smiled. "Well that's where you and I are different then."

"What he did to me was unforgiveable but very different to you and Mia. You wanted her as your ticket out of here."

"Ticket out?" Andy scoffed. "Can you hear yourself? She was a club singer, Jude, and a crutch to support me while I got back on my feet. That was all." He snorted a laugh. "You're very naïve for a forty-something woman of the world."

His words were so drained of humanity they pressed against her chest like a lead weight. "I'm not naïve. I understand what you were doing."

"Do you?" Andy leaned forward as if he was going to stroke her cheek.

She slapped him hard and his head rocked to one side. He grunted.

"Fuck," Paul said.

Andy looked at her slowly. "Maybe you do," he said quietly. "I didn't hurt Mia and I don't intend to hurt Charlie either."

He reached for the latch and she quickly let go of it then he pulled open the door and left.

Chapter 50

The clouds were so dark and low they turned the early afternoon light to evening.

Charlie braked outside the lido entrance and quickly unzipped her cagoule to check the Leica bag was still dry. Apparently satisfied she zipped back up and pulled on her hood.

"You ready?"

"Uh-huh."

"Come on, it's only rain."

She slid off the seat and he followed her across the pavement. He pushed against the fence and she slid through with a tremendous amount of grace. She pulled from her side and he struggled through and felt something snag on the back of his cagoule.

"Bugger," he said and felt water on his back. Not that it made much difference. He couldn't remember being this soaked in a long time.

"You okay?"

"Yep," he said and followed her up the steps to take shelter at the top.

Everything about the lido looked grey except the water that sprayed up over the seal wall as waves broke against it. Most of the water washed back through the hole as if it couldn't bear to be parted but some slipped down into the pool.

Movement caught his eye and he looked up at the office block but the three wide windows only reflected the dark clouds.

"What is it?"

"I thought I saw something," he said. If anyone was up there they'd either stepped away from the glass or were hidden behind the reflection.

"It could be Andy," Charlie said.

"I didn't see any cars out there. Do you think he walked?"

She gave him a withering look and unzipped her cagoule. She took the Leica out of its case and made sure to hold it where the roof protected it from rain. In a fluid movement she took four quick shots of the sea wall. "I have to admit he was right," she said. "That looks impressive."

Another wave hit the wall with a thump that echoed around the lido and the water sprayed perhaps a dozen feet into the air before slapping against the concrete.

"I think the storm's getting worse," Dan said.

Far out to sea a fork of lighting showed briefly against a dark cloud.

"I think you're right." Charlie put her camera away and zipped up her cagoule. "We'll make a run for it to the office."

"Right behind you."

"It'd be rude to stare at my bum just because my shorts are wet," she said and gave him a fierce squint before grinning.

"I hadn't planned to but now I will just because you said."

She laughed and jogged down the steps with both hands against her bum. Dan laughed as he followed.

The concrete was slippery and both of them almost fell over. They rushed gingerly across the terrace when there was a tremendous cracking noise. It was difficult to pinpoint where it came from as the sound rolled across the lido and echoed back from the funfair wall. Charlie faltered in her run and they exchanged anxious glances. It might have been something big and heavy hitting the outer wall or maybe even something falling over in the docks.

Charlie ran up the brick staircase to the office. Dan scanned the windows intently but still couldn't see anything.

The stairs ended at a small landing with a wooden door. The guttering above it was broken and a stream of water ran down the panels and made them shine.

"I hope it's open," she said. She pushed it but nothing happened. "Shit." She tried again. "Give me a hand."

Charlie pushed the handle and Dan reached above her head. The wood was greasy to the touch and moved slightly as he pushed.

"It's warped in the frame," he said. "Push harder."

"I'm trying."

It gave with a horrible groaning noise and then opened all at once with a loud crack. They stumbled into a narrow corridor and Charlie shoved the door closed as best she could.

"Phew." She pulled her hood down and pushed her wet fringe off her forehead.

Dan pulled his own hood down and wiped his face clear of water.

Three doors opened off the corridor and two windows overlooked Marine Drive. The carpet was plush and there were framed certificates on the walls. A large plant at the far end looked like it was trying to escape from its pot.

"Hello!" Charlie called and startled him.

"What are you doing?"

"Letting Andy know we're here." When there was no response she hollered his name. "It's Charlie and Dan."

"If he was up here, he heard you. Maybe he's gone down to the changing rooms."

"We just came through the only door out of the offices."

"Maybe I didn't see anyone up here then."

Charlie opened the first office door and Dan followed her in. There were great views of the lido and a half-glass stable door opened onto the sun terrace. There were so many windows the sound of rain lashing against glass created a constant low hum.

"Can you imagine the views from here on a clear day?" she asked.

Two large tables dominated the room. One had a large impressive-looking model of the lido on it with a tower of apartments where the offices now stood. The other was filled with pamphlets, brochures and a mug of lido-branded pens.

The side wall had several large photographic blow-ups of the site on either side of a closed door.

"Did you take those?" Dan asked.

"I did," she said with pride. "Do you like them?"

"They're excellent." He crossed the room to take a closer look and something knocked against the wall from next door. "Did you hear that?"

"What?" Charlie was leaning against the glass of the stable door and cupping her eyes as she looked across the lido.

"I heard a noise from next door."

"That's Paul's office but I didn't see his car either."

It might have been something falling over or even the same thing as that horrible crack they heard before. "Maybe I'm just hearing things," he said and walked over to her.

"Maybe. You know, if these windows weren't waterlogged, I could get some ace pictures but I don't want to get the Leica wet."

"If we open this door, you could lean out the top half and I'll hold a cagoule over you to protect the camera."

"That's a great idea."

There was another noise from next door.

"Could Andy be in there?" Dan asked. He felt the first touch of nerves. They hadn't been quiet since they'd got there, and Andy knew they were coming so why hadn't he come out to say hello?

"He might be," she said. "Perhaps he's on the phone?"

The door banged open.

Charlie screamed as someone wearing a yellow raincoat and a blue slicker hat came rushing through from the other office. Dan just had time to register they were carrying something before the person threw the object at them.

He grabbed Charlie's arm and pulled her towards him. The heavy glass ashtray hit the bottom half of the stable door and left a dent in the wood.

Chapter 51

Jude took the necklace out of her pocket and put it on the cistern then stripped off and dropped her wet clothes into the shower tub. Everything was soaked. She towelled herself dry and looked at herself in the bathroom mirror. Her hair was unruly and she brushed it as she tried not to think about what had just happened. It was never easy to switch off like that though.

"When did I become such a poor judge of people?"

She put on her dressing gown then went into kitchen. There was a note on the counter but she didn't have a chance to read it before there was a knock on the door. Thinking Dan had left his key behind she rushed to the door and opened it.

Paul stood in the rain. "Hey," he said.

Jude pulled her dressing gown tightly around her. "Hello."

She wanted to say so much more to him but her mind was a whirl as to what to say. Her world had shifted again with the realisation she'd been caught out at home by a liar and now she'd blundered into another situation where she didn't know the whole story. Her simmering anger was partly directed at herself for not being able to read the signs.

"Can I come in?" he asked and gave her a little pout.

"Why would you want to do that?"

"I think we need to talk and you rushed away after Andy left."

"Don't you think it would have been better to talk before?"

"I do," he said with a nod.

The wind gusted rain into her face and she stepped back. She had no desire to get wet again. "Okay."

He came in and closed the door. "Bit wet out," he said with a sheepish smile and ran a hand through his hair. It stood up in spikes.

"Took us all by surprise, eh? Like a lot of things have done today."

"Fair point," he said. "You left before things were said that needed to be said."

"I left at the right time."

"Andy was out of line."

"You both were." She went into the kitchen and clicked the kettle on. "Did you want a cuppa?"

"Are you willing to make me one?"

"I'm being polite and I want to understand what's going on."

"I haven't covered myself with glory but you surely don't think I had anything to do with Mia going missing."

Jude went into the bathroom and got the necklace. She held it up to him. "This is Mia's, isn't it? Can you explain how it got into your car?"

"I told you. We share the car."

"So who had it Monday night?

"I drove it here, but Andy told me Fiona took it home after she flared up at him in the pub."

Jude put the necklace on the counter next to the note. She didn't recognise the handwriting and quickly read it.

"Andy didn't say he was going back to the lido did he?" She handed him the note.

"That's not his handwriting."

Jude felt a chill run from her shoulders to her toes. Was this the same handwriting as the postcards?

"Well, it's someone who knows Charlie has a connection to the lido. She and Dan were going to see the police again this morning. We have to go."

"Get dressed," he said. "I'll drive."

Chapter 52

"We're supposed to be here," Dan shouted and held up his hand to show they weren't a threat.

The person came around the table looking as if they were searching for something else to throw.

"We have permission," Charlie shouted.

The person grabbed a handful of pens and threw them one at a time with force. A couple bounced off his chest and Dan put his hand up to protect his face.

A pen hit Charlie's shoulder and she managed to grab it and throw it back. It nicked off the side of the slicker hat and pushed it back to reveal a woman Dan hadn't seen before.

"Fiona," shouted Charlie.

"Who?"

"Andy's wife. She knows me."

Fiona pulled off the hat. Her eyes were wide and there was a hint of something in them that wasn't quite anger but wasn't quite madness either. She pulled open a drawer and rooted around inside it then came up with a pair of scissors.

"Shit," Dan said. She was blocking their route to the main door and backing them towards the wall.

"Fiona, it's me. What're you doing?"

"You little bitch," Fiona said with such venom it took Dan by surprise. He'd never heard anyone sound so vicious.

Even Charlie seemed taken aback.

"Hey," he said. "I don't know what you think is going on, but Charlie got a note asking her to come here."

"Oh she got a note did she? And who might that have been from?"

"Don't answer," Charlie whispered.

"Andy," he said.

"Ah." Fiona laughed and it was sour enough to sound rancid. "So she raced through the rain to get some time alone with my husband, did she?"

"That's not what happened," said Dan in frustration. Fiona was deliberately misunderstanding him. "She came to get some shots."

Charlie lifted the Leica bag up to show Fiona who shook her head.

"Were they for the nude shots?" she asked.

"Has she gone mad?" Dan muttered.

Fiona glared at him. "This is all your little girlfriend's fault. All she had to do was leave well alone and keep her fucking nose out of other people's business. But then everything's always about poor little Charlie, abandoned by mummy and daddy."

Dan heard Charlie's sharp intake of breath.

"We can't walk away from this now," Fiona said and brandished the scissors. "Why go to the police and stir things up with a stupid fucking photograph that doesn't have anything to do with anything?"

"Don't do this," Charlie said. She sounded worried but not scared. "Let us go. We'll pretend it never happened."

Fiona laughed like she'd just heard the funniest joke. Dan glanced at the door she'd come through. They might be able to make a break that way, but they still had to go through the main door and if it jammed like it had before they were well and truly stuck.

"Do you really think that'll work?" Fiona asked.

"Yes. Dan will go home, I won't have anything more to do with Andy and neither of us will ever say anything."

"You must take me for a fool, Charlie. Like Mia did before you. Did you think I couldn't see through the pair of you? Abandoned pretty girls looking for a daddy to take care of them?"

Fiona took a step closer and Dan pulled Charlie away until they were against the wall. His foot bumped the ashtray and he glanced over his shoulder to see the stable door was within reach. He tried the handle, but it didn't budge.

"I don't, Fiona, I promise. But how are you going to explain hurting us?"

"I came into my husband's office and confronted two trespassers who tried to hurt me."

"Well, that won't work," said Dan. "We haven't tried to hurt you."

Fiona punched herself hard enough in the eye he heard the smack of flesh on bone. She staggered back from the blow then did it again. Her ring must have caught her skin because a drop of blood appeared at the edge of her socket.

"Oh shit."

"Charlie hated me and you both attacked me." Fiona calmly punched herself in the other eye. "I mean, what else could I do?"

Charlie grabbed a pen and threw it like a dart. As Fiona ducked Dan reached for the heavy ashtray. He swung it towards the window of the stable door and the glass smashed instantly. Rain hit his face. He gasped and dropped the ashtray and it bounced off the lower part of the frame to knock out more glass. He took several deep breaths and pulled his cagoule sleeve over his hand.

"Come on," he said and grabbed Charlie's arm.

He punched out the remaining shards in the bottom of the frame. More jagged pieces were held in place in the upper part and looked like shark's teeth. He hoped they could fit through the gap without hitting them.

"What're you doing?" Charlie said and pushed against him.

He clambered out. Once on the other side he held out his arms and Charlie came through in a rush. She landed nimbly and zipped up her cagoule.

"Thanks," she shouted.

From somewhere on the sea side there was another horrible cracking sound that vibrated the floor of the sun terrace.

Fiona shrieked and lunged out of the window scything the scissors at them.

"Go," he shouted at Charlie.

She didn't move. In frustration he reached for her hand then saw what she'd been looking at.

Part of the sun terrace wall was missing and through the gap he could see the jagged edge of brickwork and lots of foaming water. A haphazard crack at least a foot wide ran from the edge of the hole almost to the other side of the terrace.

"We can't go that way," Charlie shouted and fear sharpened her voice. "What if we fall through?"

Fiona cried out. She was halfway out the window but her coat had caught on a piece of glass that pinned her in place.

"We can't go back either," he shouted.

He tried to catch his breath and focus – there was no time to panic. A low brick lip ran around the perimeter of the terrace and he edged to the lido side and carefully leaned over. The undercroft walkway was ten or twelve feet below and he knew what to do.

Fiona landed with a thud on the terrace.

"Let's go," said Dan. "I'll help you over the edge then you drop to the ground. It's not far."

"Are you mental?"

"It's our only way out."

Fiona got shakily to her feet. Charlie looked from her to Dan and then sat on the edge of the lip. Dan braced himself and gripped her wrists.

"Okay," he shouted.

"Don't drop me," she pleaded.

He nodded as she levered herself off the wall. She wasn't too heavy and he'd braced himself enough she didn't pull him off balance. He leaned forward to see how far down she was then let go of her wrists. She landed gracefully and managed to stay on her feet then gave him a quick thumbs up.

Dan sat on the wall and lowered his legs then turned to help himself drop. Fiona rushed towards him. Her mouth was twisted into a snarl and she swung the scissors as if hoping to slice his face.

He let go in terror and landed hard, jarring his ankles. He staggered back but Charlie grabbed his arm and pulled him into the undercroft.

"Are you okay?" she asked.

"Yes but Fiona's coming."

She landed heavily behind him and fell onto her back. It took a moment or two for her to move. Breathing heavily enough for them to hear she got herself onto all fours. The scissors were still gripped in her hand.

"She's not giving up," he said.

"This way," said Charlie. She yanked open the changing room door and pulled him into the darkness.

Chapter 53

The darkness pressed against Dan and when Charlie reached for his hand he was thankful for the connection.

"If we get far enough from the door," Charlie said, "we can see what she does. If she comes in behind us we'll have a head start and if she doesn't we'll know she's gone along the outside to the other door at the end."

"Good thinking."

Although she led him carefully into the dark he still tripped over a solid object. Water gushed through the crack in the terrace and some grey light came through to reveal debris everywhere.

There was a scraping noise and Dan turned to see Fiona silhouetted in the doorway. She stepped through and pulled the door shut and disappeared in the gloom.

"Come on," said Charlie. "Mind your step."

She set them a steady pace but the limited visibility forced Dan to take ever smaller steps. His shoulder hit something that knocked him sideways.

"What did you hit?"

"A box of some kind." He rubbed his shoulder.

"There's electrical panels and pipework all along here. We need to keep in the middle of the corridor."

"I can't see the middle of the corridor."

"Neither can I," she said tartly. "But it's not affecting Fiona."

The woman sounded as if she was coming at them quickly. Occasionally she would collide with something that made her cry out with pain but it didn't seem to slow her progress.

"I see you," she shouted and sounded shockingly close.

Dan had a sudden terrifying thought she'd swing with those scissors and he'd feel them tear across his shoulders. It didn't help that in the dark and close confines of the corridor Dan couldn't tell where she was.

"I don't think we can outrun her," Charlie said.

"You can't get away!" Fiona shouted.

Charlie pushed through a door and he followed her into complete darkness. He blinked and willed his night vision to kick in.

"It's the changing room," Charlie whispered and startled him when she touched his wrist. "There are no windows." She pressed his hand against a wet tiled wall. "Keep your hand on here. This is the lido side."

The door burst open and Fiona came through. Her harsh breathing echoed around until he couldn't tell where she was. Fear shot through him and he tried to breathe as shallowly as he could to not make any noise. Fiona came towards him or maybe towards the racks. Fingertips brushed his left hand and he pressed his right palm tight against his mouth. A body pressed into his side.

"Keep your eyes closed," Charlie whispered. Her breath was hot against his neck. "Trust me."

He heard a zip.

"Ready?" she whispered.

"No," he whispered but closed his eyes anyway.

"Hey, Fiona," Charlie called and the flash of her Instamatic lit the room so brightly he could see blood vessels in his eyelids.

Fiona screamed and clattered heavily into something.

Charlie wound the film on then held his hand. The low insistent whine of the flash recharging itself sounded very loud. They moved along slowly and he kept his free hand pressed to the wall.

She squeezed his hand and he closed his eyes. The second flash made Fiona scream again and this time it sounded like she had fallen over. She whimpered in distress.

Dan followed Charlie. Blood rushed in his ears.

Fiona whimpered as she got to her feet.

Charlie squeezed his hand and set off the flash again then quickly wound the film on. Dan heard the slap of flesh against tile and Fiona made an odd sound.

"I think she hit the wall," he said.

"Good, we're nearly at the other door."

They moved faster but it still seemed to take them a long time to reach the door. Charlie pushed it open and Dan's eyes smarted from the sudden brightness. Charlie set off the flash one more time and Dan pushed the door closed.

"Are you okay?" she asked.

Adrenaline ran through him like an electrical charge. "I think so. You?"

She nodded shakily.

"The flash was a great idea," he said with admiration.

"Thanks."

A crash and muttered groan filtered through the door.

"I hope she cracked her head on something."

"We wouldn't be that lucky," he said.

Charlie tried to push the lido door open but it didn't move. She shook her head in a 'silly-me' movement and pulled the handle instead. It still didn't move.

"Help me push," she said.

Dan put his hands on the cold and wet wood but the door wasn't going anywhere.

"It must have warped like the other one," he said.

The changing room door opened. Fiona seemed to be bleeding heavily. Her hairline was red and more blood streaked down her right leg, probably from a wound he couldn't see under her raincoat. A watery trail ran from her eye to her chin.

Charlie screamed.

Chapter 54

"You didn't get very far did you?" Fiona came towards them and the scissors caught the light. "Even after your trick with the camera blinded me for a moment and I hit the wall."

She lifted the edge of her raincoat and Dan saw the blood came from a deep-looking gash above her knee.

"You should go to the hospital," he said.

Charlie gagged.

"Are you pleased with yourself, Charlie? You seem to keep causing damage wherever you go."

"I'm not," said Charlie calmly. "You were chasing us with a pair of scissors."

"So I was."

"We're kind of equal then," Charlie said. "I tell you what – if you forget about your leg then we'll forget about everything else. Nobody needs to know."

Fiona laughed and the jagged sound echoed through the stairwell. Charlie glanced at Dan with her eyebrows raised. He lifted a shoulder in a shrug. Nothing made sense to him at the moment.

It took Fiona a few moments to get herself under control. "Is the door jammed or something?"

"Uh-huh," said Charlie.

"That's a real shame," Fiona said. "Of course it might be locked."

"I hadn't thought of that," Charlie conceded.

"Some of us plan," Fiona said.

There was another loud crash and some plaster fell off the wall below the crack. Water ran through.

"I saw your mother today," Fiona said and smiled at him. "I like her but she's too kind and understanding for her own good. She tried to convince me Charlie's a lovely girl."

"I think she's right."

"You would say that because you fancy her. I understand. Men are like that. If they think they're going to get some they're all charming and fancy. Has Charlie put out for you yet?"

"That's none of your business," he said.

"A gentleman, eh?" Fiona looked at Charlie. "I'm impressed you've held out for so long."

"What did Charlie do to offend you so much? I think you'd be better off speaking to your husband because–"

Fiona cut him off with a vicious glare. "Don't ever tell me what I need to do and please don't confuse the fact I like your mother with me owing you any favours. I know all about Charlie and I see her wheedling her way in with Andy and Paul."

"No," said Charlie carefully.

"I didn't think you knew that word." Fiona smirked. "Andy's always had an eye for a pretty young thing but I'm not about to give up this life for anyone. Especially cheap little tarts like you and Mia Garwood."

"She wasn't interested in him," Charlie said.

"I saw the paperwork for all the money he gave her, you stupid little bitch." Fiona laughed in her face. "Didn't you know? Bloody hell, you're so naïve you're going to get your heart massively broken. Nobody does anything for nothing, Charlie. This is the eighties, not the fifties. If he was giving her money, then he was getting something in return."

"That's not how it was," Charlie said. She sounded on the verge of tears.

"Do you think I'm blind? I saw the way he looked at her and how she encouraged it. I'd played her game and that bitch wasn't going to take away what I'd worked for."

"So what did you do?" Dan asked.

"I made sure she knew it."

"You killed her?" Charlie asked.

Fiona smiled and looked at Charlie as if she was memorising the details of her face then turned her attention to Dan. He felt his stomach drop. If she admitted this then they weren't walking away from the lido without something terrible happening.

"She was so easy to surprise. I borrowed Paul's car and in the fog she thought I was Andy and got in with no hassle at all. She wasn't so happy when she realised, and I hit her to calm her down. I broke her necklace and she got more upset about that than being in the car with me."

"Is that why you killed her?" Charlie asked.

"I wanted to break her, Charlie. I wanted her away. I brought her here and made her strip down to her underwear then locked the door and told her that she was going to die here. I liked it when she cried."

"You locked her in the pump room," said Dan.

"Well, look at you, a proper little Columbo. I locked her in there because it was one way in and one way out or so I thought. I took her some bread and water on Tuesday and told her nobody noticed she'd gone or cared for her. She cried again and that awful whine drove me nuts so I threw the water at her and took the bread home."

"You're mad," said Charlie, and Dan could only agree with her.

"I was acting under diminished responsibility," she said. "Mia drove me to do what I did to her."

"You didn't have to kill her, Fiona."

"I wish I had but she did it herself trying to escape."

"She went for the fire escape didn't she?" asked Charlie sadly. "She fell from the pump room."

"Who knows? One day the little cow was locked in the room and the next she'd gone. I panicked until she washed up the next morning." She gave a what-could-I-do shrug that turned Dan's stomach.

"You tortured her and left her to die," Dan said through gritted teeth.

"Oh, you pathetic little boy, I hardly tortured her and she chose to go through the fire escape door. Once the rumour started about her jumping off Julia's Point I knew I was safe. More people than I'd expected claimed they liked her but most knew she was unhappy too. Then you two started playing at being Cagney and Lacey and dragging things up. I wasn't worried until Jude told me you'd taken that bloody photograph to the police."

"You sent me the postcards."

"Give the chimp a banana," Fiona said and clapped awkwardly around the scissors. "I thought they'd put you off but they didn't and since I have no intention of going to prison I need to shut you both up."

"You're sick," Dan said.

Fiona shook her head. "Betrayed and tricked," she said. "Not sick."

"The police can do stuff nowadays," said Charlie. "If you stab us in the stairwell they'll find your blood here as well as ours."

"But we already established I caught trespassers," she said.

Charlie pulled on the door again and Dan helped. Fiona screamed so loudly he had to cover his ears and so did Charlie.

"It's locked, you morons," she said. "I've got the key. Now get downstairs."

Chapter 55

Dan pulled and pushed at the door but it wouldn't budge. He felt angry and frightened and powerless. If he didn't get out of there something terrible was going to happen to Charlie and then Fiona would turn her attention to him.

He couldn't break through the door so if he wanted to take action he had to figure out another way to do it. Dan took a deep breath and suddenly felt washed out. He forced himself on.

There was plenty of grey light in the room and water ran down the wall from the crack above the window. He didn't see anything that might help him but then thought about trying to reach the remains of the fire escape. It made him feel queasy.

A boom made him jump. It was followed by a tremendous crash that sounded like the walls were coming down. A wave slapped against the wall and frothy seawater surged through the crack.

Dan put his hand on the safety bar. His heart was thudding like a drum and a pain had settled in behind his eyes and across his forehead. This was madness but he couldn't think of anything else to do.

He pushed the door and the wind caught it and slammed it against the outer wall. Seawater splashed his face. He grabbed the door jamb to keep himself steady.

The tide was in and the waves were high. The air was full of spray. He lay on the floor and looked over the door jamb. The lido wall was sheer with no ledges or ridges he could use.

The horrifying reality that this was his only way out settled into him and made his bones feel heavy.

It was madness. He wasn't the world's greatest swimmer and didn't know how deep the water was; if the rocks were just below the surface he'd dash himself all over them.

If he didn't try something though, Fiona would murder Charlie, then him.

He felt sick because he knew he didn't have another choice.

Getting slowly to his feet he walked across to the door, counted to three then ran across the room as fast as he could and launched himself through the fire escape.

For a moment he was flying and then the cold of the water shocked his breath away.

Dan broke the surface gasping for air and frantically trod water. His cagoule clung to him and restricted his movement and his trainers felt like bricks tied to his feet.

His leap had carried him perhaps ten feet from the lido wall but each wave threatened to dash him against it so he struck out with a front crawl stroke to get him away. He aimed for the beach but got caught in some kind of undertow that meant he was swimming to stay in one place.

A wave broke in front of him and as he coughed away the face full of salt water the undertow dragged at his legs. He tried to swim against it in panic but didn't have the power.

It was a losing battle and he was going to die and so was Charlie.

More water went into his mouth and he choked. As he stopped swimming the undertow dragged him away from the lido. Panic became a cloud that settled over his head. His arms and legs ached and he couldn't take a full breath. How far out to sea could he drift?

Dan thought of his mum sitting in the caravan reading her book. Would she be wondering how his day was going? How would she cope when he didn't come home tonight? He thought of Charlie and hoped she wasn't panicking now but figuring out a way to escape.

Thinking of them both sharpened his senses. All Fiona had to do was throw Charlie onto the rocks and the water would do the rest. She'd get away with another killing and he couldn't let that happen. He needed to fight this undertow so he could help.

With his arms protesting at every stroke, he struck out again for the corner of the lido.

Chapter 56

Jude's anxiety grew the closer they got to the lido.

The roads were slick and greasy and she'd felt the back end of the Jaguar slide a few times but she still wanted him to go faster.

The pavements were almost empty and drains were backed up along Marine Drive, creating huge puddles Paul had to drive around. Out to sea it was impossible to determine where the horizon was.

"It's a bad storm," she said. "You can see why Charlie would want to photograph it."

"I haven't seen waves like this for a long time and they'll be coming in high around the lido."

He glanced at her and she thought of the cracks in the sea wall.

"Could the storm cause more damage?" she asked.

"I don't know."

She felt hot and uncomfortable. "Do you think whoever wrote that note thinks it could cause more damage?"

He pursed his lips but didn't say anything.

As they passed the funfair the lido seemed to come out of the mist and she saw the Surrey bike parked outside.

"Is that their bike?" Paul asked and steered in towards the kerb.

"It would make sense because that's how they get about. Drop me off here."

"What do you mean drop you off?"

"They might need my help."

"I'm here to help too."

"No," she said and unclipped her seatbelt. "I'll go in and see what's happening. You find a telephone and ring the police."

He started to argue and she put her hand over his. "It's my son, Paul. Do this for me."

"Okay," he said after a moment.

He pulled up behind the bike and she was out the door before the car had even stopped. The pavement was slick and her foot slipped but she caught her balance.

"Don't do anything risky," Paul shouted as he leaned over to close the passenger door.

She was already running to the entrance.

Chapter 57

Dan's arms felt like lead weights when another undertow caught him and spun him around. Panicked, he floundered but the tidal movement was strong enough to tug him back through the water, towards the lido.

With renewed hope he began to swim against the waves. From this angle he could see a narrow staircase set into the wall above the rock line that must have been for maintenance or emergency access. The rendering at the base of it was heavily cracked to reveal uneven brickwork.

A wave broke over him and as he gasped for breath he saw the rendered wall was almost in reach.

He tried to swim with the current but got caught in backwash and ended up in the same place. Another wave lifted him up and forwards.

Dan hit the wall just below the broken render and managed to grab the edge of a particularly large crack. It held and he kept his grip as the receding water tugged at his legs. The next wave lifted him bodily and he caught the bottom of the step and scrambled onto it. He pulled himself up two more until he was out of the water's reach and tried to get his breath. His adrenaline drained and he flopped in a heap with his face to the sky and his eyes closed to the rain.

It took several minutes until he had the energy to stand without feeling like he was going to collapse. He kept low so the exterior wall hid him from sight as he made his way slowly up the narrow staircase. A metal gate closed it off from the lido and he crouched down behind it. If Fiona had taken Charlie back to the office, then the bulk of the pump room stairwell would hide him from view. If they were anywhere else, he had to hope they were looking the other way.

He reached up to unlatch the gate and pushed it open slightly. The hinges squeaked but he didn't think anyone would hear it over the noise of nature. He peered around the edge of the wall.

Fiona and Charlie were halfway across the lido close to the sea wall. Fiona had a handful of Charlie's hair and was also holding one of her arms. Charlie wasn't going quietly and kept kicking out or throwing punches with her free hand. Some of the blows were landing and Fiona kept yanking her along. Charlie's crying and shouting drifted to Dan when the wind briefly changed direction.

The gate opened onto a small area bounded by the sea wall on one side and the pump room on the other. He crawled through and pressed himself tight against the sea wall. The only thing shielding him from Fiona's view were the three diving boards she'd just pulled Charlie around.

It was better than nothing.

Dan kept low and ran towards the diving boards. The floor was treacherous and he had to shorten his strides to make sure he kept his balance.

A wave broke and the spray coated him. He blinked the salt water away and trod on the edge of a puddle and his feet went out from under him.

He fell awkwardly into the diving board support and the sound of impact seemed to roll across the lido. He quickly got to his knees and peered around the edge.

Fiona saw him immediately and pulled hard on Charlie's hair until she was facing the sky.

"Don't run away," Fiona shouted.

"Shit." His terror made him nauseous.

"I don't know how you got out but I really wish you hadn't."

Dan sat with his back to the boards and tried to think of a plan that didn't involve giving himself up but his brain was twirling wheels. If he did something stupid now Fiona would hurt Charlie. If he did nothing the same result would happen.

How had he managed to fuck this up so badly? He'd endured the sea, the climb and now he'd been caught out? He had to give up. It was the only possible course of action even if it was the worst.

Dan stood with his hands in the air. "Hey," he said.

"Well, what do you know?" Fiona said to Charlie. "Lover boy came back for you."

He walked around the back of the diving boards and Fiona held up her hand. "Don't come any closer."

"What do you want me to do?"

"Nothing. I didn't even want you here. It's going to break your mother's heart if I hurt you."

"She won't be happy if you hurt Charlie either."

"See?" demanded Charlie.

Fiona pulled her hand down sharply and Charlie cried out in pain. Dan took a step forward.

"If you come any closer," Fiona shouted, "I'll kill her."

Chapter 58

Jude struggled through the gap in the fence and ran up the steps. She shielded her eyes against the driving rain but the sea wall was almost lost in a mist.

She looked up towards the office. The lights were on but she couldn't see anyone.

A sound like bricks being shredded startled her but with the echo of the rumble she couldn't tell where it came from. Could something have fallen off the lido?

She cupped her hands around her mouth. "Dan!" she shouted. "Charlie!"

There was no response and her panic grew. She had to act quickly before it overtook her and starting with the office made sense. Someone had put those lights on and even if Charlie wanted to get some great pictures she'd know it was too dangerous to be down by the sea wall. The office would give her shelter and a vantage point.

Jude rushed across the slippery terrace and up the stairs. The guttering was ruined and she could see the office door was warped before she tried to open it. She wasn't going to get in that way.

She leaned over the wall and peered through the first window but the angle wasn't good. She hit the window as hard as she could but nobody responded to it.

Jude brushed the hair out of her eyes and went down the steps. Movement from the far end of the lido caught her eye.

Two people were moving towards the sea wall. Surely they wouldn't be so silly as to risk their lives. Then she saw another person coming along behind them.

If the first two were Dan and Charlie trying to find a good angle for the photograph then did they even realise someone else was there?

Adrenaline surged through her and she rushed down the steps to the terrace. The floor was dangerously slick but she got to the concrete of the lido itself and ran.

"Dan!" she shouted but none of the figures in the watery mist seemed to hear her.

Chapter 59

Dan held up his hands in what he hoped was a placatory gesture. "Fiona, please, just let her go."

Fiona shook her head as if dismissing a dim-witted schoolboy. "It's too late for that, you fool."

"I won't say anything," Charlie said. Her head was still pulled back so she looked at the sky. "Please let me go."

Fiona laughed bitterly and yanked Charlie's hair hard. Tendons stood out in her throat and Dan felt a twinge in his stomach that he couldn't help his friend. He took a step closer but Fiona noticed immediately.

"Stay there. One more step and I'll break her neck."

"I'm not going anywhere," he said. "I just want you to let go of Charlie."

Fiona shook her head then looked over his shoulder with surprise. Worried someone was creeping up on him, Dan looked quickly over his shoulder to see his mum rushing across the lido. His surprise was quickly swallowed by concern.

"Well, well," muttered Fiona.

"Stay there, Mum!" Dan shouted. "Get the police."

"Yes," Fiona shouted. "Call the police, Jude. Tell them I found a couple of trespassers causing damage to the lido."

Dan looked at Fiona. "It's finished now. Let Charlie go and we'll figure out something to say to my mum."

"Are you mad? Jude coming here is the best thing that could have happened. She hates Charlie as much as I do and I'll say she was messing up my marriage and sticking her oar in between Andy and Paul."

Her conviction was so intense Dan could only shake his head. "She's not going to believe that."

"She doesn't hate me," said Charlie and swung a punch. It grazed off Fiona's cheek.

Fiona pulled Charlie to her knees but Charlie braced herself and elbowed her in the ribs. Fiona slapped her face with such force that Charlie stopped struggling for a moment.

* * *

Jude took things in quickly. Dan seemed to be safe but Fiona was holding Charlie's hair so tightly that even though the teenager was struggling she didn't seem able to break free.

Jude knew she'd completely misread the situation but she could deal with this. She'd spent her career working with teenagers who often seemed to be on fairly short fuses at the best of times.

"How are you, Danny?"

He gave her a quick nod. "How are you?"

A wave broke over the wall and covered them all in spray. "A bit wet," she said then shifted her attention. "Hey, Fiona, what's going on? I didn't expect to see you here."

"I didn't expect to see you either."

"So what's happening?"

Fiona laughed as if they were co-conspirators. "This is my husband's investment. I called in to make sure everything was holding up with the storm and found these two trespassing."

"Is that right?" Jude asked.

"Uh-huh. I'm sorry to have to say it because it's Dan but, you know, this is a dangerous place and they're here without permission and I need to take them to the police."

"So why are you holding Charlie like that? You look as if you're trying to break her neck."

"She went for me and I had to defend myself. She's a hard little cow, you know that."

"None of that's true," said Dan.

"I know," Jude said without looking away from Fiona. "You can let her go now, though. I won't let her get away but this place is dangerous and you're very close to the sea wall."

Fiona gave her a cold unfriendly smile. "I know what I'm doing. Once I let this little vixen go, who knows what she'll do?"

"She won't do anything," Jude said calmly. "That's right, Charlie, isn't it? If Fiona lets you go you'll be calm."

"I will," Charlie said. "I promise."

"See," said Jude. "You can let her go now."

Fiona raised her eyebrows. "Wow, Jude, I didn't think you'd be stupid enough to believe her so it shows what I know." She dragged Charlie closer to the hole in the wall. It looked far bigger than when Jude had seen it before and there were bricks lying in a wide puddle of seawater in front of it.

"I'm not stupid, Fiona, I'm trying to be practical." Jude moved sideways keeping pace with Fiona. From the corner of her eye she saw Dan moving too. "She's a teenager. What could she do to you?"

"You think I don't know? What have I been telling you about all this week?"

A pack of lies, Jude thought. "You've been telling me your fears," she said.

"They're not fears, it's actually happening. You need to back away now though, Jude, because none of this concerns you. I'll deal with it myself."

"I can't walk away while you've got Charlie."

"But you know what she's like," Fiona scoffed. "It's only a matter of time before she's making life difficult for me."

"That's ridiculous. Whatever's happening here isn't to do with Charlie so just let her go."

"You're blind. You're so blind."

"I'm not. I came here because I saw the note from Andy that Charlie got this morning."

There was the briefest of pauses.

"You see," Fiona said, "she came here because of a note."

"But you wrote the note. I saw Andy this morning and he told me everything about Mia and the lido and the money and the fact he was leaving."

"He's not leaving," Fiona snarled. "Why are you lying to me?"

"I'm not. Everything's falling apart, Fiona, and if you carry on like this it'll all be on you."

* * *

Dan didn't know what his mum was talking about but he could see it was distracting Fiona and that was enough. He took a step forward and Fiona didn't appear to notice. He took another. He was now less than six feet away from her. Charlie stared at him and raised her eyebrows as she moved her eyes towards Fiona. It looked like she was trying to draw him into some sort of plan but he had no idea what she wanted him to do.

"But he didn't tell me what happened to Mia," his mum said. "I think that's because he didn't know but I think you do."

"Shut up!" Fiona screamed.

"Don't hurt Charlie like you did Mia."

"I didn't hurt her. I wanted to scare her but she fell. It wasn't my fault."

"Maybe you didn't push her, Fiona, but it's all your fault."

Fiona must have relaxed her grip because Charlie pulled to the right towards the hole in the wall. Her head snapped back for one awful moment and then she was staggering away holding her scalp.

Dan ran at Fiona and by the time she saw him it was too late. He dropped his shoulder the way the rugby coach at school had shown them and drove into Fiona's midriff. Her breath woofed out and she seemed to fold over him. His momentum carried them into the wall and his shoulder connected with the brickwork. It felt like an explosion had gone off in the joint.

Fiona rolled away as he slid down the wall. Stars burst in the dark curtains that now edged his vision.

Charlie and Jude screamed.

He put his hand down to get himself up but the pain flared brighter. His mum knelt in front of him and cupped his cheeks. He smiled but it didn't seem to reassure her.

"Danny?"

"I hit my shoulder."

"I saw." She looked over at Fiona. "Shit."

Fiona was getting to her feet. She held her stomach and ignored them as she staggered towards Charlie.

Dan rolled to his left and quickly got to his feet. His right arm moved but hurt like a bastard and the fire spread from the joint through his biceps and down his forearm. His fingertips were filled with painful pins and needles.

Charlie was on her knees by the wall and Dan ran after Fiona but it was hard to keep his balance on the slick ground.

"Charlie!" his mum called. She sounded very close behind him.

Fiona fell onto Charlie and they slid towards the hole. Fiona tried to pin her down but Charlie fought back hard, kicking her legs and throwing punches. Dan threw himself at Fiona. She ducked but he caught her neck and pulled as Charlie scrambled to her feet. She kicked at Fiona and some of her wilder blows caught Dan.

His mum appeared in his line of vision. She hooked Charlie up into a bear hug and turned her away from Fiona.

Fiona struggled against Dan and every time her feet connected with the ground she forced them back towards the wall.

Seawater sprayed his face and the waves sounded too loud and he realised she'd pushed them to the edge of the hole. Panicked, he tried to push them towards safety but she fought him every step of the way.

Charlie shouted his name.

Fiona elbowed Dan in the stomach. Winded, he let go of her. She rolled off him but was on the very top of the hole. He reached for her arm. She screamed as her legs dropped away and grasped his hand but it was too late. She went over and he was dragged towards the hole.

Someone held his ankles.

Fiona looked up with wide and terrified eyes. Her wet fingers slipped through his and then his mum was by his side. She braced herself against the other side of the hole and grabbed Fiona's other arm. Dan and his mum pulled and even though he felt himself shift on the wet ground Charlie kept a tight grip on his ankles.

His mum tugged hard and then Fiona's upper body was back on the flat. She grabbed Fiona's waistband and pulled until the woman slid onto the lido floor.

Charlie grabbed Fiona's wrists and pulled her well away from the hole then sat heavily in the small of her back. Pinned to the concrete Fiona groaned. Charlie folded her arms and looked at Jude.

"Thank you," she gasped.

The fire in Dan's arm came raging back and he lay still until loud footsteps rang out across the lido.

"Over here," his mum shouted.

"Who's that?" he asked.

"The cavalry. But they're too late for the action."

"I think we did well enough on our own," said Charlie.

"We did," agreed his mum.

Epilogue

Early November, 1985

Jude sat at her kitchen table and looked out the window. The trees and bushes she could see were rapidly losing their autumnal fire and it made her feel cold. She retied her dressing gown and lit a cigarette.

The stairs creaked and she looked up at the kitchen door. When Paul came through, with tousled hair and sleepy eyes, he smiled. He didn't appear to feel the cold and wore only his pyjama trousers.

"Morning, gorgeous," he said.

"Morning, handsome," she said and returned his smile.

He made himself a coffee and sat across from her. "Why didn't you wake me?"

"Because it's Sunday morning and you looked so peaceful lying there I didn't want to disturb you."

Paul rubbed his face. "I don't want to waste the day though."

Jude checked the kitchen clock. "It's not even eight," she said. "I mean, it'd be nice if you could stay over tonight as well."

"Don't tempt me," he said and leaned forward to take her hand. "But it's taken so long to sort out Andy's mess, I need to meet with the bank manager in the morning so we can finalise my new business."

He was nervous about it but she'd helped him write his financial projections and business plan and was sure it would all work out fine.

"You'll be great and he'll be impressed, and you'll be a company director again very soon."

"I hope so. Couldn't have done it without you, love."

She felt the familiar rush of warmth at his words and hoped that sensation never faded. They'd taken it easy at first with a couple of phone calls and then a meeting at a pub in Cambridge, midway between Seagrave and Hadlington. Jude had wondered if she was making too much of a holiday fling but they got on so well – he made her laugh and feel good about herself and she hoped she had the same effect on him – that it made sense to take things further.

Paul stayed over for the first time a week or so later and it hadn't been as awkward as she'd feared it might be. He liked the house and took her out for a lovely meal at an Italian restaurant she recommended and then the evening was almost over and neither of them had to leave.

She went to stay at his flat the following weekend and now they alternated between homes.

Dan accepted the situation well. He and Paul managed to find some common ground and she thought they might be developing a good friendship. One night, as he helped her clear the table after dinner, Dan told her he was keen to get on with Paul because the man clearly made her happy.

"So what did you want to do today?" she asked Paul.

"I wouldn't mind calling into that record fair you spoke about yesterday. I'm still working my way through the list of Donna Summer records you mentioned and there's a couple I haven't been able to find."

Dan was away in Sheffield for the weekend, staying at Charlie's. Jude wasn't sure how serious things were getting between them but they clearly made each other happy and his eyes lit up whenever he saw her. Charlie had stayed down here a couple of times and Jude enjoyed her company.

"We can do that," Jude said. "A colleague told me about this little pub in Haverton that's supposed to do an excellent Sunday lunch, so I thought we could go there to eat."

"That sounds great. I'll finish my coffee then have a shower and we can make a move."

She gave him a smile as a thought occurred to her. "I haven't had a shower yet either," she said. "Maybe we could save some water."

He nodded his head in appreciation. "I like the sound of that, Jude. You do have some great ideas."

"I try," she said. "I try."

Acknowledgements

Mum and Dad; Sarah, Chris, Lucy and Milly; Nick Duncan, Sue Moorcroft, Julia Roberts, Jonathan Litchfield, Caroline Lake, Kim Talbot Hoelzli, Steve Bacon, Wayne Parkin, Peter Mark May, Richard Farren Barber, Steve Harris, Phil Sloman, James Everington, Ross Warren, Penny Jones, Jim Mcleod and EVERYONE who's bought and championed my books; Laura, Barry and Bob Burton; Ian Whates and the NSFWG; The Crusty Exterior and my convention friends. Huge thanks to Erik and the entire team at The Book Folks.

David Roberts and Pippa for the Friday night walks, the laughs and the plotting sessions.

And, as always, Alison and Matthew, without whom I'd be less.

If you enjoyed this book, please let others know by leaving a quick review on Amazon. Also, if you spot anything untoward in the paperback, get in touch. We strive for the best quality and appreciate reader feedback.

editor@thebookfolks.com

www.thebookfolks.com

Beth's partner Nick can't quite understand why she acts so strangely when they return to her hometown for the funeral of a once-close friend. But she hasn't told him everything about her past. Memories of one terrible summer will come flooding back to her. And with them, violence and revenge.

After separating from her cheating husband, Claire begins to feel watched. She nearly gets run over and someone daubs a hangman symbol on a wall near her house. As letters begin to get added to the game, she'll need to find the identity of her stalker before they raise the stakes.

Young single mother Rachel has no idea why an assassin is trying to kill her. Have they confused her with someone else? Did she do something wrong? Whatever the answer, it looks like they'll carry on trying unless she can get to safety or turn the tables on them. But first she'll have to find out what they want from her.

When her husband invites Jo on a couples' hiking weekend, despite disliking camping she accepts, hoping they'll rekindle their former closeness. But her hopes are shattered when the group starts to argue amongst themselves, and then the unthinkable happens… a happy holiday quickly turns into a desperate fight for survival.

A professional woman who is opposing the development of a golf course on a local nature site finds her life falling into turmoil when someone begins to blackmail her with compromising photographs. Will she succumb to their demands or can she deliver the extorter into the arms of the law?

Other titles of interest

A mother becomes increasingly at odds with her local community when she tries to deal with the bullying of her daughter at school. Yet her daughter is trying to handle it in her own way. When one bullying schoolboy goes missing, the family will have to reach the truth to remain together.

When loner Jason is invited by an attractive girl to a luxury private pool party on Nairn's seafront, he can't quite believe his luck. But when he learns the next day that someone was murdered during the event, things take a turn for the worse. As an outsider, he falls under suspicion. Can he find out who the killer is and prove his innocence?

All FREE with Kindle Unlimited and available in paperback!

www.ingramcontent.com/pod-product-compliance
Lightning Source LLC
Chambersburg PA
CBHW061802190726

48289CB00007B/2036